EBURY PRESS
DAUGHTER OF TWO RIVERS

Arun Krishnan has studied and lived in different cities across India, the US, Singapore and Japan before putting down roots in Bengaluru. He started off with a degree in engineering and a doctorate before going on to work in IT, high-performance computing, bioinformatics, computational biology and HR analytics. He is a polyglot and is conversant in Tamil, English, Hindi, Bengali, Japanese and Kannada. An amateur historian and musician, he enjoys visiting historical places and noodling on his guitar. He has previously written The Battle of Vathapi trilogy.

ADVANCE PRAISE FOR THE BOOK

'Arun Krishnan once again proves himself a master storyteller with *Daughter of Two Rivers*, an epic tale of love, loss and destiny set against the backdrop of a world in flux nearly 4000 years ago. Blending rigorous historical research with gripping narrative, Krishnan transports readers from the drying banks of the Sarasvati River to the courts of Babylon, weaving a story of courage, betrayal and the enduring power of human connection. With richly drawn characters, heart-pounding action and an emotionally charged conclusion that lingers long after the final page, it is a triumph of historical fiction. Krishnan's ability to resurrect a forgotten era and breathe life into its people makes this novel an unmissable journey for history enthusiasts and adventure lovers alike'—**Anand Ranganathan, author and scientist**

'Arun Krishnan's *Daughter of Two Rivers* is a breathtaking blend of history, adventure and romance, bringing to life a forgotten world with stunning detail. From the fading banks of the Sarasvati to the grandeur of Babylon, this epic tale of love and survival is both thrilling and deeply moving. A masterfully woven narrative, it cements Krishnan's place as a standout voice in historical fiction'—**Amish Tripathi, author**

'Richly detailed and immersive, *Daughter of Two Rivers* brings to life our ancient past in a way that is both thrilling and deeply moving'—**Ashwin Sanghi, author**

'What began as a re-evaluation of colonial history narratives is now seeping into popular culture. This gripping book by Arun is part of that journey'—**Sanjeev Sanyal, economist and writer**

'An epic journey set in a dazzling and vibrant world that once existed between the Sindhu and the Euphrates. The story grips you and never lets go, thanks to the incredible depth of research, the plethora of memorable characters and some truly heart wrenching moments—all woven together by an author at the peak of his storytelling prowess'—**Ratul Chakraborty, author**

'Arun Krishnan's latest proves why he is the boss of historical fiction. After winning over readers with South Indian history, he now goes International with *Daughter of the Two Rivers*. From the banks of the drying Sarasvati River, he takes us to the Babylonian civilization on a journey showcasing an interplay between two ancient civilizations. What follows next is an action-packed story filled with emotions. With strong characters you like instantly and an innovative plotline, this book is a must-read'—**Deepak M.R., author**

'Across land and sea, and two rivers in between, Arun Krishnan weaves a thrilling adventure that has weapons, war, conspiracies and, of course, love. A must-read for anyone interested in the history of the Indian subcontinent'— **Jeysundhar, author**

'A captivating tale of belonging, yearning, bravery and betrayal, steeped in the soul of two great civilizations on the precipice of destiny'—**S. Venkatesh, author**

'Arun Krishnan invites readers into the dawn of 1800 BCE where the mighty Sindhu–Sarasvati and the rising Babylonian civilizations flourish and tales of love, conflict and survival flow with the two mighty rivers. Arun Krishnan's mastery of weaving past with contemporary is unparalleled. Unmissable!' —**Sunanda Vashisht, author and columnist**

'From the once verdant kingdom by a long dried-up Sarasvati River in Bharatvarsha to Babylonia for an exchange that may provide what the Sumerians have wanted and what the Bharatvarsha kingdom needs. *Daughter of Two Rivers* takes the reader back in time to a timeless adventure, with intrigue, love and suspense. The story, plot and language are captivating. Arun has written an adventure for the ages that is a page-turner!'—**Abhinav Agarwal, author.**

'Rarely do we come across a book that innovates in both substance and style. On the one hand, Arun presents a teasing narrative, but the contemplation within gradually grows on you. On the other hand, the book naturally showcases the exclusivity of our civilization as it emerges through engagement with the world. It achieves all this through the experiences it creates for the reader without being burdensome'—**Shivakumar G.V., director, INDICA and author**

'Arun Krishnan's *Daughter of Two Rivers* is a molten current of history where Bharatavarsha and Babylon rise as twin echoes of a forgotten past. His prose strikes like a smith's hammer—sharp, unyielding and ablaze with intrigue—urging the modern generation to seek its roots before they fade into dust. A tempest of myth and memory, this novel is a bridge to the past, reminding us that history is not lost—it only waits to be remembered'—**Abhas Maldahiyar, author**

'Using the backdrop of ancient history, Arun crafts a gripping tale of war, valour, treachery and love. The fast-paced story traverses between Bharat and Babylonia, and weaves together two cultures seamlessly'—**Smita Barooah, author and therapist**

'*Daughter of Two Rivers* opens with a powerful invocation to the Sarasvati, setting the stage for a narrative deeply rooted in history and legend. Arun Krishnan, known for his successful historical fiction trilogy, once again brings the past to life with meticulous research and vivid storytelling. Readers of his previous works will find the same depth and richness that have defined his writing, making this a compelling addition to his repertoire'—**Dimple Kaul, poet, writer and literary strategist**

DAUGHTER
OF TWO
RIVERS

ARUN KRISHNAN

EBURY
PRESS

An imprint of Penguin Random House

EBURY PRESS

Ebury Press is an imprint of the Penguin Random House group of companies whose addresses can be found at global.penguinrandomhouse.com

Published by Penguin Random House India Pvt. Ltd
4th Floor, Capital Tower 1, MG Road,
Gurugram 122 002, Haryana, India

Penguin
Random House
India

First published in Ebury Press by Penguin Random House India 2025

ISBN 9780143472957

Typeset in Adobe Caslon Pro by MAP Systems, Bengaluru, India
Printed at Thomson Press India Ltd, New Delhi

www.penguin.co.in

MIX
Paper | Supporting
responsible forestry
FSC® C010615

अम्बितमे॒ नदी॑तमे॒ देवि॑तमे॒ सर॑स्वति । अ॒प्र॒श॒स्ता इ॑व
स्मसि॒ प्रश॑स्तिमम्ब नस्कृधि ॥

'Sarasvatī, best of mothers, best of rivers, best of
goddesses, we are, as it were, of no repute; grant us,
mother, distinction.'

Rig Veda 2.41.16

Author's Note

This story is set in a time and place roughly 3800 years ago, and rests on three facts.

The first is the presence of an object or artefact at the Bhandarkar Oriental Research Institute (BORI), which I first saw in July 2022 during a visit to Pune.

The second is the discovery made at a site that was part of the Sindhu–Sarasvati civilization.

The third is the disappearance of the Sarasvati river over time, as attested by the descriptions of the river and its flow in the Rig Veda, the Mahabharata, the Puranas and later texts.

The entire story was born out of these three facts. I have purposely refrained from stating what the artefact I saw at BORI is or even the discovery made at the site. Doing so would take away from your enjoyment of the book, but I assure you that it will be revealed to you before you finish the book.

Since the story takes place in a time where history and prehistory merge, I have had to rely on my imagination a lot. Geographically, the story spans from ancient India to ancient Babylon. A lot of the research had to be done online, and I am thankful to the march of technology for enabling this. In an earlier day and age, I would have had to spend a lot of time in libraries, finding out about distant lands and how the people in those lands lived in times past. But not any more.

I strongly believe that human actions, behaviour and emotions have remained unchanged across the thousands of years of our existence. The core emotions remain the same. I have tried to convey this through my characters. I hope you relate to them as deeply as I did while writing about them.

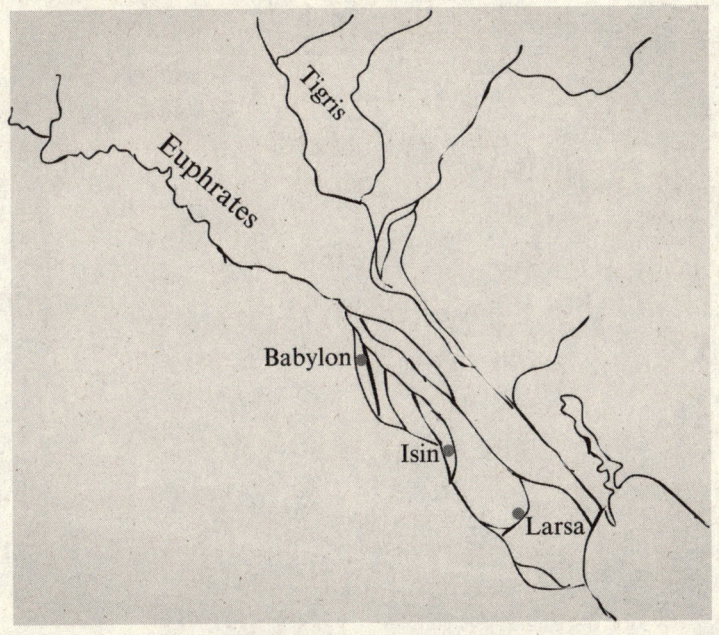

Map of Babylon, circa 1800 BCE

Credit: Avani Krishnan

Prologue

1921, Bombay, India

The middle-aged man stood at the edge of a trench, directing work at the dig. He was a member of the Archaeological Survey of India (ASI) and was involved in the survey of an ancient site that had been discovered only recently. He was wearing a loose shirt and billowy pants. He had a hat on his head to ward off the summer heat, but the humid Bombay weather was making him sweat profusely.

The site was a hum of activity. The clinks and thuds of the shovels on the earth, the grunts of the men as they came up against a particularly unyielding piece of ground, the shouts and instructions of the overseers, the steady line of workers who took away earth to dump it into a large sieving net that had been set up to sift through the mud for relics—all denoted a scene of frenetic activity.

'Careful there. Dig carefully. We don't want you to crash into some old artefacts,' shouted one of his men to those digging.

The men from the ASI were on tenterhooks as they had to constantly monitor those digging the trenches. It was a delicate activity, and any inattentiveness or negligence could lead to the loss of priceless artefacts. The middle-aged, bespectacled gentleman was seen walking around, gently encouraging the workers to be careful while they dug. He was rarely still but flitted from trench to trench, overseeing the activity. A cry from the young man manning the large sieve got his attention and he wended his way there.

'What is it, Chimanlal?'

'Sir,' said the young man, his eyes shining with excitement, 'I thought you might be interested in this.'

He held up a muddy rectangular object in his hand. The middle-aged gentleman took it from him and then started rubbing away the mud with a piece of rag that Chimanlal handed to him. As he rubbed, his eyes lit up. There seemed to be some markings on the object. Markings that seemed remarkably similar to hieroglyphics and Sumerian, at that.

The gentleman finally concluded the cleaning and gazed down at the rectangular tablet* he held in his hands. *It is Sumerian for sure*, he decided. *I wonder what it says and how it came to be here, all the way from Sumeria.*

---

* A similar tablet, discovered off the coast of Bombay, is housed in the Manuscripts Division of the BORI.

Chapter One

The Lesser of Two Evils

1795 BCE, (卄ıᴇ耳ı⊕), Rohitaka

The early morning sun shone fiercely on the brown and parched land. It was the middle of summer and the heat from the sun was already driving people into their dwellings. The young man stood in a stream, the last remnant of what had once been a mighty river. He faced east towards the sun with his eyes closed, as he muttered prayers to the Sun God. He bent down periodically to fill his cupped palms with water as he offered libations to the God who was the source of energy to our planet.

All around him, similar scenes were playing out across the land as men welcomed the dawn of a new day. Finishing his prayers, the young man waded through the stream and then trudged over the hard, packed clay of the dried river bed to the bank. *We ought to change what we call the riverbank*, he thought. *The river hasn't flown through here in decades.*

He reached the banks and changed out of his wet garments into fresh clothes that he had left there. *I really don't need to do it though. The way Surya Bhagavan* is beating down upon us, my garments are almost dry.* He then chuckled to himself. *Perhaps we ought to be propitiating God Varuna† to send us more rain so that the river can flow again as it did all those years ago.*

He blew his cheeks out in frustration as the heat bouncing off the ground enveloped him. Sweat poured down his body in raging torrents. *There really is no use in having a bath*, he thought disgustedly. *What is the use of taking a bath twice a day when I start sweating almost immediately?* He scrunched his eyes to avoid the glare of the rays reflecting off the surrounding land. He could already see heat waves shimmering ahead of him. The houses seemed to be undulating into a strange, macabre dance in the heat. He squinted through the waves at the biggest structure in town, the large temple tank.

The temple tank and the surrounding area had once been the centre of activity in the town. That had been another day and age, when the great river had flowed full, up to the banks. When water from the river used to be channeled via canals and terracotta pipes by the ingenious engineers, right through the town and into the houses. The tank, he had been told, used to be full of people, both young and old, though primarily monopolized by the young. While it was supposed to be used strictly for

---

* Sun God
† Rain God

washing one's feet before entering the temple, the priests had been indulgent, allowing young people to use it for sport and relief from the heat.

All this was hearsay, of course. He had heard it from his grandfather who, in turn, had been told by his grandfather and so on. The tank had been dry for well over two hundred years, its use now a distant, somewhat wistful memory, passed down from generation to generation.

It was a wistfulness tinged with regret and the knowledge that it would never again be the way it was reputed to have been in its heyday. The tank, now a hollow shell, served as a playground for local kids and a haven for young couples seeking privacy in its nooks and niches after dusk.

The young man walked past the structure on his way up to the walled, inner city where he lived. People on the streets recognized him and shouted out their salutations or bowed to him as he passed by. He made his way through the bazaar that lined the street leading up to the inner city. The shops were set in recesses along two broad colonnaded structures. These had been built by the rulers, keeping in mind the weather conditions prevalent here, with extremes of temperature, both during summer and winter. During the winter, fires were lit at intervals to heat up the interiors of the promenade, which was walled on all sides except the one open to customers. The structure was made of stones piled nearly a meter thick, to act as insulation against the heat in summer and to retain the warmth during winter.

The young man noticed that the customers had already thinned out, with citizens hurrying to their homes to beat the heat. He could see many traders preparing to shut shop for the rest of the day. The shops would reopen in the evening once the sun went down and the heat became somewhat bearable for folks to venture out again.

As the young man approached the gates of the inner citadel, the guards atop the walls signalled to their comrades behind the gates. With a coordinated effort, they heaved at the ropes, making the gates swing open almost magically as the young man drew near. The inside of the citadel was laid out, like the rest of the town, in rectangular sections. At one time, there were gardens with paths laid out around them. Those gardens were but a memory, given the lack of water. The 'gardens' were now merely bricked sections with clay statues of the various Gods and the kings placed in them.

The young man smiled wryly as he walked past one such statue. It was of a fierce-looking warrior holding a sword and sporting a simple band on his head. It was his grandfather, and he smiled because his grandfather's physique was nowhere close to the one that the artisan had given him. He was thin and wiry, but the artisan had let his imagination run wild, giving the statue a particularly muscular appearance while retaining the facial exactness.

The perks of being the ruler, he thought. *I wonder if they will have my statue somewhere once I am done with my life.* He actually couldn't care less whether they did or not. *What interest do I have in what they do once I am gone?*

He saw the head priest entering the palace doors, accompanied by a delegation of what he surmised were traders. The priest, noticing him, stopped at the door. The traders followed suit. The young man neared them and bent to touch the priest's feet in respect. The priest placed his hand on the youngster's head in a gesture as old as this land and, having uttered his benediction, raised the young man up.

'Hot day, isn't it?' he asked, perspiring freely.

'I seem to have forgotten when it was not hot,' said the young man.

The priest laughed. 'Arjuna, you at least have the advantage of youth. When you get to my age, the body seems to like a temperature that we get for only a couple of months of the year.'

Arjuna laughed politely, and then asked, 'Are you all going to see the king?'

'Yes, we are going to see your father,' the priest said, indicating towards the traders. 'They have a particularly tricky issue, for which they need to see the king,' he added.

'May I come along?' Arjuna asked.

'Of course, my boy,' replied the priest.

The young man led the way into the palace and to the council room. While he was grandiosely called the king, his father was more like the head of the ruling council, which was made up of the chiefs of several principalities all around their town.

The council room was empty, except for a couple of scribes diligently etching onto clay tablets with sharpened styluses. Arjuna told the man guarding the council room to inform the king that the head priest had come seeking an audience with him.

In a short while, a distinguished individual with white hair and a trimmed white beard, with a golden band on his head, signifying his office, entered the room. The men in the room bowed to the king, except for the priest, to whom the king offered a bow. The king looked surprised to see his son in the room but took his seat, gesturing for the others to do the same around him.

'I heard that you wanted to see me, *Bhagawan*[*],' he asked, looking at the priest.

'They,' he showed his hand towards the traders, 'needed to see you. I just accompanied them, *Rajan*[†].'

The king looked towards the others enquiringly. One of the traders, the chief of the guild by the looks of it, cleared his throat and said, 'Rajan, we are in trouble.'

The king waited for him to continue. After a brief glance at the others, the man resumed.

'This place is dying,' he spread his hands out to indicate them all. 'We, are dying. We have somehow kept going for the last few decades, even as the river has progressively dried up. We are struggling with agriculture, and it is getting tough to even raise cattle.'

The king sighed. He knew. They all knew. The river's drying up had turned a once vibrant, rich city into an impoverished town. Many of its citizens had moved out in search of a living. The traders had to travel farther and farther from the city to be able to find buyers for their meagre produce.

'Yes, I know. But what can we do?'

'We need to think of the unthinkable, Rajan,' said another guild member.

---

[*] A term of respect
[†] King

The king looked at the speaker, a large man with powerful arms. It was representative of the blacksmith's guild.

'No,' he remonstrated.

'Yes, Rajan.'

'I repeat, No! The reason we have been ascendant over all the other states is because of the special advantage that we have from our wonder metal.'

'We don't have to sell our technology, Rajan, but we can sell some of the instruments of war . . .'

'No!' came the king's vehement shout once again.

'Rajan,' said the priest gently. 'We have only two options left.'

The king looked at him with enquiry.

'We might have to seriously think about leaving the city. But . . .'

'But?'

'But before we do that, we might have one last throw of the dice.'

'And that is?'

'We have had a representation from our Sumerian friends.'

'That again?' asked the king, exasperated.

'Yes Rajan. I know that they have been after us to share the technology. But this time, they aren't asking for technology. Just the fruits of it.'

The king stayed silent, musing.

'We really do need this, Rajan,' persisted the blacksmith.

'Rajan,' said the priest. 'What use is our technology if our city dies? If we don't have enough wealth to safeguard it?

Things change. Circumstances change. When the decision was taken, several centuries ago, to not share our technology, it made sense then. Not anymore. In any case, we will only be providing the instruments of war to a kingdom that is far from our own. There isn't any danger of the weapons being used against us.'

The king was lost in thought for a while. Conversation in the council chambers petered out slowly and then died out completely as the others waited for a decision from their ruler. The king was sunk deep in thought, his eyes closed, his fingers steepled together. Eventually, he opened his eyes, sighed and nodded. 'All right, I don't like it, but this is just a short-term solution in my opinion.'

The guild members smiled, their faces lighting up in hope. The distant future might still be dark, but there was light in the near term. And men can't live their lives worrying about the distant future.

They trooped out of the citadel, a spring in their footsteps. They were going to make the Sumerians very happy.

Chapter Two

End of the Road

1794 BCE, (𒐏𒈦𒐋𒅀𒁁)
Māt Akkadī, Babylon

The travellers made it up the hill and could, at last, catch a glimpse of their destination. They were a mixed group of traders and soldiers, yet surprisingly similarly attired. They were wearing the long, loose robes, characteristic of this region, with turbans on their heads, one end of which was wrapped around their faces. They came from a hot land themselves, but compared to the heat here, theirs could have been the mountaintops of the Himalayas. It was a searing, dry heat that sucked the moisture from their bodies and their breaths.

It had taken them close to eight months to get here from their home, nearly two and a half thousand miles away. Their route had taken them through the forbidding Upariśyena* mountains and the land of the Avestans.

---

* Now known as the Hindu Kush mountains.

9

While this was a very old trade route and had been used for millennia, it was still a lonely route for the most part. They had to fight off hunger, cold and raiders, sometimes all at the same time. They had, however, not lost any soldiers in these skirmishes. Their weapons saw to that. The first contact that any enemy had with their weaponry seemed to miraculously teach them the values of prudence, brotherhood and peace.

They had only managed to cover an average of a dozen miles every day. *Given the treacherousness of the path and the need for constant vigilance against raiders and dacoits, I should think that we have made good time*, thought Arjuna.

He had cajoled his father, the king, into letting him go on the trip. His life, till then, had been a sheltered one. For the most part, there was peace in his lands, and while he had been trained in the various martial arts, he had never experienced war. For a young man of his age and disposition, that chafed. He had always wanted to go out and see the world. It had been his invariable practice to seek out traders and listen to their tales when they returned from trips to faraway lands.

However, he had noticed that, over time, the advent of traders from distant kingdoms to his corner of the world seemed to be decreasing, and with it, the chances of hearing about those lands. He had thus jumped at the opportunity to take a consignment of weapons to Sumeria along with the traders. While his father had sent a trusted sergeant, Shrutasena, as the leader of the pack, he had prevailed upon the king into allowing him to accompany the group as a member of Shrutasena's troops.

The king had instructed Shrutasena to not go easy on the prince, and he had obliged. The sergeant had seen to it that Arjuna had earned his keep along the journey. He was usually the first up and the last to go to bed. He was the one who had to prepare the camp and to vacate it as well. He helped in gathering wood and cow-dung for the fire. He was also in charge of hunting fresh game for food. He polished the swords and spears, mended the bowstrings and was generally made to do almost everything that a young cadet would do.

Arjuna had, however, proven himself in battle time after time. He was utterly fearless, perhaps an advantage conferred on youth, and had become very accomplished with the sword. He had been at the forefront of every single skirmish and had earned the respect of the other soldiers. They had begun the journey treating him as a nuisance to be tolerated and had resented his being a part of the entourage just because his father happened to be the king. By the end of the journey, he had become one of them, a proven soldier and warrior, and someone they knew they could depend on to have their backs in the midst of battle.

The long journey had also melted any residual fat off their bodies and left the soldiers in peak condition. The traders looked a little worse for wear, but they had done this trip many times, and the sight of the city seemed to perk up their spirits. The Sumerians who had come with them pointed excitedly towards the city and egged their horses on into a trot, their homesickness clearly evident.

The Rohitaka traders and soldiers followed their example, and it was a short while later that they came up to the eastern gates of the fabled city of Babylon. The city was situated on the banks of the Euphrates River, with the river forming a natural barrier on one side. Water from the river was fed through canals into the moat all around the city. Bridges that could be raised or lowered gave access to the city across the moats.

The bridges were down at this time of the day, with soldiers stationed at either end to carefully vet those entering the city. The visitors were stopped by the soldiers, but a few whispered words from the leader of the Sumerian delegation, followed by the flashing of a clay tablet with some sort of an insignia imprinted on it, led to the soldiers moving aside hastily. The group trotted their horses across the bridge and through the eastern gates, into the city.

The fabled city of Babylon! Arjuna dug his heels into the flanks of his horse, urging it into a gallop, his excitement barely contained. He had heard so much about the place and was eager to get his first look at it. As they entered, the skyline was dominated by the towering *ziggurat*[*] at the centre of the city. Arjuna's eyes widened as he noticed the scale of the building. *And I thought that our temple and the tank were huge, but this!*

Their Sumerian guide, Sabium, who was roughly of the same age as Arjuna and with whom he had developed a friendship over the course of their long journey, pointed

---

[*] Babylonian temple

out the temple with some pride, saying, 'That is the main temple to Bal* Marduk, the patron deity of our city. It is called the Etemenanki. There is a shrine for the Bal at the top of the temple. Huge, isn't it?'

Arjuna looked in awe at the structure. The ziggurat seemed to have multiple levels. Each level had a profusion of trees and shrubs growing in it. He could see a path that seemed to wind its way in a spiral up the different levels, but it was soon lost to his view. From afar, the gardens on the ziggurat appeared ethereal, as if they were floating in air. He shared his thoughts with his friend.

'Those gardens look like they are just hanging up there.'

Sabium laughed delightedly. 'Yes. We call them the Hanging Gardens of Babylon.'

'Very original,' said Arjuna dryly. 'Couldn't you guys come up with a better name for it?'

Sabium shrugged his shoulders and grinned.

'Is that the only temple for him?'

'Oh no, if you look to your left, to the south, you will see another temple, called the Esagila.'

Arjuna turned and could make out the very top of a smaller temple. 'That is much smaller, isn't it?'

'In comparison to the Etemenanki, yes. Heck, everything else in the city is dwarfed by that! But the temple complex itself is bigger than that of the Etemenanki. I shall take you there later this evening,' said Sabium.

They rode through the city in a wide semi-circle around the Etemenanki. To Arjuna, the city seemed to

---

* Lord

be overflowing with people. They passed through wide
bazaars filled with men and women from many different
regions. He could make out the Chinese and even some of
his fellow men from Bharatavarsha. He, however, observed
many whom he grouped under the broad category of
Yavanas—a catch-all term his countrymen used for anyone
arriving from the lands west of their own.

He saw a variety of attire: loose, flowing robes favoured
by people from desert regions and more tailored tunics
worn by others, likely hailing from colder climes. The
bazaars themselves were filled with wares that included
food and vegetables, toys, clothing, pots and pans, gems
and jewellery. Babylon was famed for its gem trade with
their artisans having achieved a high degree of versatility
and precision in working with small stones. The land itself
was bereft of large stones and rocks and hence, pebbles
and gems were gathered, nurtured and worked upon with
a great deal of passion and care.

There was all manner of food being sold, steamed and
fried fish and chicken being among the favourites. Kids
ran in and out between the carts in the bazaar, playing with
little balls, unaware or simply uncaring of the hazards of
being trampled underfoot by horses or chariots. A young
street urchin tugged at Arjuna's leg, trying to interest
him in some esoteric dancer-shaped clay statue. Arjuna
had a hard time convincing the lad that his interests lay
elsewhere.

He noticed several mounted policemen strategically
positioned along the path, maintaining some semblance
of order, in an otherwise seemingly chaotic place. He was
struck by the size of their horses.

'The horses here are much bigger than those in my land,' Arjuna remarked to Sabium. 'I think I shall take a few of them on my way back to Rohitaka,' he added.

They eventually arrived at what appeared to be a guesthouse and, following Sabium's lead, dismounted from their horses. Arjuna stretched his arms and back, easing the stiffness in his muscles.

'You will stay here tonight,' said Sabium. 'Tomorrow, we shall go to meet the king.'

'Will our goods be safe here?' asked Shrutasena.

'You noticed the policemen along the way?' asked Sabium with a smile.

Shrutasena nodded.

'They notice everything. The city thrives on trade. Robbery is very bad for business and our king is keenly aware of that. You can rest assured, no one will touch your belongings here.' He led them into the guesthouse and got them settled in a few rooms adjacent to one another on the ground floor.

Arjuna took Sabium aside and asked, 'Hey, I thought you said we could go to the Esagila temple in the evening?'

Sabium grinned. 'I will be back in the evening. But I need to go now and meet my family. It has been a long time, you know.'

'Your parents?'

'First my parents and siblings, yes.'

'And then?'

Sabium's grin widened. 'There is a girl,' he said with a wink.

'Ah-ha!'

'She would have missed me terribly.'

'You think?' teased Arjuna. 'Maybe, she has given up on you and found someone else in the meantime.'

Sabium's smile faded, replaced by a look of concern.

Arjuna laughed. 'Oh, I was just teasing, my friend. Perhaps she has been whiling away her time, thinking longing thoughts about you and writing some bad poetry.'

'I should certainly hope so,' Sabium replied with a sheepish grin.

'All right, I shall see you this evening, then,' said Arjuna, before Sabium proceeded on his way.

The evening saw the little group of Bharatiyas led by their guide, Sabium, entering the Esagila temple complex. The complex was huge, with the main temple at the centre. There were several smaller structures inside the complex.

Arjuna pointed at them and asked, 'What are those?'

'Shrines to various Gods,' said Sabium.

The complex itself was ringed on the inside by long, colonnaded corridors. The visitors approached the columns and could see the frescoes, reliefs and paintings in bright, vivid colours adorning the pillars and the walls.

'This is gorgeous,' muttered one of the soldiers, as he drew in his breath sharply.

'So, what is the story of your Bal Marduk?' asked Arjuna. 'I mean, is he your main God? The Creator?'

Sabium paused before replying. 'He is somewhat akin to your own Brahma.'

'The Creator then?' Arjuna asked.

'Something like that. According to our story, there was undifferentiated water first, swirling in chaos. Out of this water were born two Gods, the sweet Apsu and the salty, bitter water goddess, Tiamat. From their union were born the younger Gods,' Sabium replied.

'Interesting. And then?' Arjuna asked, eager for more details.

'Well, Apsu decided to kill the younger Gods because they were disrupting his work. But Tiamat heard about his plans and told the younger Gods, who then killed Apsu.'

Arjuna pursed his lips dubiously, but didn't say anything.

'Anyway,' continued Sabium, 'Tiamat, on the advice of her minister, Quingu, then tried to kill the younger Gods. But one of them, our Bal Marduk, killed her with an arrow which split her in two. From her eyes, flowed the waters of the Tigris and the Euphrates.'

'So Marduk then becomes the God of everyone?' asked Shrutasena.

'Yes. From Tiamat's corpse, he created the heavens and the earth.'

'So, what about us humans then?'

'He used that useless Quingu's corpse for that.'

'Not so useless after all, eh?', asked Arjuna with a smile.

Sabium laughed.

'Our creation story is not this definitive', said Arjuna.

'I thought Brahma was your Creator and created everything.'

Arjuna shook his head and said, 'The oldest story we have begins somewhat similar to yours. Where there is nothingness. From that nothingness, everything seems to have been created.'

'But surely, someone must have created that nothingness? Some God? Brahma maybe?'

'Nope,' Arjuna said, shaking his head. 'The writer leaves our creation story with a question, asking, "who knows where the Gods came from?" Even they came after the creation.'

Sabium scratched his beard, now trimmed, giving him a very dapper appearance.

'So, you don't have a God who actually created everything?'

'Not that I know of.'

'Hmmm . . .'

'Anyway,' said Arjuna, changing the topic. 'Did you meet that girl of yours?' A sly smile spread across Sabium's face as he bent low and began telling Arjuna about his meeting with his girl. They continued their walk around the temple with Sabium pointing out various frescoes and reliefs of interest. Shrutasena, Arjuna and the soldiers were captivated by the beauty and size of the temple. The traders, on the other hand, had been there before and were more perfunctory in their appreciation. One can appreciate the same thing only so many times, was their rather mundane conclusion.

They eventually left the area, and while everyone else voted to go back to the guesthouse and get some rest, Arjuna, Sabium and Shrutasena went down to the river that ran to the south of the temple complex. Boats, some with single sails and others powered by oars, were plying up and down the river.

'Mother Euphrates,' said Sabium reverently.

Arjuna and Shrutasena looked at each other in surprise and then glanced back at Sabium.

'What?' he asked.

'You called the river "mother".'

'Yes. We all do. She is one of the two mothers of our land. Why are you so surprised? You folks do too. I have heard you refer to two of your rivers as Mother Sarasvati and Mother Ganga.'

'We thought we were the only ones who did that,' said Shrutasena, a bit sheepishly.

'We might have more in common culturally with you than we thought,' added Arjuna.

As they exited the temple gates, they noticed a line of three boats, flying what Sabium identified as the Royal Insignia, gently docking at the bottom of the steps leading to the river.

'The queen,' whispered Sabium, quickly going down on his knees and bending low, with his head touching the ground. He gestured to the other two to do the same.

Arjuna sneaked a quick peek at the royal personages disembarking from the boats. He saw a woman in very expensive-looking clothes, obviously the queen, in the middle of the group with various other women with tight-fitting tunics and veiled faces bunched around her. There was another ring of men around this inner group, ensuring that people kept away from them.

The leader of this outer escort of men kept shouting something at periodic intervals.

'What's he saying?' asked Arjuna in a whisper.

'He is warning people that the queen is coming, and asking them to bow down to her,' Sabium muttered back.

'Can I take a look?'

'Absolutely not,' said Sabium in a most insistent tone.

Arjuna, however, was ever curious. He had never seen another queen apart from his own mother, of course. As the entourage passed them, he quickly lifted his head to steal a glance at the queen. That was his undoing. A soldier passing by brought the end of his lance down sharply on Arjuna's back. Arjuna reacted predictably. He twisted his torso and knocked the lance away with his left hand while grabbing hold of it with his right and pulling. Arjuna was a strong lad. Things just naturally came into his hands when he pulled at them. The lance did likewise. The enraged soldier grabbed at the lance with both hands while simultaneously trying to land a kick with his leg. Arjuna loosened his grip on the lance, causing the man to fall backwards just as his left foot was raised to kick.

There was only one possible conclusion. The man went down hard on his back. Seeing their comrade's fate, two other soldiers came quickly to his aid with lances extended. Arjuna spun around between them, bent low and delivered quick blows to their stomachs. The soldiers grunted and doubled over. A blow to the solar plexus tends to do that to men.

The entourage had now stopped moving. The inner circle of bodyguards tightened around the queen while the outer circle swarmed all over Arjuna. He put up a brave fight, but eventually, the sheer number of men coming at him overwhelmed him. He was pinned to the ground, face down. He heard Sabium apologizing profusely. At least, that's what he thought he was doing. The only word that he could make out in the tirade in the Akkadian language was 'sorry'.

He was pulled roughly to his feet while men held his arms in vice-like grips. The outer ring parted and one of the veiled women came towards him; her eyes blazing in anger. *Pretty, green eyes*, thought Arjuna even as the woman raised her hand and slapped him across his face. Arjuna stood there, unflinching. This seemed to goad the woman into a frenzy as she repeated the dose, asking him questions in a staccato.

Arjuna could taste some blood at the corners of his mouth. He heard Sabium saying something, perhaps trying to answer the questions. A stiff breeze seemed to have sprung up and that, along with the exertion of slapping Arjuna, broke the veil free from its clasp on her head. Arjuna found himself looking at the most beautiful woman that he had ever seen. Her doe-shaped green eyes, ablaze with anger, were set underneath finely shaped eyebrows. Long, curled lashes swept down over the eyes. The ones at the bottom touching her cheekbones.

Her nose was thin and straight but had an alluring tilt at the tip. Her lips were soft and full, her lower lip caught endearingly between her even teeth, except for one snaggle-tooth that enhanced her beauty. Damp tendrils of hair clung to her face like vines wrapping around an alabaster statue. Annoyed as they fell across her eyes, she pursed her lips and blew a puff of air at them.

Even as Arjuna let his eyes play over her face, the woman swiftly reattached the veil with the clasp, snapped

a curt order at the soldiers before hustling the group and
the queen toward a waiting chariot.

The soldiers, however, dragged Arjuna along with
them. Arjuna looked back at Sabium and Shrutasena.
The sergeant had a helpless look on his face while Sabium
seemed absolutely petrified.

Chapter Three

His Royal Highness

There were guards everywhere, and those escorting him led him down a flight of stairs to an underground dungeon, shoving him none too gently into a dingy cell. After all, they were still smarting from the blows that he had managed to land on them.

The cell itself was small, perhaps eight feet by ten feet, and there were already a dozen people in it. The place reeked of urine and faeces, and Arjuna noticed that one corner of the cell remained conspicuously unoccupied. That corner, it appeared, was the unofficial toilet which the inhabitants of this cozy world used to relieve themselves. Flies flitted over the faeces and roamed around the cell, spreading the filth.

Arjuna wrinkled his nose and tried to get as far away from that corner as possible. A couple of drunks protested when he squeezed in behind them, but fell silent the moment they noticed his physique backed up by the scowl etched on his face.

Night was spent in those cramped quarters, and morning brought no respite from the miasma that clung to the place. Arjuna desperately wanted to relieve himself but decided not to risk going over to the far side of the cell. As he was wondering about how to get out of there, he heard footsteps. A fat man with unkempt, dirty hair and a scraggy beard opened the cell door and motioned to Arjuna to get up and follow him.

Arjuna pushed the drunks off him and then made his way out of the cell. The fat guard locked the doors and then went up the stairs. Arjuna followed. The harsh light of the early morning sun hit Arjuna's eyes at the top of the stairs, and he squinted to adjust them to the light.

'Arjuna!' He heard Sabium's voice.

Arjuna flashed a grin but quickly wore a neutral expression when he caught the stern look on Shrutasena's face. He noticed that there were a couple of other official-looking men with Sabium, and the prison guards were being rather obsequious towards them. The two men barked a series of orders at the guards who bowed down to them and then gestured to Arjuna that he was free to go.

Arjuna heaved a sigh of relief as he joined his friends. 'Boy, am I glad to be out of that!'

'I think you had better stay a few feet behind us. You stink,' said Sabium in his forthright manner, holding his nostrils tight with his fingers.

Arjuna glanced at Shrutasena, and while the older man was not making an issue of the assault on his olfactory senses, he did keep a distance and had turned his face away from him. Arjuna grinned and decided to be nice to his friends by walking a few paces behind them.

He asked Sabium the question that had been uppermost on his mind.

'Oh, they?' asked Sabium, pointing to the official looking men who were striding ahead of them. 'They are the king's personal bodyguards. I had to find some way to get you out of there. So I went to the palace. I do have some clout here being part of the traders guild, you know? I met the general and told him that you were a prince and that you had come here with the weapons from Meluhha. He sent these men with me to help get your release.'

Arjuna gave a nod of gratitude, then asked, 'Meluhha?'

'That's what we call Bharat! Anyway, we had better get back to the guest house quickly. Have a bath. Have a couple of baths, actually. You will need them to get rid of that smell. We can't have you stinking up the palace.'

'The palace?'

'Why yes. I told you last evening that we would be going there this morning. We are going to meet the king, and you are going to personally present the weapons to him.'

The palace of the Babylonian king, Sin-Muballit, was an impressive structure made of brick, mud and wood. Stone was scarce in this part of the world, and hence most structures were a combination of these three materials. The Palace was three-storeys high and spread across an acre of land.

Sabium, Shrutasena and Arjuna, followed by men leading donkeys bearing the bags filled with weapons, reached the palace gates and were let in by men waiting there to greet them. Sabium had already sent word of their arrival. It was apparent that this was an event that had some significance. As they entered the palace enclosure, Arjuna was surprised to see the number of men gathered beneath a large open tent that had been set up in the palace grounds.

In the middle of the tent was a large throne and on it sat the king of all Babylonia, Sin-Muballit. The king was a man in his mid-forties, overweight, with unhealthy spots on his face. He looked sickly and ill. *Possibly a trifle too fond of somarasa**, thought Arjuna. Near the king, stood a well-muscled man with narrow eyes and bushy eyebrows.

Sabium, who kept up a steady stream of whispers, supplying Arjuna with tidbits of information about those present, said, 'That well-muscled oaf standing next to the king is Dagan, head of his bodyguards.'

'I take it you don't like him?' asked Arjuna.

'He has been troubling Mylitta.'

'Who?'

'Mylitta. My girl. The one I was telling you about.'

'Aah. Troubling? In what way?'

'Paying attention to her,' said Sabium shortly.

'Ahha! A rival for her affections. No wonder you are annoyed with him.'

'Rival my foot! She loves me. Not that big, dumb lump of meat,' he said, disdainfully.

---

* Liquor

By then, they had reached the centre of the tent. Sabium was presented to the king first, followed by the others, starting with Arjuna. Sabium delivered a lengthy speech before presenting him, and Arjuna quickly asked what he had said.

'I told him that you are a prince from Bharat,' he said.

Arjuna quickly turned back towards the king, bowed and then indicated to the man leading the donkey pack to bring over an elaborately wrapped package. The man handed the package to Arjuna, who then bowed once more and held it out in front of him.

'A gift from our king, my father, to you and the great people of Babylon, Sire,' he said, haltingly, in Akkadian.

Sin-Muballit looked pleased at a foreigner speaking his tongue. The king smiled, nodded his head and asked one of his men to accept the gift. Arjuna quickly untied the knot securing the package and took out a large iron sword, its grip and pommel encrusted with gold, enamel, and agate.

The king's eyes lit up when he saw this. He stood up, shooing away the man he had originally tasked with accepting the gift. He got off his throne and walked slowly towards Arjuna, his eyes fixed on the gift. *Like a child who has seen a toy shop for the first time*, thought Arjuna as he watched the king come closer. He then raised the sword with both hands, bowed his head to it, and presented it to the king. Sin-Muballit's eyes glowed with pleasure as he hefted the sword reverently. He ran his fingers up the blade, and then his eyes followed his fingers to the guard and from there to the grip and pommel. He gasped as the beauty of the workmanship hit his eyes.

Sin-Muballit transferred the sword to his right hand and held it the way a sword is meant to be held. He gave a couple of experimental swishes of the blade. Sabium and Arjuna prudently stepped back from this warlike demonstration.

'Careful, Sire,' said Arjuna. 'The edges are very sharp.' The king only smiled in return as he continued swishing the sword.

A strapping, clean-shaven, young lad of about seventeen, standing next to him, asked Arjuna, 'How do you speak our tongue?'

'I learnt it from him on our long journey here,' he said, indicating Sabium. He spoke haltingly, searching for words as any new speaker of a language does. 'I do not speak it very well and can only understand if it is spoken slowly. At least some of it.'

The young man nodded and then noticed that Sabium was bowing to him and tugging on his hand to do the same.

Arjuna decided to follow suit, and as he bowed, he whispered, 'Who is he?'

'I am the prince actually,' replied the young man with a smile on his face. 'And you don't need to bow to me. You are a prince, too, after all.'

Arjuna smiled at him and held out his hand. The two princes gripped each other's arms.

'My name is Sin-Murabi,' said the prince, 'but you can just call me Murabi.' Arjuna nodded.

'So, when are you going to show us all the weapons or have you only brought a ceremonial sword with you?'

Arjuna, in response, turned and clapped his hands at the attendants. They started unloading the bundles from the donkeys and then placed them in a line in front of the king and Prince Murabi. At a word from Arjuna, they slit the ropes that tied the bundles. As the bundles fell back to reveal their goods, a collective gasp arose from the crowd.

The bundles revealed numerous swords, spear tips, spears, arrow tips and battle axes made of iron. The crowd moved nearer to get a closer look at the weaponry. Murabi stooped down and picked up a battle axe. He ran his thumb over the edge and winced as the sharp edge drew blood. A smear of red appeared on his thumb, and Murabi brought it up to his mouth to suck the blood, grinning awkwardly at Arjuna the entire time.

'I told you it was sharp,' said Arjuna.

Murabi grinned again and then hefted the axe a couple of times. 'How good is it against our armour?' he asked.

Arjuna looked uncertainly at Sabium. 'What was that last word? I didn't quite understand that.'

'Armour,' translated Sabium, his hands mimicking it being worn on the upper part of his body.

'Aah!' Arjuna smiled in response. He picked up an axe and walked towards one of the guards. Then, turning back, he asked Sabium in his own tongue. 'Can you ask this man to take off his armour?'

Sabium obliged, and the man gave a quick glance towards prince Murabi. Then, satisfied that there would be no repercussions from this act, he removed his armour.

'Can you ask him to put it on a wooden post?'

Sabium translated, and in a short time, two men arrived with a wooden post and some crowbars made of bronze. They dug a hole and affixed the post into it. The soldier then walked over and put his armour over the post.

Arjuna turned to look back at the prince, checking if he had his attention. He needn't have worried. He had the attention of everyone gathered there.

He turned, hefted the axe a couple of times to get used to its weight and feel, and then, in a flash, his hand darted back and forth. The sun's rays glinted off the blade of the axe as it rotated and whistled through the intervening distance to the post and embedded itself with a 'thraaackkk' into the wood, having sheared through the armour like a hot knife through butter.

The crowd gasped as the implications of the demonstration sank in. Murabi was the first to react as he walked over languidly to the post, and holding the handle, pulled the axe out, not without some difficulty, since the weapon had been buried fairly deeply into the post. He examined the destruction of the armour closely, then looked wonderingly at the blade, which showed hardly a scratch.

He slowly raised the axe aloft in his hands and gave a whoop of delight and some sort of a battle cry or at least that's what Arjuna thought it was. The cry was taken up by all the men and women gathered there.

Sabium came over and slapped Arjuna on his back with joy. It was then that a voice cut through the tumult. A woman's voice. A veiled woman's voice to be precise.

Everyone stopped to look at her, but she had eyes only for Arjuna. *Those green eyes again,* thought Arjuna.

'What did she say?' he asked Sabium. 'She speaks too fast. I can't make out what she says.'

'She says that's all very well but in a real fight, the heavier weapon will be very unwieldy against the lighter bronze sword.'

'Is that so? Hand me an iron sword, will you?'

Sabium fetched an iron sword and handed it to Arjuna, who hefted it in his hand and then swished it around a couple of times. The muscles in his arms rippled. The woman looked at him and then laughed scornfully. She unsheathed her sword and, holding it in her left hand, walked towards him.

The assembled crowd automatically formed a circle around them. *It doesn't matter where a fight happens, the crowd always forms a circle,* thought Arjuna abstractedly, even as he tried to pick up some hints, from her movements, on how the woman would fight.

She walked towards him. No, she strutted towards him and then suddenly leapt to her right and tried to land a blow with her sword arm, her left arm. Arjuna, however, was ready for such a move. He turned sideways and let the sword pass him by harmlessly, and then, negligently slapped away her sword with his own.

This seemed to infuriate the woman as she launched a fast and furious attack. Her sword was a blur as she swished and swung her weapon at him. Arjuna was reduced to making a series of defensive jabs, turning one way and another to keep away from the reach of her sword. He soon found himself at the edge of the circle, and someone from the crowd tripped him. Arjuna landed with a thud on his back and found his opponent standing above him with her sword held loosely in her hand, pointing down towards him. She then gestured with the sword for him to get up as she walked back towards the centre of the ring.

Arjuna stood up and brushed some of the mud off his garments and his arms and then moved towards her. As she again started her sword flourishes, Arjuna moved forward to counter them, instead of merely reacting defensively. Iron contacted bronze again and again, and eventually, Arjuna, having decided that he had had enough of this, swung his sword with all his might. Iron won. The bronze sword shattered as the iron blade sliced through the top half of her sword. The piece that had broken off, flew and landed near the edge of the circle of spectators, causing the men in the immediate vicinity to step back hastily. The woman's eyes followed the arc of the broken-off piece, then swivelled to look disbelievingly at the remnants of the sword in her hand. She examined the broken edge of the sword closely before her eyes sought the weapon Arjuna held.

A harsh, loud laugh broke through the tumult of the crowd. Dagan looked particularly happy at the fate that had befallen the head of the queen's bodyguards. She looked first at Dagan with fury in her eyes and then at Arjuna. Eventually, she bowed her head to him with ill grace, threw her sword down between them and stormed off.

Chapter Four

A Secret Meeting

That same evening, roughly fifty miles south of Babylon, just off the road linking the city of Isin to Lasra, a few men were gathered at a drinking tavern. The tavern was a squat building with a sloping roof reaching low to the ground. Men had to stoop to enter it. Openings on three sides allowed air to circulate freely while the fourth was walled off and contained vats of liquor, from which the tavernkeeper dispensed the elixir to his thirsty customers. The inside was decidedly cooler, and customers usually preferred to sit there on the mats that had been spread on the floor.

The evening was cool enough for the men gathered there to be sitting on cots placed outside the tavern. The cots consisted of a wooden frame and used ropes made of natural fibres knitted across the frame. The road being deserted, clientele at the tavern was limited. There were only two other men in the tavern apart from the group sitting outside.

The men sitting outside, however, did not seem to be in any hurry to get drunk. A casual observer would make out that there were two distinct groups among them. A keen observer would have noticed the undercurrent of hostility and antagonism running through their interactions.

It was also obvious who the leaders of the two groups were. They were curiously alike and, at a passing glance, might even have passed off as siblings. Similarly attired in tight fitting garments, of average height and stocky but well-muscled, the two men sat opposite each other, flanked by their companions. They both had long hair that flowed down to their shoulders. The one difference, though, was in a wicked scar that ran along one man's face from forehead to chin. A scar that had not healed properly, with the skin raised along both edges of the scar, giving the owner a rather sinister appearance.

This was Erra and he hailed from Isin. Opposite him sat his counterpart, Zabaya, who hailed from Lasra. There was no love lost between the two kingdoms, and it showed in the behaviour of Erra and Zabaya towards one another. None of the bonhomie that manifests itself at places that serve liquor was on display. They sized each other up with distrust bordering on hostility; a distrust untempered by the undrunk wine in the wooden cups, which they held in their hands.

It was Erra who eventually broke the tense silence. He motioned to his men to move inside the tavern and leave them alone. Zabaya did likewise. The two opponents sat across from each other; their faces serious.

'Shall we salute Ninkasi*?' Erra asked, raising the cup. Zabaya raised his cup in response and took a sip from it, all the while locking eyes with Erra who followed suit.

'You called me here,' said Zabaya.

'For good reason.'

'Which is?'

Erra took a long sip from his cup and said, 'How is your kingdom doing?'

'About the same as yours,' said Zabaya guardedly.

Erra looked at him, his eyes calculating and then, as if having reached a decision, remarked, 'All right, let's stop fencing, shall we?'

'Your call,' said Zabaya.

'The king is old and probably dying.'

'Your king?' asked Zabaya.

'I meant the king of Babylon.'

'Aah. Yes, we did hear something about the fatso having spoilt his liver due to his devotion to Ninkasi.'

'Doesn't that suggest something to you?'

Zabaya took his time responding. 'It might suggest any number of things. Which particular suggestion do you have in mind?'

'The kingdom is vulnerable,' said Erra.

'And you think . . .' Zabaya left the question hanging in the air.

' . . . that we might be able to do something about it.'

'We?'

'Yes. We. Isin and Larsa.'

---

* Mesopotamian Goddess of beer and brewing

'Aah,' said Zabaya, a small smile appearing on his face. 'I suppose the humiliation from three years ago* still rankles, does it?'

'What do you think?' asked Erra.

Zabaya smirked.

'You folks might have forgotten your humiliation from eight years ago†, but we Isinians do not forget in a hurry. We have chafed at being the vassals of Sin-Muballit. I suppose you Larsans have accepted it?' Erra asked, a disparaging tone in his voice.

He could see Zabaya bristle at the not-so-subtle insult.

'We haven't forgotten our defeat either,' he hissed through clenched teeth.

'So then, will your king be willing to work with us?'

'You want us to go to battle together against Sin-Muballit? Doesn't he have a young son as well?'

'Yes, he does. But the lad is only seventeen and has never even seen battle. Their army is still much larger than both of ours combined,' said Zabaya.

'That is so,' said Erra, a note of caution in his voice. 'Which is why a direct attack against them will not be feasible.'

'What else can we do?'

'Subterfuge.'

Zabaya didn't respond to this immediately. He picked up the flagon of wine and filled Erra's cup before pouring his own. The tavern owner had placed roasted lamb chops

---

* Three years before this story, Sin-Muballit had conquered Isin.
† Eight years before the events of this story, Sin-Muballit had defeated Larsa.

in front of them. He picked up a leg, took a bite out of it and washed it down with a sip from the cup.

'I like it,' he said finally. 'Very little risk.'

'That's what we thought and that's the reason my king asked me to reach out to you.'

'What does king Enlil-Bani* want to do exactly?'

'Eliminate the Sin-Muballit family,' said Erra calmly.

Zabaya raised his eyebrows. 'Interesting,' he said. 'And how does your king propose to do that? We can hardly get into the palace and murder the lot of them?'

'We only need to kill the young prince Murabi. Old fatso won't last the year, the way he is drinking, or so my spies tell me.'

'All right. Let's say I take your proposal to my king Nur-Adad†. His question will be about how we are going to achieve it.'

'The New Year festival, my friend,' said Erra, a slow smile spreading across his face.

'Aah.'

'You know that the festival is two weeks from now, at the time of the new moon.‡'

Zabaya nodded.

'The royal family will have to come out of the palace. First to the shrine on top of the hanging gardens and then on to the Esagila. We will hit them en route.'

Zabaya pursed his lips.

'How many of us?'

---

* King of Isin
† King of Larsa
‡ The festival is held on the first new moon after the spring equinox.

'We can keep it small. Perhaps ten members each from my side and yours?'

'And how do we make our way out after we succeed in killing him. *If* we succeed in killing him,' Zabaya corrected himself.

'There will be a lot of confusion. We will have boats waiting on the Holy Euphrates.'

Zabaya looked unconvinced.

'What makes you think we can get near the royal family, even on New Year's Day? Won't there be bodyguards and soldiers to protect them?'

'There is a way to get close to them.'

'How?'

Erra leaned forward, put his head close to Zabaya's, whispering to him. Zabaya's face, which had registered a sceptical expression for most of the conversation, slowly began to lose its scepticism. At the end of it, as Erra leaned back, Zabaya broke into a wide smile, raised his cup, and said, 'The end of the Babylonian empire, my friend.'

'The end of the Babylonian empire,' said Erra, tossing the contents of the cup in one gulp.

Chapter Five

Preparations for the New Year

Arjuna's daily routine had been set for the past several days. The king had asked him and Shrutasena to help train his men in the use of the arms. Arjuna understood why. Iron weapons were much heavier than bronze, and as a result, the techniques used to wield them were also different. The added weight made it easier to be thrown off balance or to overextend, leaving one unable to recover as quickly as they could with a lighter weapon.

They would go to the palace every day and start drilling members of the elite palace guard in the use of the new weapons. Arjuna found that members of the queen's guard were also present during these drills and took active part in learning their usage. *She* was also there, of course. She still had that veil covering her face, like all members of the queen's guard, but she couldn't hide those eyes of hers. *Those vivid, expressive green eyes.*

He had finally found out her name. Lilith. He had asked her what it meant, and she had smiled with hard eyes and replied that it meant a demon or a ghost. *Well,*

*she certainly doesn't look like any demon or a ghost that I have
heard of.* He wasn't to know that she had been named thus
for her prowess in battle.

She trained a lot with Shrutasena, and Arjuna could
see from the look on the veteran soldier's face that he was
suitably impressed by her fighting abilities. She made it a
point to never learn directly from him, but he knew she
observed him as he taught the others. Later, he would
notice her practicing the moves when she thought he wasn't
watching. She didn't know that he was always watching
her. Or perhaps, she knew, like every woman does, when
someone finds them interesting, that he was watching her
and decided to feign ignorance.

She was easily the best fighter of the lot. The ease
with which she moved, and the overall flexibility and skill
that she demonstrated, spoke volumes about her fighting
abilities. He discerned soon enough that she had learnt all
that he had to teach her, and so, drawing up his courage,
requested her to assist him in teaching the others.

She merely nodded her head at him and then started
helping to train her own squad.

Arjuna was puzzled by her attitude towards him. He
sensed an animosity that couldn't be explained by their
earlier run-in at the temple, or the bout later in which she
had come out second best. If anything, he ought to have
harboured a grudge against her for slapping him at the
temple. He sensed an aloofness about Lilith, whenever
he found himself next to her. It was not like she was a
naturally introverted person. He had seen the way she
behaved with her team. He had observed a great deal of
easy camaraderie among them.

He tried to clear his head of the jumble of thoughts about her, as he refocused on his charges.

'Stop doing that!' he yelled at one person, practising with an iron spear. 'See how far ahead you have pushed your arms? It is heavy, so when you do that, your arms will tire, and the spear tip will dip downward. Try keeping your elbows to the side of your body. Let's go again,' he snapped as the soldier started to repeat the moves.

Arjuna noticed prince Murabi come out of the palace and walk leisurely towards him. The prince had also been practicing with the soldiers every day and Arjuna had been surprised to not see him this morning with the rest of the men. Murabi supplied an answer to the unasked question,

'My apologies. The New Year's Day festival is the day after tomorrow and I have been involved in the arrangements. Just managed to get away from all those boring bureaucrats,' said Murabi.

Arjuna laughed. 'Don't you know that a prince ought never to apologize?'

'Aah, but I only apologized to another prince,' said Murabi with a wide smile.

'I guess that makes it all right then.' Smiled Arjuna in return. 'Now, let's get to practising.'

❖

'Arjuna! Hey Arjuna!'

Arjuna turned to see Sabium approaching, huffing from the exertion of running. He bent over to catch his breath as Arjuna, with a gesture characteristic of friendship, slapped him on his back and made it worse for him.

Sabium stood up straight, still gulping in large breaths of air as he said churlishly, 'What did you do that for?'

'Oh, it was just to help you get some more air into your lungs', said Arjuna, a twinkle in his eyes.

Sabium still huffed and said, 'Gosh, I am not as young as I used to be.'

'You are not as fit as you ought to be. All that easy living and being pampered by that girlfriend of yours, I suppose,' said Arjuna with friendly candour.

Sabium grinned. 'Well, where have you been? I hardly see you these days.'

Arjuna pointed to the heavy iron sword hanging at his waist. 'Have been tasked with teaching your soldiers the art of fighting with these heavier weapons.'

'Is she there as well?' asked Sabium with a sly grin.

'Is who there?'

'You know who I mean. The girl who slapped you.'

'Her? Yeah, she is there.'

'And?'

'What?'

'And? Anything? Did you talk to her?'

'She hates my guts.'

'Oh, you don't mean that. I mean didn't she apologize to you for battering your face the other day?' asked Sabium.

'Um-um. She hardly even talks to me.'

'Did you at least get her name?'

'Yeah.'

'Well? What's it?'

'Lilith.'

'Lilith? The demon?' chortled Sabium. 'The name fits her, doesn't it?'

Arjuna's eyes narrowed and Sabium tried vainly to stifle his mirth.

'Well, I mean, from the way she treated you, of course. Not her looks or anything,' he concluded lamely.

'Anyway,' said Arjuna, trying to change the topic, 'What is this I hear about some New Year festival?'

Sabium's face brightened.

'Aah yes. That's our biggest festival of the year. Lots of fun. There is a royal procession to both the temples. There will be enormous quantities of food. Also loads of entertainment—jugglers, games and the like. Oh, and yes, the slave market will be free that day. So, if you want a wife, let me know.' He winked as he said that last bit.

'A free what?'

'Slave market.'

'You guys actually have a slave market?' Arjuna's eyes had narrowed, and he twisted his mouth and nose in an all-too-familiar gesture of revulsion.

'Yes, don't you?'

'You have been to our country. Have you ever seen a slave market there?' asked Arjuna.

'Well, I have always thought that you guys were missing out on things.'

Arjuna snorted in disgust.

'No, really,' continued Sabium. 'We have two different types of markets for women. One is a proper slave market. You know, for slaves.'

'And what is the other "women's market" for?' asked Arjuna sarcastically.

'That is where we get our wives. Those of us who can't get girlfriends, I mean.'

Arjuna shook his head disbelievingly. 'And how does it work?'

'Well, all the unmarried women are brought to the market, and the auctioneer ranks them by beauty and starts by auctioning off the most beautiful of them first. Usually, the rich get the most beautiful women, and as they go down progressively in looks, the poorer people can then afford themselves some wives.'

Arjuna had a disgusted look on his face as he listened to this narrative.

'You don't look happy,' Sabium remarked.

'Do I seem happy to you? Did you even hear yourself as you told me about these markets? Don't you find them distasteful?' Arjuna retorted.

'No, why?' asked Sabium with childlike innocence. 'That's how it has always been.'

Arjuna shook his head once more in revulsion.

'Anyway,' continued Sabium, 'the whole festival is great fun. I shall show you all the sights.'

'Not the slave markets, though,' said Arjuna.

'Oh, come on. Look at it this way. At least you will have something to tell all your friends back home. About how barbaric us Babylonians are', said Sabium with a grin.

Arjuna laughed. He couldn't really be angry at the artless Sabium for long.

❖

The burly man looked furtively around as he walked his horse through the southern gates of the city. The men manning the gates recognized him, but did not give it any more thought. It was not their business where the powerful men of the land went.

The gathering dusk masked the man's face from the other travellers as he walked his horse slowly southwards. His destination was the outskirts of a village, roughly five miles south of the city, and he was in no hurry. He knew that the men he was going to meet would wait for him. After all, they needed him more than he needed them.

It was a couple of hours later that the man reached the outskirts of the village. The moon was a barely seen sliver in the sky. The stars shone bright and a more poetic man than the furtive traveller might have stopped to marvel at the sight that the cosmos presented.

The rider, however, paid no mind to such trivialities as the cosmos' light show. His unwavering focus was fixed on a well near the edge of the village. As he directed his horse there, egging it on with his knees, he saw a few dark shapes sitting on the walls of the well. A couple of men were standing up, and as he neared them, they held up their hands, asking him to halt. The horse came to a stop, its shod feet clicking on the stones, its tail idly flicking flies off its body.

'You took your time coming,' said one of the men standing. He had a scar running down the side of his face.

The man on the horse grunted as he got down.

'Are we all going somewhere in a hurry?' he asked.

The others remained silent.

A man got off the wall of the well and made space for him to be seated. He looked at the two men, mere silhouettes, standing in front of him.

'Can we have some light?' he asked.

Erra gestured to another man who took out his flint and after much effort and cursing, managed to get a torch lit.

The single flame danced and threw flickering shadows across the faces of the men.

'Well?' asked Zabaya.

'Well, what?'

'Are you ready for *Akitu**?' asked Erra slowly, as if questioning a particularly dense person.

'Do you have the money ready?' countered the man.

Erra hefted a small sack he had placed next to him on the ground, and tossed it across to the visitor. The bag clinked as he caught it.

'Half now, half after the event,' reminded Zabaya.

The visitor nodded.

'So, what's the plan?' asked Erra.

The visitor took his time, bouncing the bag of coins up and down in his hand, the contents jingling musically.

'Come into the city the day before Akitu. I shall get you access to the route between the temples.'

'How?' asked Erra.

'I shall get you into the guard detail that mans the route. There are soldiers from different units. You all can blend in.'

Then, looking at Erra, he said, 'Not you though. That scar of yours is too prominent.'

Erra nodded even as the ghostly shadows cast by the flame danced across his scar, giving it a macabre appearance.

---

* New Year

'I shall be on the boat,' he said curtly.

'All right then, once this is over,' continued the visitor, 'you make sure that you don't forget the rest of the money.'

'Don't worry,' said Zabaya, 'you will get what's owed to you,' a sinister tone in his voice that the visitor failed to note.

The visitor got up with a groan and stumped over to his horse. Catching the pommel, he hoisted himself onto its back and then, giving a wave in their general direction, made his way back towards Babylon.

Chapter Six

The Attack

The morning of the New Year's Day, or Akitu as it was called, found Arjuna, Shrutasena and Sabium walking through the crowded streets of Babylon, somewhat aimlessly. Shrutasena had sent the soldiers back along with the traders eager to return to Bharatavarsha, after purchasing a large quantity of gems at incredibly low rates. They knew these gems would be in high demand back home, promising a hefty profit, provided, of course, they made the return journey safely—surviving the gauntlet of kidnappers, smugglers, brigands, and ruffians. Hence the need for an escort of soldiers.

The three men wandered through the crowd, the visitors soaking in the sights and smells. The streets had been turned into impromptu bazaars. People were out selling all kinds of food items, some that smelled appetizing to the Bharatiyas, like chicken, mutton and fish, while others offered less appetizing options, such as snails and snakes.

There were jugglers, fire-breathers and acrobats entertaining the crowd with their tricks. They were particularly enthralled with the fire-breather who drank oil and then sprayed it out in the form of a flame, lit by a torch that he held in his hands. They stopped, next, in front of a man who was swallowing swords, long ones at that. The soldiers clenched their fists as they watched the man begin to swallow a long sword, knowing that even the slightest mishap could mean his death. It didn't happen and they clapped enthusiastically as he pulled the sword out of his innards and bowed to them. Arjuna gave him a few coins, perhaps overpaying him outrageously.

'You paid too much,' protested Sabium. Arjuna merely shrugged his shoulders and said, 'That's all right. I am an ignorant foreigner after all.'

Toy sellers were doing brisk business, as children hounded their parents to buy them at least a small proportion of the many toys on display. Most of them gravitated to the ones with wheels, mostly war chariots. The toy chariots had small threads attached, which could be used to pull them along the road. They were a complete nuisance to the other pedestrians, who had to either dodge them or avoid stepping on them.

Flower sellers were not doing too shabbily for themselves either. Gaggles of giggling women bought garlands from them or single flowers, adorning their necks or tucking them into their hair, casting coquettish glances at men—both single and married. There was outrageous flirting by both men and women, and Arjuna remarked to Sabium that it was being done regardless of marital status.

'No one cares on Akitu,' he explained.

'The men, I can understand,' said Shrutasena. 'But the women too?'

Sabium showed his teeth as he grinned wide. 'Yes.'

'Shouldn't you be thinking about what your girlfriend is up to then?' asked Arjuna.

Lines of worry creased Sabium's forehead but were quickly replaced by his usual insouciant expression.

'Where can she find someone like me?' said Sabium.

'I would like some of that confidence,' Arjuna said to Shrutasena, prompting even the taciturn Shrutasena to burst into laughter.

They threaded their way through towards the centre of the city. The skyline was dominated by the Etemenanki.

'I always feel so insignificant when I stand in front of this,' murmured Shrutasena.

'Truly,' agreed Arjuna as Sabium looked on with pride. 'It is big, isn't it?'

'Big? It is enormous. Humongous. Gigantic. I don't know how you folks get any work done with that staring you in your face all the time.'

'We get used to it, I suppose,' said Sabium.

At the centre of the city, just in front of the ziggurat, a huge platform had been set up. A swarthy man with a pointed beard and a wispy thin moustache was standing at the front. Behind him were arranged several tittering women in various stages of undress.

'Can't really call what they are wearing "a dress" now, can we?' said the prudish Shrutasena.

Sabium laughed aloud. 'Aah. Here we are. This is what I was telling you about the other day,' he said, turning to Arjuna.

A large group of men were crowded around the stage. Sabium led his companions off to one side and climbed a few stairs up the ziggurat to enable them to get a better view of the proceedings. They saw the man with the pointed beard ask one of the women to step forward and to then turn around. She did so slowly, preening a bit and there were many appreciative wolf-whistles from the crowd. This seemed to enthuse the young lady who, rather than being embarrassed, seemed to revel in it as she smiled alluringly at the men, paying particular attention to the richer looking ones.

Bids rang out from the crowd, and as the auctioneer skillfully drove the price higher, the number of bidders dwindled. The contest finally narrowed to two men, each hesitantly pushing the bid higher. Eventually, as it happens in life, there was only one man with the highest bid, and the auctioneer handed the woman over to him and received his payment in return.

'I thought you said that it was a free auction,' said Arjuna.

'The auction is free, of course. The auctioneer does not make any money. The money collected is deposited in the shrine up there,' he said, pointing to the top of Etemenanki. 'The money is used for the upkeep of the temple and as an offering to Bal Marduk,' he added.

The auctioneer had called up another woman to the centre, and Arjuna said, 'I think I have seen enough of this ...'

The last words were lost in the sudden fanfare that the heralds blew on their trumpets.

'Oh, the royal family is here,' announced Sabium, excitedly. They could see two chariots roll up to the ziggurat with the king and queen in the leading one, followed by Prince Murabi and his sister Sybella in the second.

The king's troupe of bodyguards had precedence over that of the queens and they closely surrounded the king and queen. The queen's own bodyguards formed a ring around Murabi and the princess. Arjuna spied Lilith among them. He could recognize her even from a distance.

The royal party moved up the path leading to the shrine at the top of the ziggurat. As Murabi and Sybella passed them, the prince saw them and gestured to Arjuna and his companions to join him. Arjuna needed no second invitation as he pushed past the soldiers barring their way. Lilith had noticed the prince motioning to them and made a way through the crowd for them to join Murabi and his sister.

Murabi introduced Sybella and another pretty girl, who seemed to be her companion, to the group. The princess and the girl acknowledged them, but Arjuna noticed that she seemed to be paying special attention to Sabium.

'You know her?' he asked his friend.

'She is my girlfriend, Mylitta,' he murmured.

'Aah. Now I understand why you weren't worried about who she would be flirting with. What does Mylitta mean, by the way?'

'Mother of the child,' he whispered.

Arjuna punched him playfully on his arm while Sabium smiled and continued to walk alongside Mylitta, their hands touching occasionally and their fingers searching out each other's. Arjuna tried to catch Lilith's gaze, but she had moved behind them, bringing up the rear.

The party wound its way up the path. The Bharatiyas looked in awe at the gardens at each level until they reached the top of the ziggurat. As impressive as the structure was, the shrine itself was a bit of a disappointment, especially after having been to the Esagila a few days earlier.

The chief priest of the shrine led the royal party inside the sanctum where a large idol of Bal Marduk looked down on them. The group went down on their knees in front of the idol as the priest intoned his benedictions. The royal party then moved out of the shrine and started slowly on their way back down. Sin-Muballit was seated inside his palanquin carried by four bearers on their shoulders.

Arjuna and Shrutasena tarried a bit as they wanted a view of the city from the top. Sabium seemed reluctant to leave his lady love's side and Arjuna motioned to him to continue as he and the sergeant walked over to the wall at the top and took in the spectacular view of the city. The people below looked like so many ants energetically going about their business. They could periodically make out the royal entourage slowly winding its way down. They were hidden from view by the overhanging trees more often than not.

'The view is impressive, isn't it?' asked Shrutasena.

Arjuna nodded, unwilling to break the spell that the scene cast on him. After spending some time admiring the view, they began their descent, walking briskly in hopes of catching up with the royal party.

Zabaya stood on the pathway leading up to Esagila; his men gathered around him, careful not to draw attention. They had streamed into the city, singly, the previous evening as planned, and had put up at different guest houses for the night. They had walked down here a couple of hours earlier and their nocturnal visitor, a senior official, had placed them there, explaining to the sergeant that these were special troops who would take care of the path leading to the temple.

He had been standing here ever since. He had a clear view of the river and the boats. One boat caught his interest. He knew Erra would be on it. The boat, flying a flag with an ostentatious Babylonian insignia, was moored at the end of the stairs leading down to the river. It was the same size as the other boats, but much sleeker, as if built for speed—which it was. As he turned around, he heard a voice calling him.

'Hey you!'

Zabaya looked at a large sergeant and pointed to himself as if to ask, 'Me?'

'Yes, you idiot. Who else would I be talking to?'

'Yes, sergeant,' said Zabaya, acting suitably chastened.

'Go and check on the boats there.'

'Yes, sergeant. Do you want me to check on that long boat as well?' he asked.

'Are you kidding me? Can you see that big royal insignia on it?'

'Yes.'

'Now tell me again if you think that I would want you to check on that boat.'

'Uh, no, Sir.'

'Right. Go ahead and check the other boats,' he said as he wandered away. Zabaya smiled to himself as he sauntered over in the direction of the boats.

Arjuna and Shrutasena caught up with Murabi and the others just as they reached the bottom of the ziggurat. He noticed that the royal family did not get back onto the chariots but started walking towards Esagila. The king, of course, was borne in the palanquin. The warriors formed around the entourage as they made their way to the larger temple.

Arjuna and Shrutasena were in a group behind Murabi and princess Sybella. Mylitta had got permission to detach herself from the royal retinue and was walking behind them, hand in hand with Sabium, alongside the Bharatiyas. The king's bodyguards were all around the palanquin, leaving the safety of the queen in the hands of Lilith and her group of warriors. Arjuna's eyes followed Lilith as she kept moving from the front to the back, her head swivelling one way and then the other, trying to sniff out any danger.

Arjuna didn't know why, but he felt that familiar prickling sensation at the base of his neck. A sensation that he got only when there was danger lurking. He looked off to his left and noticed the soldiers lining the road. He turned back to the front and then whipped his head back towards the soldiers again. Then it struck him.

While most of the soldiers were keeping an eye on the crowds, there were some whose eyes were fixed on the royal entourage. *Why will soldiers, tasked with keeping the family safe, focus their eyes on them rather than on the surrounding crowd?* he thought.

He didn't have much more time to think this through because there was a sudden explosion of activity. Dagan, the head of the king's guards had positioned himself just behind the palanquin. Even as Arjuna's unbelieving eyes looked on, he yanked out his sword and ran it quickly through three of the guards around him.

At the same time, a new threat manifested itself from the soldiers lining the road. Arjuna saw a stocky, well-built man slash the throat of a fat sergeant, who dropped dead at his feet, gurgling blood from his mouth, nose and throat. The soldiers immediately started towards the bodyguards protecting the queen and the princess.

'Lilith!' shouted Arjuna, drawing his own sword and moving forward to offer help. Lilith, who had been on the side farther away from the attackers, quickly swung around, her iron sword whistling out of its scabbard. She was the only one carrying the iron sword since the others in her group had not been deemed competent enough with the new weapons. Arjuna barely had time to see Lilith take on two of the soldiers before his attention was diverted towards those approaching him as he prepared to engage.

Shrutasena, like any good, experienced soldier, had moved forward, past Murabi and princess Sybella to protect the king. Dagan, now backed by hired goons, had wiped out most of his own cohort of bodyguards. The palanquin bearers had put the palanquin with their charge inside, down on the ground, and fled in panic. The two remaining members of the king's guard were standing in front of the palanquin and fighting desperately to protect their monarch. They were, however, no match for Dagan and his henchmen.

The arrival of Shrutasena in their midst tilted the balance in their favour. Dagan, recognizing the danger, focused his attention on the Bharatiya veteran. He smiled as he showed Shrutasena his sword. It was the new iron sword that the Bharatiyas had given the king. Shrutasena responded with a grim smile and stepped into the fray. The clash of iron on iron rang differently compared to the sound of bronze swords striking each other. Dagan pressed hard, forcing Shrutasena back against the palanquin.

Shrutasena suddenly switched from a single-handed to a double-handed grip on his sword. He could see Dagan's brows wrinkle in confusion. *I bet you have never seen this*, thought Shrutasena as he swung his sword, each strike now powered by more muscle. Dagan faltered under the onslaught as his single-handed strokes had to contend with the added punch that the double-handed grip gave to Shrutasena. He fought desperately as he came under increasing pressure from the veteran Bharatiya.

He tried to use his shield to knock Shrutasena's sword away while simultaneously trying to launch an attack on him. His actions were becoming increasingly ragged as realization hit him that the veteran was perhaps more than a match for him. His sword swings became progressively wilder. Shrutasena had been waiting for just this moment. As Dagan swung his arm back fully, Shrutasena stepped forward and to his left, away from the shield arm, and drove his sword forward. Dagan raised his shield to protect himself, but Shrutasena's footwork had taken him outside the line of the shield. His blade slid inches past the shield and plunged into Dagan's chest, past his rib cage and into his heart. Dagan was dead before Shrutasena could draw his sword out again and fell to the ground, motionless.

Meanwhile, Arjuna was having a difficult time of his own. He had jumped into the fray in support of the queen's bodyguards. His sword whistled through the air, clanging sharply against his opponents' blades. Their bronze swords were no match for his heavy iron sword with the curved blade. He shattered several of them before hacking off the hands that held the swords.

There were more men who were streaming towards them. Already, nearly half of the bodyguards lay wounded or dead. Lilith was fighting hard against two men. Arjuna noticed that one of them was creeping around to get at Lilith's back. He knew he didn't have any opportunity to warn her. He rushed his way past the already fighting bodyguards and slid down on his knees towards Lilith. He intercepted the downward stroke of the enemy's sword at just the right time. The enemy's sword shattered in half, and Arjuna drove his own blade through his opponent's belly.

He stood up, his back to Lilith, who, sensing someone behind her, half-turned to check if it was a new threat.

'It's only me,' yelled Arjuna as he met the attack from another soldier. Lilith turned back to face her own opponents. Arjuna noticed Prince Murabi caught up in his own skirmish with an attacker. The young man, displaying remarkable skill, swiftly dispatched him. As he turned, Arjuna beckoned Murabi towards him and the three of them—Lilith, Murabi and he—stood with their backs to each other in a triangle.

They fought hard. One of the men suddenly came at Lilith with a sword in one hand and a knife in another. She fought warily, more worried about the smaller knife than the larger sword. A knife can be used for slashing as well as throwing with just a little change in the grip. Lilith's strokes were met confidently by her opponent who used the other hand to slash at her. One of those slashes ripped across her forearm and Lilith grunted in pain. Blood dripped down her left hand. She redoubled her efforts now, waiting for a similar move from her opponent. Sure enough, the man attempted it again, but this time, she was ready. She moved her body to the right and then slashed down at the man's wrist. The heavy iron sword cut through flesh, muscle, ligaments and bone, cleanly shearing his hand at the wrist.

The hand holding the knife fell on the ground as blood gushed out of the stump that was his hand. The man yelled in agony and clutched his right hand with his left, dropping his sword in the process. Lilith wasted no time but nearly sliced his head off with one final devastating stroke.

'Die *Mlechcha*!' she yelled.

Arjuna swivelled his head around for a moment on hearing her scream. He barely had time to register the import of her words when his attention was diverted to another opponent who was coming at Murabi. Arjuna jumped in front of the prince and dispatched the enemy quickly with a short thrust of his sword through his ribs.

The tide of battle seemed to have turned with more and more soldiers coming to their support. There was, however, chaos everywhere with men, women and children running helter-skelter, trying to get away from the fighting. Amid this chaos, the trio of Arjuna, Lilith and Murabi realized that they had winnowed through their enemies. There were no more people left to fight.

They looked around and saw the king getting out of the palanquin slowly, being helped by Shrutasena. 'Sergeant,' shouted Arjuna. 'All well?'

Shrutasena raised his sword in response. It was then that they heard Murabi yell, 'Sybella!'

Chapter Seven

Taken Away

At the first sign of the attack, Murabi had instinctively pushed Sybella behind him, shielding her. Just behind them, Sabium had tried to pull Mylitta along with him, away from the centre of the clashes. Instead, she had dragged him towards where Sybella was, unwilling to leave her princess' side. There, the three of them had cowered, while battles raged all around them.

Sybella had taken comfort from the fact that her parents were well protected by their bodyguards. As she watched, wide-eyed, at the action, she felt someone tugging at her hand from behind. She turned and looked into the eyes of a group of three soldiers. The one in the lead said urgently, 'Princess. This way. We want to get you out of the fighting zone.'

'But my brother and parents ...'

'They,' he gestured towards the other bodyguards, 'will take care of them. My duty is to ensure your safety.'

The princess tarried briefly and then, pulling Mylitta's hand, started following the soldiers. Sabium had also tagged along behind them as they skirted the skirmish and moved towards the river.

'To the royal boat, princess,' urged the soldier.

Sybella looked at the boat and a little frown puckered her brow.

'That does not look like any of our royal boats . . .' she said.

She had barely finished speaking when she felt herself seized and lifted onto the soldier's shoulders. Another one picked up Mylitta. Sabium, stunned at this turn of events, tried to stop them by yanking on the arms of the man who had picked up Sybella. A trader is, however, no match for a trained soldier. The soldier shrugged Sabium off and started running towards the river. In shrugging Sabium off, the end of the turban that had been wrapped around his face came loose, allowing Sabium a clear look at the man.

Sabium got up again and ran doggedly after them, gaining on the soldiers, all the while yelling, 'Stop. Stop them! They are carrying away the princess.'

He lurched suddenly as a sharp shooting pain radiated up his left shoulder, just above his shoulder blades. He clasped his hand to that region, and as it came away from there, he looked incomprehensibly at the blood that stained his palm. He felt a deep gash on his shoulder. He had been running and perhaps that act had saved him. The blow that had been aimed at his neck had found his shoulder. The enemy soldier who had stabbed him had, however, run past him without seeing the damage that he had wrought.

❖

'Where's Sybella?' Prince Murabi asked again, swivelling around in every direction, desperate to catch a glimpse of his sister.

Arjuna and Lilith looked at each other and then started yelling Sybella's name.

'Princess! Princess Sybella!'

They heard some commotion towards the river, and Arjuna said to Lilith, 'There. Let's go see what that's about.'

'I can't,' she said miserably. 'My first duty is to protect the queen. Take Shrutasena and go.'

Arjuna nodded, gestured Shrutasena to follow, and ran in the direction of the river. As he neared the river, he saw Sabium coming towards him; his right hand clasped over his left shoulder and covered in blood.

'Sabium!' he exclaimed as he went to his friend.

'They took the women,' he told them. 'They took the princess and Mylitta.'

'Go,' said Shrutasena to Arjuna. 'I shall take Sabium to get his wound tended to.'

Arjuna ran on, and as he reached the steps leading down to the river, he noticed a boat, flying the royal insignia, pulling away. What caught his attention were the other boats. They were all on fire. Arjuna looked on in frustration as the boat made its way towards the middle of the river, travelling south. 'Did you see princess Sybella?' he asked a bystander.

The man looked terrified as he stared at Arjuna, who, unaware of the intimidating image he presented, stood with his sword in hand, his face and body splattered with blood from the fighting. He caught hold of the man's arm and repeated the question a few more times, slowly, before he got a response. The man rattled off something too fast for Arjuna to catch. He did, however, pick up the words 'princess', 'men' and 'boat'.

He looked around to see if he could find any horses, but there were none this close to the river. He started running back towards Esagila and saw Prince Murabi rushing towards him with a mingled look of worry and anger on his face.

'Did you find her?' he asked.

Seeing Arjuna's shoulders slump, Murabi held him by his arms and asked again.

'Did you find her?'

Arjuna shook his head and pointed towards the distant boat. Murabi's face clouded in rage.

'Can we get a horse?' asked Arjuna.

'Why a horse? Let's take one of our boats and chase them.'

'They burnt all the boats. Well, almost all. The smaller ones, they didn't deem fit to burn. We will never catch them with those boats.' Murabi's face darkened as he watched the burning vessels on the river.

'Let's go then,' said Murabi, turning on his heels and running back towards the centre of town. He saw several soldiers sitting on horses. They jumped off their perch with alacrity as they recognized the prince. Murabi and Arjuna grabbed a horse each, jumped on them and left at a gallop towards the river. Having reached it, they turned their horses southward and rode them hard. They could still make out the boat as it moved downriver under sail.

However, the boat seemed to keep pulling further ahead of them as the two had to avoid the men and dwellings along the riverbank.

They eventually lost sight of the boat as it rounded a bend. Murabi drew his horse up in frustration and Arjuna followed suit. The prince sat there looking in the direction in which the boat had disappeared, anger borne out of his helplessness, suffusing his face. Arjuna was quiet, unwilling to intrude on his grief. Presently however, he placed his hand gently on the young prince's back and said, 'Murabi. We will find her. I promise.'

Murabi sat still, his body rigid, still looking into the distance.

'We aren't doing any good by staying here and it could be dangerous for you as well. Let's head back and sit together with the king and the soldiers. We will figure out a way.'

Murabi finally seemed to come out of his trance-like state. He looked at Arjuna with gratitude and nodded. The duo started walking their horses back towards the palace.

Night descended on a sombre city. The festivities that usually attended the first new moon after spring had been suspended. The city mourned, not just for the sacrilegious attack on the royal family but also because news had spread about the kidnapping of two of their women, one of whom was the princess, Sybella.

Three men, one of who had his right shoulder bandaged, came out of a large building, a stone's throw away from the palace. Arjuna and Shrutasena had gone there to enquire about Sabium. They had met their friend sitting on his bed, his shoulder heavily bandaged.

Arjuna glanced at the physician attending him and raised his eyebrows in a query.

The physician had smiled, and said, 'He'll live. He is a lucky man. The knife passed very near the artery on his neck.'

Arjuna had let out the breath that, unbeknown to him, he had been holding in. Shrutasena, a man of few words, had clapped him on his shoulders as the two looked down on their friend. Sabium smiled at them. A smile tinged with worry.

'You rest and get better,' said Arjuna.

'The princess . . .' said Sabium.

'We know. The boat.'

Sabium nodded. Then, leaning back and wincing as the muscles flexed and a shooting pain went up his arm, he asked, 'And . . . Mylitta?'

'She was also taken,' said Arjuna.

'We will get them back, my friend. I promise you that,' said Arjuna, after a pause, somewhat more confidently than he felt at the moment.

'When you do go after them, promise me that you will take me along?'

'I promise,' said Arjuna.

Sabium looked at the physician and asked, 'Can I leave now?'

'Absolutely not,' said the physician, adding, 'The wound on your shoulder is deep. You need some rest . . .'

' . . . which I shall get at my own place,' said Sabium.

The physician shrugged in resignation and walked off. He had other patients to look after. Those with life-threatening injuries.

Sabium, his shoulder heavily bandaged and favouring his left side, walked out of the hospital along with Arjuna and Shrutasena. At the entrance, they found a soldier waiting for them.

'The king has requested your presence at the palace,' he said.

Arjuna turned to Sabium and said, 'You go home and rest. I shall come and get you once we know where they have taken the princess and Mylitta.'

Sabium nodded and set off for home while the two Bharatiyas followed the soldier to the palace.

The palace presented a gloomy appearance in keeping with the events of the day. The gloom was more in spirit than in terms of the availability of light. A profusion of torches had been lit in the royal hall where the king, his ministers and generals were seated.

Arjuna noticed Lilith standing to one side, her left arm heavily wrapped up in a cotton cloth. He could see the bandage coloured by the red of her blood mingling with the yellow and green of the paste that had been applied on her wound. He saw her glance at him but as he made eye contact with her, she looked away and back towards the king.

The king was speaking and paused briefly as they entered and then carried on. Arjuna understood perhaps one word in four of those spoken, and stood around uncertainly. He slowly edged over to where Lilith was standing and whispered into her ears in Sanskrit, 'Can you translate for me?'

The instinctive 'yes' from her in the Devabhasha told him all that he needed to know. She knew that she had given herself away and looked at him in confusion, but he kept his face neutral and pretended to concentrate on what the king was saying.

'So, what's he saying?'

'They are having a discussion on what needs to be done. Some of the generals are sure that it is the work of the Isin kingdom since we had just subdued them a few years ago. He thinks that this is their way of taking revenge.'

'And what does he propose to do about it?'

'He is suggesting an all-out mobilization and war against Isin,' Arjuna pondered on this and then whispered softly to her. 'Do they know who apart from Dagan was involved in this?'

Lilith shook her head. 'I don't think there was anyone else apart from Dagan, but one can never be sure, of course.'

'If we do anything precipitate, the princess' life could be in real danger. Assuming that this is the work of Isin, and we attack them, what is going to prevent them from bringing out the princess and displaying her on top of the city walls? Will we still attack them?'

Lilith kept quiet. Presently, she said, 'I agree. This suggestion won't work.'

'We need to find the princess first.'

Lilith nodded and then spoke up. Again, Arjuna didn't get all of what she said, but he heard enough familiar words to understand that she was repeating their recent conversation.

The king and his ministers listened to her for a while before the king interjected.

'What should we do?'

Lilith looked back enquiringly at Arjuna who said to her, 'Ask that men be sent out to find where that boat landed. Then, once they find that out, and only then, do we send out a small party to start tracking the kidnappers. If they have indeed been taken inside Isin, a small party can get in under disguise and try to rescue her.'

Lilith nodded and translated Arjuna's words for the king. While Sin-Muballit digested this in silence, Arjuna said to Lilith, 'Oh, and one more thing. Send some soldiers to the other side of the river. They might well have crossed the river and disembarked on the other bank.'

The king looked at him in surprise as Lilith translated.

'Will you go?' asked King Sin-Muballit.

Arjuna nodded his acquiescence. Murabi immediately stepped in front of his father and said, 'So will I, father.'

'And I,' said Lilith.

'You are injured,' pointed out the king.

'It doesn't matter. I hold myself responsible for what happened. Your Majesty, please give me a chance to atone for my mistake.'

'Aah, Prince Murabi,' said Arjuna, adding, 'I don't think it is a good idea for you to come with us.'

'Why not?' asked Murabi, a trifle belligerently.

'Because it is quite obvious that the entire royal family was the target of the attack. By going, you would be putting yourself in harm's way, and as the crown prince, that would not be the most prudent thing to do.' Arjuna chose his words carefully, striving to express his thoughts without upsetting royalty in any way.

The king gave him a long, measured look before turning to his army chief.

'Send men out immediately to check where the boat landed. Two men per group. On both banks of the river. I want one of the men from the group that finds the boat to return with the news as fast as possible.'

The army chief nodded, got up, bowed to the king and rushed out.

Chapter Eight

A Barrier Broken

'Lilith, can I talk to you?' asked Arjuna.

They were in the large garden inside the palace grounds. Shrutasena had returned to their dwelling to get some rest. Arjuna had declined the offer of going back immediately since he wanted to ask Lilith questions that had been troubling him all day, ever since he had heard her scream 'Die Mlechcha' as she fought the enemy soldiers.

The court had dispersed soon after the king's orders to his army chief. Lilith had tried to make her way out quickly to her own quarters that were in a row besides the palace, but Arjuna had intercepted her. They had walked towards the large garden and were now seated on one of the wooden benches that dotted the garden.

Lilith sat looking into the distance, her hands wrestling with each other. Arjuna struggled to figure out how to broach the subject. After what seemed like an interminable silence, he asked, 'At the battle earlier today, I heard you say something.'

The nervous hand-wringing stopped as she turned towards him, her green eyes asking the question. She had discarded the veil once inside the palace. Arjuna understood that the veil was part of the uniform for the queen's bodyguards. Her petite nose and the full lips, centred perfectly below her nose, captivated him. He tore his eyes away from them and looked back into her eyes.

'Mlechcha.'

Lilith remained silent.

'I didn't think anyone in Babylon would even know that word unless . . .' He left the words hanging in the air.

'Unless?' she asked.

'Unless the person was a Bharatiya.'

'Couldn't the person have picked it up on travels to your land?'

Arjuna shook his head. 'Not the way it was used, no. And certainly not in the heat of battle.'

Lilith passed her tongue gently along her lower lip before catching it with her teeth.

Pretty teeth, noted Arjuna in passing.

She presented a very alluring sight. Her green eyes locked on his, her lower lip caught between her teeth, her nostrils flaring slightly from whatever emotion was eating her up from the inside. Arjuna moved his hand and placed it on both of hers. The nervous wringing that had started again between her hands when he had asked her about the use of the word mlechcha stopped. She, however, didn't withdraw her hands from his touch and Arjuna took that as a good sign.

'Well, you are, aren't you?'

'What?' she whispered.

'A Bharatiya?'

Lilith nodded as she dipped her head and taking her right hand from under his, buried her face in it. A few seconds passed. Seconds that felt like aeons as she struggled with her memories. Seconds that tore at wounds that had healed and exposed them once again.

When she raised her head to look at him, those green eyes were full to the brim with unshed tears. Arjuna instinctively took hold of her right hand, this time with more firmness.

'Yes, I am a Bharatiya. Or at least I was. Now I don't know what I am. Maybe just Lilith. But before I became Lilith, I was Chitrangadha.' Arjuna drew his breath in. *What a name to go with her face.*

'Where in Bharatavarsha are you from?' he prompted her gently.

'Surashtra. You know of it?'

'Yes. I have heard of it.'

'It isn't a big city like Rohitaka,' she said, the beginnings of a smile on her face.

Arjuna shook his head. 'Rohitaka is not what it once was. Ma Sarasvati is abandoning us.'

'I have heard. Ours is a port town. Lots of ships and boats come there from many distant lands.'

Arjuna nodded sombrely. 'I have heard of it, though I haven't visited it. Anyway, how did you end up here?'

Lilith sighed. Her eyes took on a faraway look as she gazed into the distance.

'Do you really want to hear all that? I haven't told this to anyone in a long time. I had, in fact, suppressed these memories from my mind.'

She sighed again. 'Oh, well. Would you be surprised to know that I, too, am a princess? Was a princess?' She corrected herself.

'No, it wouldn't surprise me at all,' said Arjuna, adding, 'You are more of a princess than any princess that I have ever met, and that includes Sybella.'

Lilith smiled as she gently placed her right hand on his arm. 'Flattery is not going to get you anywhere.'

'It wasn't flattery,' he said indignantly.

Lilith laughed a throaty little laugh.

'Anyway, like I said, I was a princess from Surashtra. My father was the king. I was, however, an only child, and you know that when the only child is a girl, the king and the kingdom are subject to all kinds of intrigue.'

Arjuna nodded. The laws of primogeniture were very strict and only the male son of a king could take over from him.

'There was an uncle.'

'Aah,' said Arjuna, a wealth of understanding in that one word.

'Aah indeed. My father's younger brother. Very ambitious and more importantly, had a few sons.'

Lilith looked at Arjuna.

'You see where this is going?'

'I think I do. Your uncle's jealousy. His ambition for his sons. The fact that your father did not have a male heir. What did he do?' he asked, curiously.

'Kidnapped and sold me to the slave traders,' said Lilith matter-of-factly.

'I didn't know there was a slave trade from Bharatavarsha?'

'Citizens of Rohitaka live very protected lives, I think.'

'But how?'

'He came to me one day and asked me to take a ride with him to a nearby temple. He *was* my uncle. I trusted him. So, I went along. A day and half's ride away, we came to a camp of sorts in the woods. There were several men there. Dirty looking men with unkempt beards and in urgent need of a bath. My uncle passed me over to them and money changed hands. Then he was gone. And just like that, before I could even understand what was happening, I was a slave. There were other women there, of various ages. They herded us all together, like so many sheep, as we began our long walk north, past the deserts and across the large mountains to the north-west of Bharatavarsha,' said Lilith.

Arjuna creased his brows and asked, 'Why didn't he just put you all on a ship? Wouldn't that have been easier?'

'My father knew all the captains of the ships there. It would have been fraught with danger for them to try and smuggle us on board the ships.'

'Oh ...'

'Anyway,' she continued, 'most of the women were older and at night, they were pulled out of the tents, and we could hear their cries as the men took turns with them. The sounds of their cries diminished over the next several days as it became routine, and the women simply stopped caring about what happened to them. No, that is wrong. Their tears dried up. They became hollow husks.'

Lilith paused. *Has she run out of words as well?* thought Arjuna. He felt a slow burning rage inside him. At her uncle. At the slave traders. It was, however, an impotent rage. What could he do? He took her hands in his once more and asked, 'Did they . . . did they trouble the young ones as well?'

She turned towards him and gave a bitter smile. 'No, they didn't. Not because they had finer sentiments or anything. Virgins command a higher price in the slave markets, and they were businessmen after all.' Then, after a pause, she added, 'Among other things.'

'Did you and the others ever think of escaping?' asked Arjuna.

She snorted. 'All the time. Some of us. At least in the very beginning. The older women had simply lost the will to live after the first few days. But us younger ones—we still had some spirit. Once, when we were crossing the high mountains, a few of us girls made a break for it. It was at night. When they were all drunk and sleeping.'

She paused, gazing into the distance as if she had been transported back in time and place.

'It was a bleak landscape, with jagged rocks. There was not much moonlight that night, and we managed to put some distance between us and the slavers. We slipped, fell and scraped our legs a few times. My knees were bloody from all the falling. It was also very cold and after some time, we found a spot under an overhang and huddled together for warmth.

We were woken up by kicks to our feet and the sound of coarse laughter. They had found us. And they made us pay.'

'Did they?'

She shook her head. 'No. They didn't touch us that way. We were valuable virgins, remember? But they whipped our feet until we could barely stand. And they made us walk on those torn feet. It was agony. Many a time I felt like giving up, but I always had this stubbornness inside of me. An adamant refusal to give up on things. It's just the way I am.'

Arjuna squeezed her hand sympathetically. 'Chitra, do you perhaps want to continue this discussion later?'

She gave a happy little laugh. 'It has been so long since someone called me Chitra. My father used to call me that,' she said wistfully. 'I have been Lilith for so long that I had almost forgotten my original name.'

'You didn't answer my question, though.'

'No, I don't want to stop. I thought talking about it after all these years would be tough, but I find that it is strangely cathartic.'

She freed her hand from his, closed her eyes, and continued.

'After what happened to those of us who tried to escape, no one else ever gave any thought to escaping again. We walked all the way to Babylon. It took us almost a year to get here. Quite a few of the women died along the way. They were left on the paths, without a cremation or even a burial. Just left there for the animals to feed on. Some of the younger ones died too. Perhaps they just willed themselves to death. I didn't. I was one of the lucky ones to survive. Or perhaps, an unlucky one, come to think of it?'

'They brought us to the slave market here. Looking at all those men gawking at us just infuriated me. Perhaps it was all that pent up anger inside of me that made me do what I did next. My father had always treated me as both a daughter and a son. He had had teachers come and teach me horse-riding, archery, sword-fighting as well as the martial arts. As the man who had bought me came up on stage to take hold of me, I kicked him hard, right where it hurts for a man to be kicked.'

Arjuna chuckled involuntarily. A reaction that always happens when one man watches or hears about another man being hurt down there.

'And then?'

'And then, it all went downhill very fast. Some of the traders came up to me to get me under control. But all those months of watching them demean and whip us into submission, memories of women being raped and left for dead—something snapped inside me. All those hours of training came back to me. I laid into them. The slavers fell on stage, blood spurting from their faces, their noses smashed. I broke quite a few arms and cracked any number of ribs that day.'

'My actions seemed to have made me very popular among the general populace. The very same men who were bidding to buy us as slaves now started whistling through their fingers and supporting me as more slavers appeared on stage. Some of the prospective buyers even jumped on stage to help me. It was a general melee, and I must say that I quite enjoyed myself.'

'Eventually, a woman got on stage and came up to me. In my bloodlust, I tried to smash my fist into her face, but she knocked it aside quite easily and then caught my hands behind my back in a vice-like grip. "Come with me," she said, and I don't know why, but I followed her. She was dressed all in black and was veiled. I noticed that everyone in the crowd gave her a wide berth as she marched me out of the slave market. After a while, she gave up her hold on my arms and just walked ahead, knowing that I *would* follow her.'

'I think I know where this is going now,' said Arjuna.

Lilith smiled; her eyes still closed. 'She was the head of the queen's bodyguards. She took me under her wing. Became my mentor. Trained me. And at the end of all her training, I was bonded to the queen and here I shall remain bonded, until I die. Or until the queen sees it fit to release me.'

'Why were you so upset with me that first day that we met? When you slapped me?' asked Arjuna.

Lilith opened her eyes and turned to look at him.

'I am sorry about that. But for some reason, you reminded me of my home. And of the men there. It is not like I have never seen Bharatiyas after I came here. You know that your people are here all the time for trade. But for some reason that I don't rightly know, your face just seemed to bring back memories of home.'

Oh great, thought Arjuna. *I find a girl that I like, and she hates my face.*

'Would you like to come back home?' he asked.

'This is home.'

'Your original home, I meant. Don't you want revenge on your uncle?'

'What can I do alone?'

'You aren't alone,' Arjuna said with some conviction. Her eyes softened at his statement.

'Didn't I tell you that I was bound to the queen here?'

'We shall see about that,' he said, adding, 'Perhaps, if we can help get the princess back, she might consider releasing you?'

Lilith was silent. He thought he heard her say 'perhaps' but he wasn't sure. Her breathing was regular, and he realized with a start that she had fallen asleep. Arjuna sat there, just a foot away from her, unwilling to leave her alone on that bench. He thought about the wounds on her psyche and her soul. Perhaps the wounds had never healed and had always been raw, except on the outside. Perhaps time, that great healer would eventually heal her wounds. Perhaps.

Chapter Nine

The Hunt Begins

It was towards the evening of the following day that a soldier came to fetch Arjuna and Shrutasena. Arjuna had sat with Lilith while she slept on the bench, well into the night. It was only after she had suddenly woken up from her sleep that he had reluctantly torn himself away from her and come back to the guest house, admonishing her to go back to her place and give her injured arm some rest.

The king was waiting along with Murabi and his army general Gamil a heavy-shouldered man in his forties with a receding hairline and a neatly trimmed beard without a moustache as Shrutasena and Arjuna entered the room. Lilith was already there, and she gave Arjuna a quick little smile.

Sin-Muballit merely grunted and then gestured to an attendant, who went out and then came back in with another soldier. The man looked tired. It was obvious that he had not slept the previous night, but he still stood erect as any professional soldier would.

The king motioned to him, and the man started speaking, directing his monologue at the army chief. Lilith translated the gist of what was being said to Shrutasena and Arjuna.

The man said that he and his partner had crossed the river and gone south. Progress had been slow since there were no people about at night along the riverbank, and they had to ensure that the boat wasn't moored in one of the many sandbanks that adorned the sides of the river.

Daylight had quickened their pace since they could now just ask the villagers, and finally, it was a toothless old man, not a day under 100, who had told them that he had seen the royal boat on its way down the river. The two of them had then sped on until they reached the junction of the Euphrates with one of its smaller tributaries, just north of Isin. They found the boat abandoned there. They had decided it was time to deliver the message back to Babylon. This man had taken both horses and, riding them alternately, made good time back to the city.

'Well,' said Arjuna to Lilith, 'I suppose we had better get started then.'

'Do you have a plan?' asked Murabi.

'We will try and follow the route that the kidnappers took,' said Lilith.

'What if they have gone into Isin?'

'We don't know that yet, Your Highness,' replied Lilith. 'They could have gone further south as well.'

'South to where? Larsa?'

She nodded.

'That would mean that the kingdom of Larsa is behind it.'

'We really don't know, Murabi,' interjected Arjuna. Then speaking rapidly to Lilith, he said, 'There are quite a few possibilities. As I understand it, His Majesty has defeated both Larsa and Isin over the last few years. It could be either one or both of them in collusion or none of them. Although my own bet would not be on the last one.'

'Why not?' asked the king after Lilith had translated for the others.

'The attack was audacious, and it had to have the support of some king to come up with an operation of this sort. Ordinary citizens do not benefit from the chaos and confusion caused by killings of the royal family. It must have been someone with a vested interest. Who else but the kingdoms closest to you and with whom you have fought wars in the recent past and subjugated?'

Then, as another thought struck him, he said, 'It could be some internal enemies of yours too, Your Majesty. Do you think there might be someone here, some relatives who might want to do away with your family?'

Sin-Muballit looked at Arjuna with hooded eyes. Then looking at Murabi, he said, 'Check to see if any of our people could have had a hand in this. Treat everyone as guilty until their innocence is proven.'

Murabi bowed to the king.

'We shall be starting then, Your Majesty,' said Arjuna.

Meanwhile, Lilith turned to General Gamil and said, 'Sir, can we get a small platoon of five of your soldiers to accompany us? We might need to send back messages in a hurry, and they would be of immense help.'

Gamil nodded and then said, 'In the meantime, I am going to start making preparations for war. We might have to march against Isin or Lasra, and I want to be prepared for that. Perhaps we ought to have crushed those two cities when we defeated them all those years ago. We won't be making that same mistake again,' he concluded ominously.

A glum-faced Sabium sat near the bow of the leading boat, as it scythed through the waters on its way down the river. He was in pain from the wound on his shoulder, but he didn't show it. A messenger had come up to him the previous night, asking him to meet Arjuna and the others in the morning, behind Esagila. He had barely been able to sleep the rest of the night.

He was up and about even before the sun rose over the horizon. Throwing some clothes into a bundle, he had walked down to the Esagila. The temple was just opening for the day, and he went inside to offer prayers to Bal Marduk for the success of their mission. He had come out within half an hour and walked down to the river where he had sat on the stairs and waited for the others to show up.

They had come by shortly. Lilith, Arjuna, Shrutasena and five more men, all leading two horses. It was obvious what the extra horses were for. It would speed up their journey if they could keep switching between horses. They had distributed themselves across three large royal boats and were now on their way downriver to the south. They could have just ridden down the bank on their own side of the river and come up to the site where the boat had been abandoned. But it was Lilith's idea to try and follow the route that the kidnappers had taken. Lilith, who was in command of their group, felt that it would give them some insights into the minds of the kidnappers.

Sabium was in the boat along with the Bharatiyas and Lilith, but he was in a peculiar mood and didn't want to sit along with them. He wasn't in the right frame of mind for conversation. He thought exclusively of Mylitta and the place that she had come to occupy in his life. His relationship with her had been playful to begin with. At least on his part. He had no idea what she had felt or did feel about him. *After all, who knew the mind of a woma*n, he thought morosely. But she had come to mean the world to him. He had understood this during his recent trip to Hind. He had wanted to come back home, of course—but he had wanted to come back home to her. He hoped that she was all right and that the kidnappers were treating her well. If something happened to her . . . he didn't quite know what he would do. All he knew was the searing rage coursing through him. Even with a broken wing, he was ready to unleash unspeakable violence on her kidnappers.

Fifty or so miles away, Zabaya and Erra sat together over the remnants of their campfire, eating some mutton that they had roasted on the spit, the previous night. The others in their group were still asleep, including the two women that they had kidnapped.

Erra had been furious when the others had come aboard the vessel with the two captives. As the boat had sailed downriver, Erra had lost his cool at Zabaya and the others.

'What on earth have you got the captives for? Why haven't you killed them already? Let me kill them and dump them overboard,' he had thundered.

Zabaya had got in his face and physically restrained him. It had been a challenge. Erra was as strong as him and his anger seemed to have increased his strength. Zabaya had struggled with him, and eventually, as Erra's anger dissipated, so did his need to throw the women overboard. He had sat there to one side of the boat glowering at the two petrified women, his chest heaving with emotion. Eventually, he had calmed down enough to ask, 'What happened to the others?'

'Gone,' said Zabaya shortly.

'Huh?'

'Gone. As in finished. Dead.'

'Did you get the others? The king, the queen, Prince Murabi?'

Zabaya shook his head.

'Perhaps you had better tell me what happened.'

Zabaya told him about the attack, the spirited defence by the bodyguards, and then the flight—the urgent need to escape.

'It was while we were trying to get away that we thought that it would be a good idea to take a couple of captives. These were the only two we could get our hands on.'

'Who are they?' asked Erra.

'Princess Sybella and a companion I suppose,' said Zabaya.

'We will have the entire Babylonian army after us now,' said Erra.

'Not at the moment, though. You did a good job burning those boats.'

'Where do we go now? If we head to Lasra, your king might well kill us all and wash his hands off the whole matter.'

'Wouldn't the same apply to your king?' asked Zabaya.

Erra's face took on a troubled expression.

'There is merit in what you say,' he acknowledged, reluctantly. 'But that's the worry. We can't just land up at Isin or Lasra with the prisoners.'

'What do we do then?'

Erra thought for a while, passing his fingers over his forehead.

'Let's take the boat all the way down past Isin. We will do it at night so that no one at Isin will see us pass. After that, we can get off the boat on the far bank. You know that large, wooded area to Isin's southwest? We can hold them there while I pay a visit to the king. If the king threatens to wash his hands off the matter, I can at least threaten him with exposure.'

'Let me do the same with my king,' said Zabaya, adding in a soft whisper, 'but only once you are back.

I don't trust these remaining guys to hold the women if both of us are missing.'

Erra nodded as the boat sailed on downriver.

Enlil-Bani, emperor of all Isin, royal protector of the people and the land between the rivers—and countless other pompous, meaningless titles—sat pensively on a cushioned chair in his room. Before him stood the scar faced Erra. The king was a stocky, bearded man with a high forehead and piercing eyes. Those eyes were hooded as he was lost in thought.

Erra had come by shortly after noon and requested a meeting with the king. Enlil-Bani had called Erra into his own private chambers. The news that Erra had delivered had left him sitting pensively in his chair.

Erra kept quiet, waiting for his king to speak. He knew the man and the shrewd brain that his face concealed. He knew that the king would be working out the various permutations and combinations, and finally reach a decision.

Enlil-Bani eventually stirred and said, 'You know, I could always deny that I had anything to do with this?'

'Yes, my king. You could do that. But we could always return the captives to Babylon and claim that it was you who had ordered us to do it, but that we, as citizens of Babylon, were all overcome with remorse. Who do you think they will believe?'

Enlil-Bani gave a tight little smile. He hadn't expected anything different from Erra. He knew the kind of man he was dealing with. After all, no other man would have accepted the kind of order he had given.

'What does Nur-Adad say?'

'We haven't gone to him yet. Once I get back with your response, then Zabaya, the man from Lasra, will go to his king.'

'What do you think I should do?' asked Enlil-Bani.

'There might be an opportunity here, my king.'

'Opportunity. . . ?'

' . . . to renegotiate.'

'Hmmm,' said the king, thoughtfully, adding, 'There are dangers to that, too.'

'There was danger when we undertook this plan of yours, Your Majesty,' said Erra.

'True. But there was no real threat of an invasion had you carried things out according to the plan.'

'Plans tend to come up against reality and break down. That's why we have alternatives. I am sure that you would have thought of some before you tasked me with killing the royal family.'

Enlil-Bani gave a tight-lipped smile again. 'Do you think we can defend ourselves against a full-fledged attack?'

'I don't think it will come to that, Sire. Why would they attack knowing that we hold the princess?'

The king shrugged. 'What if Sin-Muballit is willing to sacrifice the princess?'

'Sacrifice his own daughter?'

'Why not? If it came between my kingdom and my daughter, I would choose my kingdom,' he said, coldly.

Erra shuddered. He thought of himself as a practical man but even he would have baulked at sacrificing his children for some cause. Not that he had any children of his own to sacrifice.

'At this point, my king, I don't think we have much choice.'

'What if we hid the princess at Larsa?'

Erra waited for him to continue.

'We could then claim, truthfully, sort of, that we didn't have the girl, and it wasn't our issue. We could always promise Larsa that we will support them if the Babylonians come at them with their army. We would then be in their rear and could launch an attack. Sin-Muballit would be caught between two armies. Yes, I think that might be a better course of action.'

Erra wasn't terribly convinced by this. 'What if Nur-Adad thinks the same and that we ought to have the princess here at Isin? After all, it was our idea, an idea mooted by you that caused us to reach out to them. Their deniability would sound more plausible than ours.'

Enlil-Bani furrowed his brows again in thought. 'Could we hide the women somewhere in between us and Larsa?'

'You know the land, Sire. There are a few wooded areas, but other than that, it is flat farmland. Where are we going to hide them? I am sure they will be sending out search parties. We can perhaps misdirect them by making it seem as if we are going further south, but then we *will* have to double back here.'

'And keep the girls where?'

Erra told him.

Enlil-Bani gave it some thought and said, 'All right. Do that. I don't like it, but I don't see what choice we have.'

Chapter Ten

On the Trail

Progress was frustratingly slow, despite the flat terrain, which was mostly fields interrupted occasionally by groves of date palms. There were some wooded areas, but these were few and far between.

They had disembarked at the exact same spot as the kidnappers—right next to the boat they had used, in fact. They had gone aboard and looked around, not out of any necessity, but more out of curiosity and to ensure that this boat had indeed carried the two women that they were looking for. It was Sabium who had spied a little bead on the boat and picked it up with a cry.

'That's Mylitta's!' he exclaimed.

'How do you know?' asked Shrutasena.

'I know,' insisted Sabium. 'I had given her a bead necklace after my trip to Bharat.'

Shrutasena took a closer look at the necklace and shrugged his shoulders. Arjuna gesticulated to Lilith to have a look. She picked it up and after a quick glance, nodded her head.

'Yes, this is from Hind. It could be anyone's, though,' she said, pursing her lips.

Arjuna had to struggle to bring his mind back to the task. Those pursed lips were very attractive.

'What is the probability that this boat, the one which the kidnapper's took, will have beads from Bharat other than those from Mylitta's necklace?'

'Very slim', agreed Lilith. 'Also, it must be deliberately done by her.'

'How do you say that?' asked Shrutasena.

'If the necklace had broken of its own, we would see more beads scattered around. I doubt if the kidnappers would allow her to pick up all the pieces of a broken necklace.'

Sabium's eyes brightened with pride. 'That's my girl.'

'Yeah, Sabium. You seem to have picked someone with beauty and brains. Perhaps to compensate for your lack of both those qualities,' teased Arjuna.

Sabium looked pleased and then the smile disappeared from his face as the import of the bead hit him. They had his girl.

Lilith, with the intuition that only women seem to possess, walked over and put her arm around him, saying, 'Don't worry, Sabium. We will get them back.'

Small words of comfort, but they were all she had at that moment, and they seemed to revive Sabium's spirits somewhat.

They had started off along the riverbanks, stopping ever so often to quiz people as to whether they had seen

a group of men taking a couple of women along. They
had initial success as those living near the place where
the boat had docked, remembered seeing a few men and
two women descend from the boat and go in a southerly
direction. However, as they went further south, the number
of such sightings decreased, and they often had to detour
into villages and speak to a number of people before they
could locate someone who had seen the group.

This made the going agonisingly slow.

Sybella and Mylitta's legs were sore. They sat down on
the ground, their backs resting against the same date-palm
tree. Their kidnappers had moved them into the palm
grove for the night. They had taken to travelling through
the fields rather than through the main roads.

They had initially moved south, keeping parallel to
the river for a day, before stealing a boat and crossing
it. The women had no idea where they were. Neither of
them had travelled this far south of Babylonia, at least
not along this path.

Sybella had been to Isin and Larsa once before, but she
was much younger then, and as a princess, had travelled by
the royal chariot. She hadn't paid any particular attention
to the roads, or the general lay of the land. It all looked the
same to her. Fields, fields and yet more fields.

They had been on the move constantly since they
had crossed the river a second time. From snippets of
conversations that Sybella could catch, she surmised that

they were south of Isin and, because the sun set to their right, she knew that they were moving further south.

'Do you think they are taking us to Larsa?' she asked Mylitta in a whisper.

'It could be, Princess,' Mylitta replied.

'Let's keep track of the directions. Also, keep your ears peeled for any bits of conversation that you can overhear.'

Mylitta nodded and then said, 'Princess. I have to tell you something.'

'What?'

Mylitta opened her hand and showed her a little bead.

'Your lovely necklace,' exclaimed Sybella. 'Oh, I am so sorry. How did it break?'

'I broke it.'

'But, why?'

'I have been leaving beads every time we have rested.'

'You mean . . .'

'Yes. I am trying to leave those who will come searching for us, something to look for. I left one on the boat that they kidnapped us in, the campsites the first two nights and also in the boat that brought us here. I am really hoping that one of them finds the beads and recognizes these as beads from Hind.'

Sybella hugged her. 'Oh, you clever, clever girl. I wish I had thought of that.'

They heard coarse laughter from their kidnappers and disentangled themselves to see them standing there, with mocking looks in their eyes.

'If you need hugs, we can provide you some,' said one of the two men that they had identified as the leaders.

'Yeah, two pretty women such as yourselves. The boys here are wondering when it is that they will be able to comfort you,' said the scarred one, with a gleam in his eyes.

Sybella and Mylitta drew back in fright. These men could very well carry out their threats and they knew it. Sybella, summoning whatever courage she possessed, passed on to her through generations of royal blood, retorted, 'You do know that my father will have people looking for us. And when they do ...'

'When they do, they will find your dead bodies, before they can even get to us,' finished the scarred one whom they had heard referred to as Erra.

'Don't have your hopes up too high, princess. You aren't going to make it back to your loved ones anytime soon,' said the other man who they had heard referred to as Zabaya.

'Perhaps we will get to know each other better over the course of the next few days.'

That same night, the women spied some ghostly shapes come into camp and stand around the dying embers of the campfire. The men squatted down on their haunches and picking up the remaining pieces of meat that were sitting on sticks on top of the fire, bit into them.

Silence reigned for some time, punctuated by the crunching sound of teeth on meat and the occasional burp as the newcomers satiated their hunger. It was only after they had started licking their fingers that Zabaya gave voice.

'Well, Gandash? Shall we get down to business now?'

Gandash grinned, revealing a mouth filled with gaps and dotted with rotting, discoloured teeth.

'What is it you want?'

'We want you and your men to lay in wait for people who come in search of us and kill them,' said Erra in a matter-of-fact voice. The expression on his face, however, could not entirely hide his disgust at having to deal with the likes of Gandash.

'And what do *we* get in return?'

Zabaya juggled a bag of coins in his hands. Gandash reached his hand out towards it greedily and Zabaya threw it to him. Gandash gave him that same rotten-toothed grin as he ran his fingers through his ugly, unkempt beard, leaving bits of meat from his fingers in it.

'What about them?' he asked, pointing to the two women. His men followed his glance and whistled appreciatively while eyeing them covetously.

'They are not part of the deal,' said Erra.

'Maybe we want them to be part of the deal,' said Gandash, getting up. He had barely stood up when Zabaya moved and in one motion, brought his sword out of its scabbard and had its point touching the underside of Gandash's chin.

'He said,' muttered Zabaya with emphasis, 'that they are *not* part of the deal.'

Gandash's beady little eyes looked at him, possibly calculating the chances of his men and he being able to overpower these men. Prudence won over greed and avarice as Gandash threw his hands up in mock surrender.

'All right. All right! If those women are for you, we understand.'

'You will get a similar bag once you have accomplished your task.'

'And where will I meet you?'

'Come near, Isin,' said Zabaya as he gave him directions on where to find him.

'How many men did you say will be part of the group?' Zabaya looked at the scar-faced Erra. 'Fifteen? Twenty?'

'About twenty, maybe,' said Erra.

'About twenty then,' said Zabaya.

'Twenty,' echoed Gandash, adding, 'You want us to go up against twenty soldiers and eliminate all of them? That is dangerous work.'

'You don't get paid this sort of money for easy work,' said Erra.

'Yes, but this is *very* dangerous work. I don't think the money that you have given is enough for that,' said Gandash.

Zabaya looked at Erra who nodded. He threw another bag of coins at Gandash. The brigand caught it and hefted it a couple of times in his hands.

'You will get another two like that once you do what we have asked you to do,' said Zabaya.

Gandash nodded and left, his eyes casting a last, lingering look at the women.

❖

'I am not sure anymore,' said the man shaking his head. He was one of the two trackers that they had—men with the gift of following signs on the ground, in the water or even in air. Or so it was said about them. The initial part of the chase, while slow and frustrating, had at least yielded results. They had been able to follow some tracks and then make their way through the villages dotted along the riverbanks. But now, they seemed to have run out of luck. They had hit the road leading south, and the trackers threw up their hands.

'They could very well have travelled up or down this road and there is no way of knowing which. We can't even follow their footprints. The earth is packed hard and as you can see, even we are not leaving any footprints on the ground.'

Lilith went down on her haunches as she scanned the packed earth that was the road. She straightened after a bit, her eyes reflecting the worry she felt inside.

'They could surely not have turned towards the north,' said Arjuna. 'It wouldn't make any sense. If, as we believe, they are from Isin or Larsa, why would they try going back up north, into enemy territory? Surely more people up north would recognize Princess Sybella, and I doubt that they would want to run that risk,' he added.

Lilith brooded on this for a bit and said, 'I agree. We can't be going everywhere aimlessly. We need to figure out how their minds might work. I do not think that they would have turned back up north. But where could they go down south? We are already past Isin, and only Larsa is further south. To get to either of these places, they would have to cross the river, right?'

The others nodded.

'So how do we know that they haven't already crossed over?'

'We don't,' said Arjuna.

'Here is what I would suggest then. Let's split up into two teams. One team can go down south checking for crossings nearer Larsa. The other team could start looking for crossings somewhere along this vicinity,' said Lilith.

Arjuna and Shrutasena looked at each other and then back at Lilith.

'That sounds like a plan. Sergeant, why don't you and Sabium go with one half of the soldiers and head on down south. Lilith here, and I, will take the other team and start scouting for some indication of a crossing north of you.'

'Oh, why don't we let the sergeant here go with Lilith and you come with me?' asked Sabium, his face showing no emotion barring a twinkle in his eye.

Arjuna stared at him flatly while Lilith turned away, a small smile on her lips.

'Why? Don't you have trust in the sergeant's ability to protect you in case of a skirmish?' asked Arjuna a trifle belligerently.

'Oh, no. No! Not at all. I always wanted to spend time with the sergeant here. Right, Shrutasena?'

Shrutasena, a man of few words, merely grunted, but the light smile playing on his lips told Arjuna that he was in on the fun at his expense. He scowled and then broke into a wide grin and winked at them, chancing a quick glance back to ensure that Lilith wasn't looking at him. She however, had her back turned on them and was glancing into the distance, studiously ignoring them.

'How do we keep in touch?' asked the ever-practical Shrutasena.

Lilith pursed her lips. Then her face cleared as she asked Sabium, 'You are a trader. Do you know that trading post between Isin and Larsa?'

'Yes, of course,' said Sabium.

'We will send a man with news from our end, every evening, say a couple of hours after the sun sets. You do the same. We will likely not move in the night, so that gives the messengers the time to deliver their messages and get back to their own groups.'

Shrutasena gave a nod of appreciation for the idea as his team started preparations to head south.

It was evening of the second day since they had divided into two teams. Lilith and Arjuna were walking a few yards in front of the others, their hands almost touching. Arjuna wanted desperately to reach out and take her hand, but while Lilith had poured her heart out to him, he didn't think that entitled such familiarity on his part. Arjuna made sure that he treated Lilith like the soldier that she was, in front of the others. Especially since she was the leader of the pack. She was known in Babylonia as one of the fiercest warriors and there was nothing but respect for her on the part of her comrades.

They had been searching for two whole days along the riverbank and had not succeeded in finding any hint of the kidnappers having come this way.

They stopped and looked around. The river wasn't very wide at this point. This was one of the many tributaries of the Euphrates before it wended its way to the sea. They could see the other bank of the river quite clearly.

A little boy was skipping stones on the water ahead of them. They paused, marveling at his skill, and soon Arjuna and Lilith, along with the other soldiers, joined in, attempting to skip stones across the river's surface. It's one of those timeless games that never loses its charm, no matter one's age. The soldiers were soon having friendly wagers on whose stones would bounce the most times on the water surface.

The weariness of a futile search magically deserted them as they seemingly regressed to their own childhoods and a simpler time. The young lad, seeing the adults trying to emulate him, started skipping stones with renewed vigour, making them bounce even more times before they sank into the river, as if spurred on by the challenge posed by the men. His eyes sparkled and he laughed out loudly as the efforts of the adults came a poor second to his own stone-slinging prowess.

Lilith approached the boy and said, 'You seem to be really good at this.'

'I have had many hours of practice,' said the lad, proudly.

'It sure looks like it. Do you live in that village?' she asked, indicating a village a few hundred yards from where they stood.

'Yes.'

'What are you doing here alone? Won't your parents be worried?'

The lad shook his head. 'They know I won't do anything stupid. Also, I am a good swimmer. I am waiting for my father.'

'Oh? Where has he gone?'

'He has gone with my uncle to the other side.'

'To buy something?'

'Buy? No. To get his boat.'

'His boat is on the other side?'

'Yes.'

'How did his boat get to the other side?'

'Some people stole his boat.'

'How did he know that it was stolen?'

'I saw it.'

'Saw it being stolen?'

'Yes. It was earlier in the morning. A few men sneaked up, untied the boat, got into it and rowed to the other side.'

'Were there any women in that group?'

The little lad scrunched up his eyes as if trying to remember.

'Yes. I think there were two women. The men were pushing them onto the boat.'

Lilith's heartbeat quickened. This could only be the kidnappers. She thanked the boy and handed him a couple of coins. He looked at her questioningly.

'Keep it. It is for how well you skip stones,' she said as she ran back to the others to share the news with them.

It is true that human beings do not understand the importance of chance or luck in the success of their endeavours. We are quick to blame chance for our failures, yet we often overlook its role in our successes, choosing instead to credit our own efforts. Lilith understood that they had been incredibly lucky in coming upon the little boy when they did.

Chapter Eleven

The Decoy

Mylitta put one foot in front of the other, mechanically. She was dazed and tired. The many hours of walking in furnace-like conditions had sapped her strength. But what had weakened her resolve more was being separated from Sybella.

Sybella and she had drawn solace from each other ever since they had been kidnapped. They had comforted one another and allayed each other's fears. They had spoken in whispers deep into the night, giving each other hope of what the new day would bring. A swift rescue perhaps. But with each passing day, their hopes had dimmed. Still, the feeling that they were in this together had given them the strength to carry on walking through the long, brutally hot days over hard, baked earth. While it was still only spring, it almost felt like summer was upon them. Spring in these parts didn't last very long, in any case.

They had been together until they had all crossed the river again. It was then that the kidnappers had separated into two groups, with one group taking Sybella and moving south, while her group had turned towards the north. She and Sybella had held each other fiercely when they realized that they would not be going together, with Sybella whispering into her ears, 'Do not, I repeat, do not cry. Do not give these savages the satisfaction of watching your tears.'

And so, she hadn't. She had watched them leave and then, prodded by her captors, had started walking. It was late in the evening, and she was yearning for a break, yet too proud to ask them to stop on her behalf. What she had done, however, unknown to them, was to provide hints to anyone who might come in search of them. She had taken to dropping a few of her beads every mile or so. She had about a hundred and fifty beads in all. She had counted them one night. She dropped them along the way, hoping against hope that those searching for her would come upon them. She had also taken to intentionally leaning against plants or trees and breaking branches surreptitiously. Surely, a good tracker would be able to follow these. She knew the chances were slim, but she wasn't ready to resign herself to her fate—at least not yet.

They had crossed over to the far bank on the same boat that the kidnappers had taken. The young lad's father was only too happy to make some money by ferrying Lilith, Arjuna and the group across. Lilith had asked him to take the boat to the exact spot that he had found it. As they stepped off the boat, one of the soldiers shouted with excitement.

'Here! I found some.'

Lilith and Arjuna hastened over to see that he held three red beads in the palm of his right hand.

'Mylitta!' exclaimed Arjuna even as the tracker in their group went down on his haunches, peering at the ground. This close to the river was probably one of the few places where they could observe footprints.

The tracker looked keenly at the ground and then said something to Lilith in a dialect that Arjuna found hard to grasp. He noticed the disturbed look on the faces of the other soldiers.

'What'd he say?' he asked Lilith.

'He says there is only one woman in the group,' Lilith replied.

'But that means ...'

'Yes. They have split them up into two groups.'

'Are we sure it is Mylitta that we are following and not the princess?'

Lilith turned to the tracker and asked him the question. He gave her a short, crisp reply which she then translated for Arjuna's benefit.

'He says those footprints belong to Mylitta. He says he can make out from the tracks who it is, and this is definitely her. Mylitta's feet are longer than those of Sybella's.'

Arjuna paused to think. 'Should we try to cast around for signs of where the other team went?'

Lilith shook her head. 'We know only one team crossed over on the boat. Which means that they must have divided into two or more groups somewhere on the other side. We have no way of knowing where that could be. It would be an aimless pursuit.'

'You have a point there. So, we follow Mylitta and see where that leads us?'

'We follow Mylitta and see where that leads us.'

Gandash sat on a log as his men collapsed around him, each wearing the same weary mien. Tough, nasty specimens, and everyone in need of a good bath. They exuded a smell that assaulted the olfactory senses of other members of the human species. They themselves, however, seemed completely oblivious of it. Or perhaps they had just grown used to it.

Gandash was not sitting around aimlessly. He was waiting for word from scouts that he had sent out along the riverbank to pick up the trail of those who were following his paymasters. It was a fairly long stretch of land, and he wasn't in any hurry. He knew he couldn't do anything until he found out where the men that he was chasing had landed.

He was not generally a patient man, except when he waited for prey. Then, like any other predator of the jungle, he could be inordinately patient. He had grown up as an orphan along these very banks, surviving on scraps that the people threw him. He had grown to resent them early on in life. Resent their homes, their families, and their perfect lives. He had discovered, when quite young, that he was physically very strong. He had found a loaf of stale bread as he was rooting through the trash outside a village. A larger boy had approached him, intending to wrest it from him. Gandash had thrown him off and then pummelled him into the dust with his fists. He had left the boy on the ground, bloodied and unconscious as he dug his teeth triumphantly into the stale bread, his only meal for the day.

Since that day, he realized that he could wield his Marduk-given strength to his advantage. He had found it easier to feed himself by preying on people and had become quite good at understanding who he could and couldn't attack at that age. As he grew, the number of people he couldn't overpower physically dwindled, and with it came a corresponding rise in the audacity of his escapades. He had soon attracted some of the other urchins around him; orphans like himself. There had been no doubt in anyone's mind who the leader of the pack was.

Gandash gave a contented smile as his mind flitted through his memories, absently patting the money pouches that had been given to him by those kidnappers. He, however, did not have the self-awareness to wonder why despite his obvious physical advantages and the years of preying on hapless victims, he still had to scrounge around, ever so often, for money, to barely subsist. He still didn't have a roof over his head or fine clothes to wear. In a perverse way, he looked down on those who did have houses to retire to or wore fancy clothes. His lips curled into a sneer as he thought of the dandies and pansies who paraded around in their finery. *Little better than weak women*, he thought.

His reverie was interrupted by the clip clop of hoofs. He looked up to see a man getting off a horse. It was one of his scouts.

'Well?' he asked.

'Found where they got off the boat,' said the scout, a short, thin man with a squint.

'How far away?'

'About five miles or so. They are not moving too fast. If we leave now, we can come upon them in a few hours.'

Gandash nodded. The thing seemed to be working out for him. He loved the night. Night-time was good for ambushes.

The crescent moon seemed to make its way cautiously up the sky. The gem-encrusted sky looked brilliant as the great swathe of stars cut across the heavens. Lilith, Arjuna and the other soldiers in their group were seated in a little grove, beside a pond. They sat with their backs to the pond. They had a fire going, and some meat was roasting on the spit. Beside their fire lay the remnants of an older, long-extinguished blaze. Perhaps a day or two older. Inside the blackened and charred remains, they had found three little beads. Mylitta was still guiding them, as she had guided them throughout the day.

The kidnappers had initially followed a path parallel to the main road leading to Isin but later veered off, cutting north-east through the fields. It was only because of the keen-eyed tracker that they had spotted the three little beads that Mylitta had dropped when she understood that they were leaving the path. There were long stretches where they couldn't find beads or any other signs from her. The tracker, when asked, had pointed out to them that the clever Mylitta, probably trying to conserve her beads, was only dropping them when their direction of travel changed. She did, however, leave other signs.

The tracker had pointed out a place where her foot had seemingly slipped on the raised earthen bunds between fields, breaking off a bit of the bund and leaving a clear imprint on the wet ground. He also showed them where she had fallen down and had crushed a sugarcane plant. In doing so, she had artfully managed to arrange the leaves in such a way that they all pointed in one direction.

'This one is very smart,' was his only comment.

In yet another place, they had been passing through a grove, and she had probably acted as if she was stumbling and had got hold of a low-lying branch of a tree and broken it. If the branch had broken naturally, it would have pointed downward; however, this one angled noticeably in a specific direction.

'See here again? She has broken it off to show us the way.'

'May Indra, Varuna, Agni, Bal Marduk and all the Gods bless this girl. Sabium is one lucky man,' said Arjuna to Lilith.

They had followed the signs to this camp and had settled down here for the night. There was water nearby and they were buoyed by the knowledge that they weren't too far behind the abductors and Mylitta.

Arjuna and Lilith lay on the ground, a few feet from each other with their legs stretched out. They were about twenty yards away from the other soldiers. They had finished their meal, settling into that drowsy little lull just before sleep takes over.

As they lay there, looking up at the sky, Lilith asked Arjuna, 'Do you believe that our fates are written in the stars?'

Arjuna turned momentarily to look at her and then looked back up. 'I really haven't given it all that much thought. I have been taught that it does. Why? What do you think?'

'For the longest time, I didn't believe in it. Especially after that whole episode with my uncle. The palace priest had told my father so many times in my hearing that I was destined to rule that land and do great things. And then, I became a slave. I figured that the old priest was a charlatan. He was only saying stuff that my father wanted to hear.'

'But now?' She turned towards him. 'Now? Now I am not so sure. Perhaps there is something written in the stars.'

'Perhaps you can still become the ruler of your land,' said Arjuna.

'Yeah right.' Lilith sighed. 'I am still a slave, you know. Yes, I am the chief of the queen's guards, but I am still a slave. Bound to her till death. Or until she releases me. Not even another member of the royal family. *She* has to release me personally. And I don't see why she would do that.'

'Not even if we were to save her daughter?' asked Arjuna.

Lilith turned back to look up at the sky.

'Perhaps. Then again, who knows how the mind of royalty works.' She sighed again and closed her eyes. The flames in the fireplace had died and even the embers had turned from bright red to a dull grey.

The clink of stone against stone, as someone stepped on them, jolted Lilith awake. She reacted instantly, calling out Arjuna's name to wake him, taking up the sword and the knife that she always kept next to her, and yelling out to her soldiers.

It was too late for at least two of them as their attackers had already plunged their heavy knives into their sides repeatedly. The leader of the attackers had not seen Arjuna and Lilith since they had been sleeping off to one side. He turned toward them now, trailed by two more men, while the remaining soldiers swiftly joined the battle.

Gandash was to soon find out that preying on hapless citizens and trying to ambush well-trained soldiers was an entirely different game. Lilith and Arjuna, seeing three men come towards them, had moved apart so as not to get in each other's way. Gandash signalled to the men behind him to advance and attack the pair, intending to use the distraction to swiftly eliminate his opponents under the cover of the assault. The plan was one he had used before and with success. However, the one problem with this plan was that the opponents had not been trained soldiers, especially elite soldiers like Lilith and Arjuna.

Even as his men approached them, the two stepped inside their line of attack. The opponents' smaller swords hissed past their ears as they parried the blows, then smoothly plunged their own swords into their attackers' bellies. So smoothly was this done that it almost looked choreographed and rehearsed. Which in a sense it was, since they had been practising moves with the heavy iron swords together for a number of days.

Gandash, who had been preparing for his own attack, was suddenly taken aback at the sight of his men's crumpled forms sprawled before him. He looked up and saw two figures. One was larger and bulkier, and the other was slimmer, shorter and somewhat wiry. The second figure also had one arm bandaged and was closer to him. Gandash figured that he would be the easier to attack and moved towards the shadowy figure now waiting for him. The other figure, he noticed through his peripheral vision, had moved towards where the larger group was fighting with his men.

He stepped slowly towards his opponent and picked up the sword of one of his men who had gone down. He twirled the two swords slowly in his hands as he advanced. He noticed that his opponent stood very still, waiting for him to make the move. Gandash flashed his rotten-toothed smile, but the night kept it hidden from his opponent. He was only a few steps away now. Behind him, he could hear the shouts of battle. The clangs of swords. The rasping breaths of men fighting for their lives. The grunts of men straining their every sinew. There was the susurration of feet on leaves, and thumps of bodies as they fell to earth. There were also the muted whispers of knives and swords slicing through layers of flesh and muscle. These were inevitably followed by cries from the victims.

Gandash heard all of this and yet his mind was focused on the opponent standing in front. As he took his right hand back and over, preparatory to taking that next step and bringing it down on his foe, he thought that it would be too easy. This frail person in front of him didn't have a chance.

The frail person suddenly exploded into action. Gandash's brain at some level had registered that this person was a woman. Even as his brain processed that bit of information, the woman had moved smoothly and had thrust aside the sword he held in his left arm with a stroke of her own. As his right arm came down, his opponent's sword seemed to ricochet off his other sword and its tip gashed his right forearm. A spurt of blood erupted from that arm. Gandash looked up in surprise and tried to slash at her with the sword in his left hand, but she had danced away, out of range.

He came at her again, more slowly now. Less assured. His right forearm dripping blood. She stood still and once again, at the very last moment, as he attacked with both swords, she slid down to her knees. His swords whistled over her head but hers bit hard into his right thigh, severing several muscles there. Gandash's feet nearly gave way, and it was only the sheer, brute strength of the man that kept him upright. He collapsed to his right knee, his leg refusing to support his weight. He dug the short sword of his into the ground to gain some balance and then looked up at his opponent.

She was standing rock still as she waited for him to take his fighting stance again. This time, however, she didn't wait for him to make the move. She rushed in quickly and twirled her wrists in effortless motion. The blade of her heavy sword came down upon his left arm and severed it completely, leaving a bloody stump in its place. Gandash looked at it in surprise. The pain hadn't hit him yet. The pain from the severed hand was overwhelmed by the other pain where her sword, doing an intricate dance in the air, was thrust into his belly. It went in smoothly and came out through his back. As his opponent pulled again at the sword, it ripped out his innards. That is when the pain hit Gandash and he screamed in torment.

Arjuna had rushed to the help of the other soldiers. Their fight had been short but hard. They had initially been overwhelmed by the attackers, but Lilith's timely shout had alerted them, and they had regrouped. The attackers were a motley bunch. The Babylonian men soon realized their opponents were not trained soldiers and countered with greater vigour. Gradually, training and skill won over bravado and the element of surprise.

They soon cut down on the remaining attackers while a couple of them managed to flee. Arjuna sneaked a quick look back to see how Lilith was doing. He saw her standing over the large man who had attacked her, her sword pointed at his throat.

'Lilith, wait!' he cried urgently as he ran to her side.

'Get me a torch,' he yelled at one of the soldiers. The man quickly lit the torch from the embers of their fire and brought it over to Arjuna who held it up over the stricken man.

Gandash looked back at him, his eyes reflecting the pain that he was under. His breathing was short, shallow and stertorous. His hands clutched his abdomen and sweat streaked his face. Arjuna bent down as did Lilith. Gandash's eyes flickered from one to the other.

'You . . . you fight well . . . ' he rasped out the words slowly, painfully.

Lilith looked on with steely eyes. Arjuna looked across at her and then down at the man.

'What's your name?'

'Gandash . . .'

'Well, Gandash. Who put you up to this?'

Gandash smiled and then tried to laugh. His laughter turned into an extended bout of coughing. Coughing that brought blood frothing out of his mouth.

'Do you really want to protect the men who sent you and your men to certain death?' asked Arjuna, a trifle brutally. Gandash took in a few deep gulps of air. The shadows cast by the lone torch flickered around him.

'Isin,' he said.

'Isin? Not Larsa?'

Gandash shook his head. 'Get paid . . . in . . . Isin,' he spat out the words with difficulty. His eyes were starting to close.

'Where in Isin? Where Gandash?' insisted Arjuna.

'Palace . . . outside . . . Isin.'

'Which side?'

Gandash's eyes closed, and his breath gurgled in his chest. A thin stream of blood ran out of the corner of his mouth.

'Which side, Gandash?'

Gandash's eyes flickered open. 'Eastern . . . gate . . .'

And then he was gone. His breath gurgled out of his lungs one last time and he lay still.

Lilith's eyes met Arjuna's. 'We know where to go now,' she said.

Chapter Twelve

Despair and Hope

Shrutasena and Sabium had not had much success. They had spent two days riding south along the riverbank, stopping frequently to question people, but they had not come across anyone who had any news about the group that had kidnapped the princess.

It was towards noon of the third day since they had split from their group, that Sabium had finally spoken to a man who claimed to have seen a group of men with a woman take the boat to cross over. However, the man was drunk and Shrutasena had not been inclined to believe his claims. Sabium had spent a considerable amount of time questioning him about the woman who accompanied the men and how she looked. He had come back to Shrutasena and the others and said, 'I reckon he is telling the truth. The description he gave of the woman matches Princess Sybella's.'

'What's on the other side?' asked Shrutasena.

'Why, Larsa of course. About five miles south, that is.'

'So, they took her to Larsa? And didn't our messenger get back this morning with news that Lilith and Arjuna are on their way to Isin to free Mylitta?' Sabium nodded.

'That is kind of strange, don't you think?'

'Not really. It just means that our enemies have tried to unite,' said Sabium.

It was Shrutasena's turn to nod.

'So, what do we do now?' asked Sabium.

'We need to follow them. But we can't follow them looking like soldiers now, can we? If they are going to Larsa, don't you think that they will have people on the lookout for us?'

'I suppose so . . .'

'Can you ask the soldiers if they can maybe buy or borrow some clothes that don't scream "soldier" at passersby?'

Sabium smiled that ready smile of his and had a brief conversation with the soldiers. He took considerably longer to get his point across to the soldiers than Shrutasena had spent in telling him.

'What's the problem?' asked Shrutasena.

'They don't like wearing non-soldier clothes and they don't necessarily like taking orders from a civilian like me.'

'Tell them the orders are from me.'

'You aren't a soldier, at least here.'

'Did they agree to what you said?'

'Yeah, they did. I had to use the name of Prince Murabi a couple of times, but they finally understood that they had to listen to you and me because Lilith had left us in charge.'

'Well, let's go get ourselves a boat then and be on our way,' said Shrutasena, getting up from the ground where he had been sitting cross-legged, in the fashion of the people of his land.

About five miles south of them, and across the river, Zabaya was striding through the palace, a guard leading the way as they approached the king's council chambers. Zabaya and his men had reached the city a few hours earlier. They had brushed past the guards at the gate and commandeered a closed bullock cart. Zabaya had roughly pushed Sybella into the cart and got in alongside her. He had asked the cart owner to drive the cart towards the far side of town. A far seedier side than the one he was in now. There was an old, dilapidated and abandoned house there that Zabaya was headed for. The house was in the possession of a ruffian whom Zabaya occasionally employed for tasks unfit for his soldiers.

The house had a serviceable dungeon, and more importantly, had an escape route that only he knew of. He had deposited the princess in the dungeon, and after having cleaned up, left for the palace.

The king was seated in the council chambers along with some of his close ministers and advisers. But when he saw Zabaya, he signalled to him to stay put. He brought his meeting to a close quickly and then waved his hand at Zabaya to approach him.

'My King,' Zabaya said, kneeling and bowing his head.

'Well?' asked Nur-Adad.

Zabaya took his time to respond.

'Well?' asked Nur-Adad again in irritation. He was an elderly man with grey hair, rapidly balding. He also had the rich man's paunch.

'Things did not quite go according to plan.'

Nur-Adad took a date from the bowl, popped it into his mouth, and sucked on it. After a moment, he said, 'Why don't you tell me everything.'

As Zabaya recounted the story, the king sat there going through the bowl of dates. At the end of it, he spat out the seed of the date he had been sucking on and said, 'So, you guys messed it up royally. I was afraid of that. I will have to deny all knowledge of this, of course.'

'What? The girl is already here with us.'

'Did I ask you to bring the girl here? You were the one who came to me with this cock and bull plan of trying to eliminate the Babylonian royal family. I accepted, but had warned you even then, that if anything went wrong, I would have to wash my hands off the whole affair.'

'Yes, but . . .'

Nur-Adad cut him off. 'Things have not just gone wrong; you have made a proper meal of it. What got into your head that you had to kidnap the girl? Why couldn't you have killed her then and there?

Zabaya had been asking himself this same question. He had not been able to come up with a reason that sounded convincing even to himself.

'Be that as it may,' he said, adding, 'we now have her here. They are bound to eventually come for her. We have a great bargaining chip in our hands. Think about it.'

Nur-Adad gave him a disgusted look.

'And what exactly do you think I can get in exchange for her?'

'Freedom from paying taxes to Babylon?'

'Do you think Sin-Muballit will ever forgive me for this?'

'What can he do?' sneered Zabaya. 'He is old and diseased and rapidly nearing his end. And that young pup of his has barely lost his milk teeth. Do you think we can't take them now if push comes to shove?'

Nur-Adad was lost in thought for a while.

'And think about a Babylonian army caught between us and Isin if it comes to that!' said Zabaya, pushing home his advantage.

A slow smile spread across Nur-Adad's face.

Sybella sat on the hard floor, her hands on her knees, her head resting on them. The floor was filthy, and the stale smell of sweat, urine and faeces enveloped the little cell. She had gone to sleep almost instantly after they had bunged her into the cell. The days of walking had tired her out and even her hunger couldn't keep sleep at bay. It was night when she woke up, and pitch dark. She could hear the squeaks of rats as they scurried across the floor. She was terrified of rats and moved closer to the iron gate since the rats seemed to prefer the back of the cell.

Presently, she heard footsteps. A light cut through the darkness had crept into the cell under her door. As the sound of the footsteps grew louder, the light grew brighter. She put her head on the floor and peered through the gap under the door. Eventually, she could see the elongated shadow of a man on the floor which shrunk as the man carrying the light came near her cell. She heard the plate being placed on the floor and then the clinking of keys. The key was placed in the lock, and she heard the click as the lock opened. The man pushed open the door and light streamed into her cell. She threw up her hands over her eyes to give them time to adjust to the sudden brightness.

The man bent down and placed the plate on the floor. She noticed some fruits, a flat piece of bread and a bowl containing what looked like watery soup. He slid the plate on the ground towards her. He started to get up and gave a gasp, as he caught sight of her face.

'Princess!'

Sybella, who had been eyeing the contents of the plate, looked up quickly.

'You . . . you know me?'

The man gave a stiff little bow.

'Yes, Princess Sybella,' he whispered. 'I am from Babylon.'

'Oh, are you? Can you help me, please? I have been kidnapped. Can you get me out of here? I will give you anything. My father will pay you handsomely . . .'

The man shook his head vigorously as she said this. He then cut in.

'I am sorry, Princess, but I can't help you escape. They will kill me for sure.'

'But you work here.'

'I do. I don't really have a choice. Not anymore. I fell in with them, and I have done a lot of things that my mother would be ashamed of.'

'Atone for it,' begged Sybella. 'I am giving you a chance to atone for it.'

'I can't release you or help you escape,' said the man with a dreadful finality in his voice.

Sybella whimpered when she heard this. She had someone here who knew who she was, who might even have been kindly disposed towards her, but couldn't help her. She wracked her brains as she thought about what she could say to him to change his mind.

'Can you . . . can you at least get a message out that I am being held here?'

The man looked uncertain.

'I don't know . . .'

'I am not asking you to release me. I am merely asking you to pass the word around to someone.'

'But who?'

'Some trader, perhaps? A Babylonian trader?'

The man gave a curt, 'I'll see what I can do' and left.

Sybella took up the plate and started wolfing down the food. Hope is indeed a wonderful thing. Even the watery gravy tasted better now.

Chapter Thirteen

The Ruined Palace

Arjuna and Lilith walked their horses along the road leading to Isin. They were dressed like the others on the road in loose fitting lower garments and tunics that were common to that part of the world. They also had turbans wrapped around their heads to ward off the heat from a sun that seemed to relish beating down fiercely upon the land. Lilith's turban differed from the men's in being more gaily coloured and artfully arranged on her head.

Arjuna's well-muscled frame was evident even through the loose dress, drawing admiring glances from members of the opposite sex. However, it was Lilith who turned many heads. Men are usually more open in their show of admiration for beautiful women and this woman was gorgeous.

Both Arjuna and Lilith ignored the glances that came their way as they rode on their horses, their bundles tied to the saddles and hanging to the sides.

A mile or so before they reached the southern gates of the city, Lilith nodded to Arjuna while nudging her horse

with her knees off the road and into a wooded area. Arjuna
followed suit.

Lilith got off her horse and wiped her face with the
end of the turban that was hanging to one side of her head.

'Hot day,' she observed.

Arjuna's lips curled into a smile.

'Stating the obvious now, are we?'

Lilith's eyes narrowed in mock anger as she turned to
lead her horse further into the woods, away from the eyes
of those on the road.

The attack by Gandash and his band of brigands,
along with the man's dying revelation of where Mylitta
had been taken, forced a re-evaluation of their plans. Lilith
had immediately dispatched one of the soldiers to Babylon
with the message to the king and to prince Murabi to start
with their forces for Isin.

They had then discussed how to go about rescuing
Mylitta. Lilith felt that their only hope in rescuing the
princess was to get their hands on some of the kidnappers,
and that meant going after those who had taken Mylitta as
well. Arjuna was the one who had suggested that they split
up. The attack on them was indication enough that other
groups might be waiting for them. Splitting up gave them
the opportunity to blend into the local populace and make
their way towards Isin.

So here they were, Arjuna and Lilith, waiting for the
others to join them. The woods that they were in ran
parallel to the city walls and then curled around to the
north. Somewhere to the east lay the abandoned palace
Gandash had mentioned as the location where he was
supposed to collect the reward for having killed them.

The plan had been for the members of their group to make their way towards Isin and then gather in the woods opposite the eastern gate. Lilith led the way as she and Arjuna walked their horses through the woods, eastwards. It was certainly cooler here under the canopy provided by the trees than out on the road, and they made good time to cover the couple of miles that Lilith estimated would bring them to the outer edge of the southern wall. She then veered to the north.

After traveling for half an hour, Lilith stopped and tied her horse to a tree. Arjuna followed her example.

'We don't want the sound of the horses to give us away,' she whispered, moving forward silently.

The sun had begun to set, and the shadows had lengthened inside the forest. The birds were flying back to their nests and there was a great clamour in the upper reaches of the trees. The tittering of birds provided them with ample cover as they proceeded north, keeping behind trees.

As they neared the treeline, Lilith got down on all fours and crept forward. Arjuna copied her and soon they had crawled to the very edge of the woods, making their way gingerly through the bushes and foliage.

They spied an abandoned mansion a few hundred yards in front of them. The mansion looked old.

'It looks older than the city walls,' said Arjuna.

'It can't be,' said Lilith.

'Why do you say so?'

'Because, it would have been on the other side of the walls, in the case.'

'It still looks mighty old,' said Arjuna.

To say that the mansion was crumbling would have been an understatement. It must have been stately at some point in time, but that must have been a long, long time ago.

The house was dark and grew darker by the minute as the sun went down over the western horizon. Lilith and Arjuna lay in the grass patiently, peering and listening intently for any signs of habitation in the mansion. The forest started taking on that peculiar stillness that comes with night as the tittering of the birds finally stopped. An owl hooted somewhere and the sound of its ghostly wings flapping softly came to them. A cicada or two started their high-pitched buzz, intermittently. They could hear the whisper of some animal, perhaps a boar, moving through the jungle.

A solitary light sprung to life in the lower left corner of the house. A torch or a lantern had finally been lit. More likely a lantern with a protective covering so that the throw of the light was much reduced. The inhabitants inside were obviously taking care not to advertise their presence to outsiders.

'You think it's them?' asked Arjuna in a subdued whisper.

'Mmhmm. It looks about right. I doubt any reputable people would want to live in that dilapidated structure, and moreover, to keep their movements from the eyes of the others.'

'So now we wait for the others to join us?'

'Now we wait,' said Lilith.

❖

The light from the lantern barely penetrated the all-enveloping darkness that was in the room that Mylitta had been locked in. She sat with her back against a wall, facing the entrance. A thin sliver of light showed under the wooden door.

The door suddenly swung open, and the sliver of light expanded into a band, into which intruded the shadow of a bulky figure. The man to whom the shadow belonged walked in and, yanking her by the hair, dragged her out of the room with a snarl, 'Come here, you wench!'

Mylitta wanted to shriek in pain, but the men had gagged her and tied her hands to her back. Her shriek died in her throat and brought involuntary tears into her eyes. They were tears of pain and not of submission, a lesson the man learnt quickly enough as Mylitta kicked his shin with her foot. The man grunted in pain and then straightened and slapped her across the face. Mylitta's head rocked back under the blow, and she fell down. The man grabbed her hair again and dragged her into the outer room.

Erra looked at Mylitta as she lay on the ground. He asked his henchman to step away and the man moved to one side, bending down to massage his shin. Erra walked over to Mylitta and looked into her eyes, his right hand holding something small between his thumb and forefinger. He reached out and removed the gag from her mouth with the other hand.

Mylitta looked at it. It was one of her beads.

'I see that you recognize your bead,' he said and then dipped his hands into a pouch tied to his waist and brought a few more of the beads out.

Mylitta's eyes widened.

'So,' said Erra in a sibilant whisper, 'you have been a naughty little girl, haven't you?'

She stared back at him, her eyes blazing.

'He,' Erra indicated one of his men, 'found these when he went to pick up some food for us. He had noticed the necklace around your neck when we had picked you and the princess up. It wasn't very difficult to figure out what you have been doing.'

Mylitta's head tilted up in a gesture of pride and defiance.

'If you have found it, others will too.'

Erra looked at her, unblinking. Her eyes were drawn to the scar on his face. Erra, noticing, rubbed his scar along its length, menacingly.

Mylitta gave a mocking little laugh.

'Is that supposed to scare me? All that means is someone was good enough to give you a scar. Perhaps there will be another one on the other side of your face soon. It might provide some symmetry.'

Erra's lips tightened and he brought his face down near hers.

'The scar,' he hissed, 'means that I am still alive and the one who gave me that is dead. I will be waiting, for whoever wants to attempt to rescue you.'

He gestured with his hands to the large henchmen with the hurting shin, who hobbled over to where she lay and then, grabbing her upper arm, dragged her back into her cell and locked the door.

Mylitta sank back onto the floor, and this time, the tears flowed—tears that spoke of hopelessness.

❖

Prince Murabi glanced impatiently at the palace gates. He was expecting to see his father, the king, walk out so that they could commence their journey to Isin. The soldiers were all assembled outside the southern city gates. Sin-Muballit had insisted on coming with them to Isin. The kidnapping of his beloved daughter had enraged him like nothing else before, that Murabi could remember.

He was anxious to get started and Sin-Muballit's delay was making him irritable. He had already snapped at a couple of soldiers. *I shall apologize to them later*, he thought. He knew that the king's slight delay wouldn't significantly change their time to reach Isin, but that was scant consolation to him.

Ever since the soldier sent by Lilith returned with news that she and Arjuna were pursuing the kidnappers to Isin—and that Lilith was certain of Isin's culpability—he had been chomping at the bit. Ready to go out and render retribution to the Isin dogs.

He had already sent the soldier who brought Lilith's message back to her with news of their campaign's commencement. He started pacing the front of the palace again, impatiently, as he waited for his father.

Sin-Muballit eventually emerged from the palace and stepped into the chariot that was waiting in front of the gates. Murabi mounted his horse and trotted it alongside the chariot.

'Do you need to come along, father? You haven't been keeping good health, and this might just exacerbate the situation.'

Sin-Muballit grunted dismissively.

'My daughter was taken. That is an affront that I cannot swallow. That dog Enlil-Bani must pay for what he has done.'

Murabi had no response to this. He knew how much his father doted on Sybella, as he himself did. She was older to him by a couple of years, but she had always mothered him. He nodded to his father and rode alongside him, silently.

The army followed the king and the prince, a mass of burnished bronze—except for the front lines. The front lines were made of elite soldiers, and they carried the black swords, spears and arrows that had been brought from Hind. The new metal that was as superior to the bronze weapons they had always fought with as bronze had been to sticks and stones.

They marched, determination writ large on their faces. Sybella's kidnapping, from inside the city, which they had sworn to protect was looked on as a personal affront by every soldier. They marched now, not just to obey their king's orders but also for their own honour.

Lilith lay hidden in the grass, along with Arjuna and the rest of her men. The men had trickled in during the course of the night and had found Arjuna and her the next morning. They had pulled back from the tree line into the forest, avoiding the risk of a stray glance from the men in the ruined palace. They had been taking turns ever since, with only one man crawling up to the tree line and keeping watch at any given point in time. A new man would replace him every hour or so.

The palace was guarded. That much was apparent. Not only were there guards at the palace doors, but a few men also lounged along the path leading to it. The presence of the guards told Lilith everything she needed to know. You only placed guards if you had something to guard in the first place.

'Well, at least Gandash spoke the truth while he lay dying,' she said.

Arjuna looked at her speculatively.

'What do we do about it? A frontal attack?'

'Without knowing how many people they have or knowing anything about the internal lay of the land?'

Arjuna scratched his beard irritably. He usually liked to be clean shaven, but ever since they had been on the road, he had not had the luxury of having his face shaved. The beard itched and he hated that.

Lilith noticed the scratching and said, 'It gives you a distinguished look.'

'What, this?' he asked, scratching his beard again.

'Yes. Stop worrying about it. It won't itch once it grows out.'

'And what do *you* know about beards?'

She chuckled that warm, throaty chuckle of hers but didn't rise to the bait.

Arjuna's eyebrows went up and then he smiled back at her, while still running his fingers through his beard.

'Getting back to the topic,' he said, 'how do you propose we get to learn more about the number of men they have inside that building and the layout?'

'One of us has to go in.'

'Oh? And I suppose you are thinking of doing that yourself?'

'Well, you certainly can't do it. You won't pass off as a Babylonian or an Isinian.'

'What if I sneaked in at night?'

She considered it and then shook her head.

'Too dangerous. Your chances of getting caught would be very high. No, we need to figure out a way to get in without raising any suspicions.'

She did her familiar biting of the lower lip with her teeth that Arjuna had come to recognize over the past few days as indicative of her being in thought. He thought of telling her to stop it as it was too distracting for him but refrained. While Lilith had opened up a little more to him since the night when she had shared her past, he didn't think that she was the sort that would respond kindly to him flirting with her. He sank into silence beside her, trying to think of some way to get them into the palace.

After what seemed a long time, he noticed Lilith stirring. She looked at him and said, 'I think I know how to get into the palace.'

Chapter Fourteen

Into the Lair

The trader sat with his wares in the central marketplace in Larsa. There was a large umbrella made of straw above his head, working to keep at least some of the heat off him and largely failing. While it did protect him from the direct rays of the sun, it could provide no protection from the heat radiating off the earth and the buildings nearby. It was almost noon, and the sun was at its fiercest. The man, who traded in pots and vessels had been in Larsa for a week now. He was a Babylonian and traded with both Isin and Larsa frequently. He could usually sell all his wares within two or three days. But this time, it was taking him longer. He was finally down to the last of his stock, and was hoping to sell it off today so that he could start back home early next morning.

His eyes, always roaming and searching for the next buyer, had been tracking a man for a while. A bearded, dirty, scruffy and thoroughly unscrupulous-looking man. He had been stopping and staring at the wares at practically every stall, somewhat aimlessly. He didn't seem to have anything specific that he was looking for. He gave equal attention to a vegetable stall as he did to fruits, pots, pans and toys. This perplexed the trader. Usually, it was women who did this. They would walk through the marketplace, looking at all the wares, not necessarily to buy immediately but as a sort of mental inventory that they seemed to keep for later retrieval.

Men, in his experience, were more to the point when it came to buying things. A man would visit the marketplace with something specific to buy on his mind and would go directly to the stalls that sold the product that he was looking for, buy quickly and leave.

This man's behaviour was very distinct in that sense. He seemed to peer at the goods only cursorily. The trader noticed that much of his time was spent in looking at the traders. He knew the man would come to his stall for sure and the trader decided to wait. He kept calling his wares. A couple of women came over and bought some pots after beating him down on price to about half of what he had quoted, which still left him with a healthy profit. He noticed out of the corner of his eyes that the man was two shops down from his. He again called out his wares aloud, this time, trying to attract the attention of the customer.

The man walked over to him and looked at the remaining pots and pans.

'How much is this?' he asked, sitting on his haunches, and picking up a shallow-bottomed vessel.

'Fifty,' said the trader.

'Too much. Too much,' muttered the stranger.

'What will you give for this?'

The stranger looked up at him, his eyes narrowing. 'You from Babylon?'

The trader hesitated. While he knew that traders were never harassed irrespective of where they came from, as a Babylonian, he had grown accustomed to being guarded. After all, no one loves people from a kingdom that has defeated their own.

'Ye . . . es' he said, hesitatingly.

The stranger gave a quick glance to the left and right, at the other traders sitting in the stalls next to his.

'I have a message to pass on,' he whispered, keeping his head down. 'Can you meet me near the stables there in half an hour? Please?'

The trader hesitated again, unsure of the reason for this strange request and suspecting some ulterior motive. The stranger discerned his feelings and said, 'It is not a trap, my friend. Please trust me. The stable is in full view. You can come there without your money. I have no interest in it.'

The trader thought for a second and then nodded. He would leave his purse with the trader next to him, a man he had known for many years and whom he could trust. He nodded his head, and the stranger moved on.

A half hour later, the trader got up from his seat and, handing his purse over to his friend, made a pretence of going to relieve himself. He walked away in the direction of the stables which were at one end of the marketplace. When he reached there, he heard a low whistle and quickly ducked under the awning of the stables. The stable roof was sloping and low so as to keep the interiors cool. Rows of horses stood there, tethered to wooden poles, munching on hay and drinking water from mud troughs in front of them.

The trader stood uncertainly, letting his eyes adjust to the dim interior, when he heard the whistle again—this time, accompanied by a hoarse whisper: 'Over here. To the back.'

The trader walked over slowly, cautiously, between the rows of horses and saw the bearded man sitting on the edge of an empty trough at the back.

'Thanks for coming,' said the man.

The trader nodded in acknowledgement.

'What did you have to tell me?' he asked.

'I have some important news to pass on. For King Sin-Muballit.'

'What news could *you* have for my king?'

The stranger noticed the emphasis on the word 'you' and smiled, baring brownish teeth.

'Only the most important kind, my friend.'

The trader gave a quick look around the stables, still wary about the intentions of the stranger sitting in front of him. The man, noticing this, laughed.

'Do not be afraid. If I had to take your money, I would have found other means.'

'Well? What's your message?'

'Pass the message on to the proper authorities that the Princess Sybella is being held here.'

'What? The Princess? Here? How? What's going on?' asked the stranger, his confusion apparent.

'How long have you been away from Babylon, my friend?'

'About two weeks. I spent a week in Isin before coming down here.'

'That's why you don't know.'

'Don't know what?'

'About the attack. On the royal family.'

'What!?'

'Yes. There was an attack on the royal family, and our princess was kidnapped.'

'Our princess?'

'Well, of course. I am from Babylon too. Couldn't you tell?'

'You disguise your accent very well,' said the trader.

'I have to.'

'So how do you know that the princess is being held here?'

'I can't say. But I know she is here. I have spoken to her.'

'Where?'

'In an abandoned mansion, near the back end of the city.'

'Is this on the level?' asked the trader. 'You are not having me on, are you? If I go and give this information and they find out that it is false, I shall possibly be put to death.'

'What do I have to gain from feeding you false information on this?'

'How do I know? Maybe you don't like tradesmen. Or tradesmen from Babylon. Or you don't like my face. Any number of reasons.'

'Look, I am running a considerable risk coming here to tell you this. I was trying to look for a Babylonian tradesman to whom I could pass on this information.'

'Is that why you were going to every stall?'

The stranger nodded.

'And you say you have spoken to the princess? She is safe?'

'Yes, to both questions. She asked me to pass on the message.'

'And why are you doing this? What's in it for you?'

'I may not be the most reliable person in the world. But I *am* a Babylonian, and she *is* my princess,' said the stranger, somewhat vehemently.

The trader nodded, thanked the stranger and left the stables. He walked over to his stall and, retrieving his purse from his friend, asked him to take care of his goods for him since he had to go somewhere urgently. Then, untying his stunted excuse of a horse, he mounted and left towards the city gates at a fast trot. Once outside, he started flogging his beast of burden in the direction of Isin and Babylon.

Arjuna was disgruntled. He had tried to dissuade Lilith from her foolhardy plan, but she had pulled rank on him. He was only a civilian here, even if he was a prince back home. She was the head of the queen's bodyguards and the soldiers in their little group automatically deferred to her. He had tried appealing to her as a friend, but to no avail.

He had eventually given in to her, albeit with ill grace, but had stubbornly insisted that if she were going through with this nonsensical plan of hers, he would go along with her. She had given in easier than he had expected.

So here they were, walking through the forest back towards the road—Lilith, him, and another soldier. They made their way to the road and then Lilith asked someone the way to the closest nunnery. She was directed to a large, squat, unattractive building some distance away from the city walls to the west.

'Who or what is a nunnery?' asked Arjuna

'These are women who are married to the Gods,' she said.

'What? So, they are actually married to them?'

'Yes, in a ceremony. They spend their life in this nunnery.'

'And what do they do here?'

'Oh, they can do anything. Run a business. Work. Pray. Whatever they want.'

'All right, and why are we going there?'

'As I explained, I need to disguise myself as one of them, and these clothes', she gestured to her own, 'won't help me do that.'

'Is their clothing very distinctive?'

'Yes. They only wear white clothes, tinged with gold and a golden wreath on their head.'

'Won't they be targeted by bandits?'

'No, for two reasons. One, everyone knows that these women have extraordinary powers because they are attached to a temple of their God, whoever that is. Secondly, there is a royal decree across the land, regardless of the kingdom. An attack on them is punishable by death. And not an ordinary death. The attacker will be flayed alive in the centre of town over several days. In all the time that I have been here, I haven't heard of a single case where the *entu** were attacked.

'Aah,' said Arjuna. 'And what of us? What do we do?'

'The entu never travel alone. They are always followed by temple guards. You are it. Oh, and the temple guards guarding the entu are supposed to be eunuchs,' she said, with a sly grin.

'Anything else?' asked Arjuna, looking annoyed.

'I think we will make you a mute eunuch,' she said, her eyes twinkling. 'We can't have you talking and giving us away, can we?'

Evening saw the trio walking along the path leading to the eastern gates of the city. They had deliberately chosen this time as they figured that dusk and her attendant companion, night, would help create some confusion for their enemies.

Lilith looked transformed and stately. She was wearing a long, flowing white gown and had a golden wreath on her head. She had pinned her hair up at the back and her long neck gave her a very statuesque appearance.

She had gone into the nunnery alone and had explained to the women their predicament. They had immediately come to her assistance. The sisterhood of women is strong, and the news of women being kidnapped brought not only

---

* The priestesses married to a God.

condemnation of the dastardly act but also immediate offers of assistance.

Lilith had requested for some clothes and the golden wreath, and these had been provided to her without any hesitation. The sisters had also helped in decorating the faces of Arjuna and the other soldier with the markings peculiar to the protectors of the nuns.

As they made their way towards their destination, Lilith kept up a constant stream of instructions out of the corner of her mouth.

'Walk erect. Look fierce. Make eye contact with anyone you come across. Do not make way for anyone! Everyone makes way for the entu.'

She herself had worn a forbidding expression that would have discouraged anyone from crossing her. About four hundred yards or so from the building, they saw one of the men guarding the place, stand up straight as he saw them walking towards him. Lilith's pace did not slacken as she bore down on the man who glanced around nervously to see if there was anyone else to support him. Finding himself alone, he shied nervously and gave a deep bow as Lilith and the two men neared him.

Lilith's expression was haughty and impatient as the words cracked out of her mouth, 'Well? Why are you blocking my way?'

The man looked fearfully at her. He had heard stories about the entu and the kinds of magic that they were capable of. There were always stories about the entu in his village. His orders, though, had been clear. To ensure that no one walked past him towards the house. But he had not been told what to do when it was an entu on her way to the house. On the one hand was the wrath of Erra. On the other, the wrath accompanied by who knows what magic from the entu. He decided that he would rather face Erra than this steely woman. He stepped aside in a hurry.

Lilith glanced disdainfully at him as she swept past, followed by her two attendants. They walked at that same fast clip towards the house. The scenario with the guard was repeated a couple of more times. The guards stepped aside with alacrity as they saw who it was. They finally came to the door of the mansion.

'Move aside, oaf,' barked the soldier accompanying them to the man guarding the door.

'I have been asked not to allow anyone into the house,' he said fearfully.

'Do you want my mistress to turn you into a beetle or something? Do you not know the power of the entu?'

The man gulped. He was out of his depth.

'Please wait here. I shall get my master,' he said and went in through the door. He was back soon.

'Aah, revered entu. My master is not here,' he said.

'So?' asked Lilith with arched eyebrows.

'What . . . what business . . . ' the man stuttered.

'You dare ask me, *me* what business I have?'

Lilith started to move her hands around in circles, murmuring incantations under her breath in a foreign tongue. It took all his willpower for Arjuna to maintain his composure and not crack a smile. He understood the incantation that Lilith was mouthing. It was the *Gayatri Mantra*.

The man almost fell at her feet blubbering.

---

* The ancient Rig Vedic invocation to the Sun God.

'Mistress, please forgive me. I meant no disrespect. Please come in and be seated inside till my master comes.'

Lilith stopped moving her hands and looked at him, her eyes blazing in anger. She then flicked her wrist at him to tell him to move aside and stepped into the mansion.

❖

Lilith noticed the men scattered around the room. There were ten of them. They had obviously been told by the guard at the gate as to who the visitor was, and they backed fearfully away from her and went to the farthest corner of the room to create as much space between them and her as they could.

Lilith scanned the room and, spotting a lone chair, sat imperiously, back straight. She swiveled her head to glare at the men cowering to one side. She raised her hands dramatically in the air and made some swirling motions, muttering something under her breath.

The men backed further away from her, if that was at all possible. Lilith lifted her head up and sniffed the air. Then asked the men, 'Do you hear noises at night? Rustling noises?'

The men looked uncertainly at one another and then nodded their heads.

'What about the strange smell that I am smelling? Do you guys notice that?'

The men looked at each other once again and then shifted nervously as a few of them nodded again.

Well of course you would hear something at night. There are leaves around and they rustle. And then with so many of these unwashed men in the house, it is bound to smell, thought Lilith, suppressing a smile.

'Do you know what it is due to?'

'No, mistress,' answered a man.

'Spirits.'

'Spirits?' asked the man, his voice quivering.

'Yes, spirits. Bad ones. This house is haunted by the followers of *Pazuzu*,' she said.

A few of the men moaned. Pazuzu was a powerful demon, and they knew that ill befell those who got on his bad side.

'How . . . how did you know, mistress?' asked the one man who seemed to be capable of speech.

'Because,' said Lilith, pausing for effect, 'I am an entu of the moon God Nanna. He came in my dream and tasked me with ridding this house and the woods out there of the demons. Have you all been going into the woods?'

'Sometimes,' said the man.

'You are lucky,' she said abruptly. 'Have you heard any sounds or noises from there that you haven't heard before?'

Another man, standing towards the back, spoke up.

'Yes, mistress. We have heard what sounded to us like the neighing of horses.'

'Aah, the horse-demons,' murmured Lilith.

'Horse-demons?' stuttered the man, nervously.

'Yes, very common and quite indicative of the presence of the demons. The horse-demons are always sent ahead of the main demons when Pazuzu wants to destroy a place.'

---

* The Babylonian demonic God and son of Hanbi, the king of the demons of the underworld.

The men visibly shrank back further against the wall.

Lilith noticed a room at the other end, directly opposite from where the men were standing.

'Is there anyone in that room? I sense a feminine presence there,' she said.

The men looked furtively at one another. Before any of them could respond, they heard footsteps coming from a door directly opposite the locked door that had captured Lilith's interest. A light appeared, followed by a man. A man with a scarred face.

He took in the scene in front of him. His men cowering to the far side of the house. A strange woman sat in his usual chair, flanked by two fiercely painted, armed men.

He raised the torch further up until he could see the woman's face and asked, 'Who are you and what are you doing here?'

Lilith studied the man who, it was quite apparent, was the leader of the pack.

'I am an entu,' she said.

Erra's face darkened. He had never liked the entus. He could take his Gods or leave them. He didn't particularly feel any fear of them. The entus, he looked upon with disdain, as freeloaders who fooled a gullible public.

'Yeah? What of it?'

Lilith rapidly reassessed this man. He was dangerous. And he couldn't be frightened like his followers had been.

'I was sent to rid this house of the demons infesting it.'

'Who sent you?'

'The God Nanna.'

'Yeah? How do I know you aren't simply making it up?'

Lilith rose from the chair and drew herself up, her tone icy.

'You dare to question an entu?'

'I will do more than that. If you and your two henchmen don't clear off in another minute, I will make sure that you never leave here.'

Lilith started chanting some incantations again. She raised her arms above her head and then made a motion as if throwing something at the soldiers in the other room who all moaned in terror and shrank back against the wall. She turned back to Erra and made the same gesture, but his lips curled up in a sneer.

'Get out!' he barked.

Lilith turned, her eyes flashing, and walked towards the door. As she reached it, she glanced back at Erra's men and said, 'Your master is a cretin who will doom you to your death because of his own foolishness. Nanna remembers and will not forgive this affront.' With that, she swept out of the house, Arjuna and the soldier close behind.

Chapter Fifteen

A Plan in Action

Shrutasena and his men were each lost in their own thoughts. They had spent the last two days walking futilely on the road along the river, questioning passersby ever so often, about whether they had seen a group of men with a single woman.

They had had very little success. Shrutasena had a splitting headache from the sun and had ordered some strong wine from the tavern in which they were sitting. He sat massaging his head with both hands, as he waited for the tavern owner to bring him the wine.

The others in the group looked equally discouraged. The futility of their search was weighing heavily on them. With each passing day that they failed to uncover the location of their princess, the soldiers seemed to feel the metaphorical weight on their shoulders more and more. The problem, they felt, was like trying to identify a particular feather in a forest full of birds. People travelled all the time between Isin and Larsa. They couldn't expect them to remember a particular group among all the different groups that passed between the cities.

The tavern keeper brought them their drinks, and Shrutasena gratefully clasped his hands around the cup and took two or three large gulps. He licked his lips and looked down the road towards Larsa. Traffic was light at this time of the evening, and he could see a lone traveller walk his horse towards them. The horse's head bobbed up and down, mirroring the traveller's as he sat hunched in the saddle. It was clear that both the animal and the human were completely knackered.

The man got down from the horse with a weary grunt and tied the mount to a railing next to a water trough. He walked over to a pile of hay, hefted a bundle in his arms and then went over to the horse and dropped it in front of the animal. The horse, which had been slurping water from the trough, immediately switched its attention from the drink to the food and started munching on it.

The traveller sat down on one of the free, stringed cots with his body resting on his arms. He stretched and let out an audible groan. He motioned to the tavern keeper and then said, 'Wine,' seemingly unwilling or unable to rouse himself to say more than that.

Shrutasena, stopped staring at him and turned his attention back to the cup in front of him. He asked Sabium sitting beside him, 'How much farther do you reckon it is to Larsa?'

'Another fifteen miles or so.'

Shrutasena grunted. 'I wonder if we shouldn't send back word to Lilith or even to Babylon to send some more soldiers. Will make the task easier, I think.'

Sabium did not respond. His mind was on Mylitta. Only the Gods knew where she was. Well, the Gods and the kidnappers, of course. Actually, he hoped that both the Gods and the kidnappers had been joined by Lilith and her group in knowing the whereabouts of Mylitta. He knew he had a task on hand, but half his mind was still wondering about how Lilith and Arjuna were doing. His arm hurt badly, and he hefted it into a more comfortable position as the sling bit into the side of his neck.

He dragged his attention back to the present and said morosely, 'What if we can't find them?'

Shrutasena understood that his friend needed some reassurance. He draped his arm around Sabium's shoulders and said, 'Don't worry, my friend. We will find them. Lilith doesn't seem to me to be someone who will give up easily, and I am a stubborn man myself.'

He offered Sabium a warm smile, wishing he felt even half as confident as his words suggested.

Some of the other soldiers were talking and snippets of their conversation reached Sabium and Shrutasena.

'What are they talking about?' asked Shrutasena.

'Oh, the same as us. Worrying about not having found the princess and wishing that they could go back to Babylon.'

As he said this, the stranger sat up straighter and looked keenly at them. Shrutasena noticed this from his peripheral vision but continued drinking from his cup. The man seemed to want to come over and talk to them, but hesitated. Shrutasena could make out the struggle that he was going through. Eventually, the man decided to risk it, got up from his seat and came up to them.

'Excuse me,' he said, hesitantly. 'Are you people soldiers from Babylon?'

Shrutasena understood what he asked but given his lack of felicity in Babylonian, let Sabium respond.

'Who asks?'

'I am a trader.'

'From where?'

'Babylon.'

'Returning from Larsa?'

'Yes.'

Sabium looked him over slowly and then asked, 'Why did you ask if we were soldiers from Babylon?'

'Are you?' asked the trader.

'We might be. Depends on you. You still haven't answered my question. Why did you ask if we were soldiers from Babylon?'

The man looked at them indecisively and then, finally coming to a conclusion, sat down on the cot in front of them and said, 'I have some important information that I can only give to soldiers from Babylon.'

'Well, we are soldiers from Babylon,' said Sabium.

'How do I know that?'

Sabium called out to one of the soldiers in their group. 'Sergeant, can you convince this trader here that we are bonafide soldiers from Babylon?'

The sergeant got up from his seat and came up to the trader. He pulled out the chain hanging inside his tunic and held it for the trader to inspect. The chain ended in a clay tag, a standard identifier for every Babylonian soldier, inscribed with his name, rank and unit. The trader looked carefully at it and then, evidently satisfied, said, 'Thank Marduk that I have found you. I have been riding hard all afternoon from Larsa.'

'What is this news that you said you had for us?' asked Sabium.

'It is about Princess Sybella,' he said, even as the soldiers jumped up from their seats and crowded around him.

'What about her?' asked Sabium, guardedly.

'I know where she is being held.'

Enlil-Bani stomped up the stairs to the top of the tower of the northern gates to the city. A short while earlier, his men had come to him with news that an army had appeared on the horizon and seemed to be making its way towards them.

He had expected that, of course. He would have done the same if someone had come into his city and kidnapped his child. Enlil-Bani was confident that this time, unlike three years ago when he had been soundly defeated, he could hold off the Babylonians. He still smarted from that defeat and the thought of getting some revenge on Sin-Muballit was a pleasing thought.

His confidence stemmed from the new unit he had secretly raised over the past three years. The unit was made up of Numidians, who he had reached out to for help. The Numidians were tall, strong and mighty warriors. He loved to watch them practice, their ebony skins glistening from the sweat and providing a striking contrast to their bronzed armour and weaponry.

He knew that they were a formidable force, and with them at his disposal, he was sure that he would be able to inflict perhaps a decisive defeat against the Babylonians. It was this confidence that had impelled him to give his blessings to the plan that Erra had come up with, for wiping out the Babylonian monarchy. The failure of that attempt and the subsequent complications arising from the kidnapping of the princess had momentarily perturbed him. However, he had his backup plan in place. The Numidians.

As he looked over the ramparts and to the horizon in the gathering dusk, he saw the dust cloud raised by what was evidently a large army. He could make out a chariot in front. *That must be Sin-Muballit*, he thought. *The old man still wants to come to a fight, eh? I thought he was on his sick bed.* He tried to peer through the dust cloud and the rapidly approaching night, to make out details. The Babylonian army marched closer and stopped a good arrow's distance away from the city gates. He saw feverish activity that resulted in tents springing up across the horizon. He thought he saw Muballit's fat frame get off the chariot and waddle off into one of the tents, but that might just have been his fanciful imagination.

'So, you each understand what you have to do?' asked Lilith.

They were huddled deep inside the woods. They hadn't lit a fire for fear of being discovered by the kidnappers. The soldiers were squatting on the ground while Lilith was on her haunches. She had gone over the plan a dozen times with the soldiers until she knew for sure that there wouldn't be any mess-ups.

They had returned from the house and back into the woods by a circuitous route. Lilith had ensured that they went back to the nunnery, just in case the scar-faced leader sent a man to follow them. It was good that they had done so for, the kidnapper had indeed sent one of his men after them. They had peered through the slit in the nunnery door and seen him pass by, his eyes locked on the entrance. They had waited him out patiently and only once he had gone back up the path leading to the old palace had they resumed their journey back into the woods, clothed in their own attire. Lilith had thanked the nuns profusely for their help and had returned the golden wreath and the white dress.

Now, clad in her familiar all black and with the veil covering her face, Lilith addressed her men. She made them repeat her orders once again and then, having satisfied herself that she had done all she could, looked at Arjuna and nodded her head.

'We go at midnight.'

Their plan was simple. They knew that they were outnumbered but were counting on the element of surprise. There were three men on guard—two on the path leading to the house and one man guarding the door. The door would be bolted from the inside, and they needed the man at the door to help open it for them. The other two could be disposed of, and Lilith had nominated two of the soldiers, both veterans, to attend to them.

It was a quarter to midnight when the group crept
slowly to the edge of the woods. An owl hooted somewhere
close by. Cicadas buzzed incessantly. A grunt or two gave
the indication that some wild boars were also on the prowl.
As they came up to the edge of the woods, overlooking the
path, Lilith held up her hand and the group crouched low.

A man could be seen patrolling the path directly in
front of them. About a hundred yards in front of him, was
another man. They would walk towards each other for
half a minute and then turn around and walk back. The
soldiers sat motionless, timing the walks. At a nod from
Lilith, one of the soldiers peeled off from the group and
hared back up the path, directly across from where the first
man was walking. As the guard turned to walk away from
the house, the soldier dropped on his knees and forearms
and started moving slowly across the intervening distance
of about fifty yards.

The second soldier started doing the same as he belly-
crawled his way towards his man. Meanwhile, Lilith and
Arjuna had moved through the woods to come up to one
side of the house and were creeping up on it, mindful of
the fact that there could very well be a guard placed there
for just such a contingency. Luckily, for them, there wasn't,
and they tiptoed their way around the house, their black
clothes providing an effective camouflage, allowing them
to almost merge into the wall.

The other two soldiers had made sporadic progress
towards their prey. They would move only when the two
men were moving away from each other and then lay down
like a log as the guards turned and walked back towards

one another. The two soldiers were hardly ten yards or so away from one another as they huddled on the ground, motionless.

Lilith and Arjuna waited for the cue. It would come from the men in the woods in the form of a long owl-hoot. The man guarding the door was sitting on the steps outside. They could see his head slowly make its way down towards his chest and then periodically jerk up as he struggled to stay awake. Lilith motioned to Arjuna to stay behind her. She was much better at stealth than he was, having been trained for it. Only a few yards separated them from their quarry. They could even smell the mix of sweat and body odour emanating from the man, intermingled with the smell of cheap wine. Arjuna held his nose delicately with his fingers and then mimicked a gagging motion to Lilith, who shushed him with a raised finger to her lips while her eyes conveyed her mirth.

A long hoot broke into their little world. Immediately, the Babylonians sprang into action. The two soldiers had crawled almost to the side of the road, unobserved. It was very difficult to make anything out in the night and the guards marching on the path had no idea what hit them. As they met and then turned around to walk back the way they had come, the two soldiers leapt off the ground and wrapped their forearms across the throats of their adversaries. The men immediately got their hands up to try and release the choking pressure, their feet beating useless tattoos on the ground. The soldiers, however, had already pulled them down and, with a swift, savage twist, broke both their necks.

At the same time, Lilith had also jumped into action. She had covered the intervening gap to the guard at the door and applied a similar chokehold on him. However, instead of breaking his neck, she had whispered gently into his ears, 'If you want to see this night through, you will do as I say, got it?'

The soldier tried desperately to loosen her arm around his throat, his hands like claws, raking her forearms.

Lilith merely tightened her hold and asked again, 'Got it?'

The man, desperate now for a breath of air, tapped his hands on her arm in a gesture of surrender. Arjuna, who had also materialized around her, put his large hands over the guard's mouth. Lilith gently eased the pressure on his throat, but took out her knife and thrust it, far from gently, into his side.

'This knife, my friend, is very, very, sharp. One wrong move from you, one misplaced yell, or scream or warning, and I will ensure that you die a horribly slow death. I will cut out your stomach and spill your intestines all over you and wrap them around your neck. Do you understand?'

The man might have been drunk. He was also possibly not terribly bright, but it does not take someone to be super intelligent to figure out the minimum that they must do in any situation to stay alive. Self-preservation is an innate quality in every living organism. The man had a healthy respect for his own life. His boss might kill him later for letting these two in, but that was later. These two, he was sure, would kill him now. He choose to prolong his life, even if it was by a few minutes. He nodded.

'Good,' whispered Lilith. 'Do you have a key to the house?'

He shook his head. *It was worth a shot*, thought Lilith. She hadn't really expected the guard outside the door to have the key to open it, not when his leader was sleeping inside.

'Okay then. Call out to whoever sleeps closest to the door to come and open it. Be urgent and insistent.'

Her other soldiers had run up to the house, having taken care of the two patrol guards. They stood beside her, pressed against the wall, as the guard tapped on the door and called out, 'Open up. Open up, Tayma. For Marduk's sake, open up.'

They could hear a stirring inside the house and then, the sound of the bolt being pulled back. As the door opened inwards, the guard outside, perhaps out of loyalty to his comrades or fear of his leader, yelled out,

'Watch it. It's a trick. We are under attack!'

Chapter Sixteen

Rescue and Ruins

Arjuna, who had had his knife out, immediately slit the guard's throat from ear to ear. He shoved the gurgling body aside and threw his weight against the door to prevent the man inside from slamming it shut. The force of his push flung open the door and he, Lilith and the other soldiers poured in.

Inside, the kidnappers were still trying to figure out what was happening. The yell from the guard outside had woken up at least some of them and they stood up with weapons in their hands. The others, however, were still scrambling to make sense of what was happening.

Arjuna had gone through first and had run the man who had opened the door through with his sword. He stepped over him and looked for the leader. It had been decided that he would tackle him. Lilith and the others moved to mow down the other kidnappers.

The clash of steel and bronze echoed in the house. The cries of the injured and dying men added to the clamour. From the door opposite the locked door that Lilith surmised contained Mylitta, stepped the scarfaced man, his face contorted in fury, his sword drawn. Moonlight poured in through the windows and illuminated the scene scantly.

Arjuna moved towards him, his sword extended in front of him, but not at full stretch. His elbows were bent slightly so as to enable him to thrust forward in attack or to bring up the sword quickly in defence. Scarface leapt towards Arjuna, his sword slicing through the air towards him. Arjuna parried it away with his own sword. He thought he caught a flicker of surprise on the man's face as steel met bronze, but he couldn't be sure in the dim light.

Arjuna saw his opponent moving warily, losing that initial swagger. Perhaps he realized that Arjuna was not a mere civilian but a well-trained soldier.

Behind them, the battle was proving to be short and brutal. The surprise attack had all but won the day for them. Several kidnappers littered the floor, their throats cut or entrails spewing out of their bellies. A few of the ruffians had given up the fight and had darted through the open front door and escaped. Lilith, however, was engaged in a furious fight with one of the few kidnappers who had managed to maintain some presence of mind despite being abruptly woken from his sleep.

As she fought him, her sword whistling through the air—first parrying his thrusts, then aiming to sever his head—they heard a rumble, followed by the earth shaking beneath them. The shaking was so violent that the fighters were thrown off their feet and crashed onto the ground. Masonry started falling from the ceiling of the already dilapidated house, first in small trickles and then in larger chunks. Lilith got up and tried to steady her feet, even as her opponent did the same. It was then that she heard a cry from Arjuna, 'Chitra! Watch out!'

Arjuna was himself thrown to the ground along with his opponent from the violent shaking of the earth. He had experienced an earthquake a few times back home in Rohitaka, but nothing as severe as this. As he unsteadily rose to his feet, he caught sight of Scarface in his peripheral vision, beginning what would have been a fatal thrust with his knife on his shoulders. He didn't have time to turn around and parry. He merely reversed the grip on his sword and thrust it back and up.

His opponent was caught completely by surprise. His hands were both raised up in a striking motion and he had no way to defend himself as Arjuna's sword went smoothly through his abdomen. His sword fell from his hands as they grabbed at his midriff to cover the wound caused by Arjuna's sword. He looked from the wound to Arjuna and back, and then, wordlessly, crumpled to the ground.

The ground was still shaking heavily, and as Arjuna looked towards where Lilith was fighting, he noticed a portion of the ceiling directly above Lilith start to collapse. That's when he had shouted out the warning and then watched in horror as the entire ceiling came down on them. He heard cries from the people trapped underneath the debris and the cloud of dust that arose from the masonry.

'Chitra!' he cried, as he rushed to help her, fearing the worst.

It was hearing the word 'Chitra' that saved Lilith. If Arjuna had yelled out her Babylonian name, it might not have registered with her. However, the novelty of hearing her original name had given Lilith that extra split second to react. When the ceiling started caving in, she had gone down on her knees and slashed her opponent's belly with her sword. As he started to crumple on her, she had grabbed hold of him and pulled him down on top of her, just an instant before the ceiling collapsed. A brick had however caught her a glancing blow to her head, and she had lost consciousness.

She heard a voice calling from what seemed like far away.

'Lilith, Lilith. Wake up. Lilith.'

She tried to shoo the voice away. To tell it to leave her alone, but to no avail.

The voice grew ever more insistent. There was a weight on her, and she couldn't move. She tried to push against the body lying on top of her, but it was too heavy.

Arjuna dug desperately through the debris, trying to get to where he had last seen Lilith. There was a pile of rubble there. Some of the soldiers on their side were trapped under it along with Lilith. But right now, his actions were focused solely on getting to her. He dug with his bare hands, his nails tearing in the process. He kept calling out her name but heard no response. This only made him dig even more feverishly, his hands working in a frantic blur as he moved brick, mortar and rubble out of the way. Eventually, as he moved a large piece off, he saw her face, her eyes closed, and dust caked. Someone was lying on top of her. He kept calling out to her to wake up, hoping against hope that she was still alive.

All the while, his hands kept working of their own volition, mechanically, moving debris to one side. A few of the soldiers on the outer edges of the collapsed masonry had managed to dig their way out. They were bloodied and seemed a little woozy, but alive. One of them came over to him to help him move the rubble. They worked frantically, until finally, they got the last of the masonry off the man lying on top of Lilith. Arjuna pulled the man away, leaving his entrails on Lilith.

'Lilith! Lilith. Wake up! Wake up!' he yelled desperately.

He put his ear against her nose and was relieved when he felt her breath on it. He lifted her up in his arms and, moving to the other side of the room, laid her gently on the ground, with her head in his lap. Eventually, he was relieved when she opened her eyes and looked up at him. She gave him a thin smile.

'Worried?' she asked.

'Like you wouldn't believe,' he said, relief writ large on his face and in his eyes.

'What happened?'

'That,' he said, indicating the missing ceiling.

The main earthquake seemed to have stopped although there were still smaller tremors.

'Mylitta?' she asked.

'Oh Rudra!' he said as he looked towards the still shut door of the room opposite them. Lilith struggled into a sitting position as Arjuna left her and went to the room. He unbolted the door and walked in with trepidation, unsure of what he would find. Thankfully, there was no damage to the ceiling on this side of the building. He saw a visibly shaken Mylitta sitting towards the back of the room, peering fearfully at him. As recognition dawned on her, she got up with a sob and flung herself into his arms.

'Oh, thank you. Thank you. Thank you. Thank you,' she said, sobbing on his chest.

Lilith walked into the room and Mylitta gave a gasp of joy and hugged her.

'Is Sabium . . . ?'

'No, he isn't here,' said Lilith. 'He and the others have gone in search of the princess.'

'You haven't found her yet?' asked Mylitta, her eyes tearing up.

'Not yet. But we will,' said Lilith.

They walked out of the room and saw their soldiers sitting down. They had lost two men when the ceiling came down on them and the general feeling among the soldiers was one of gloom, even as they recognized that they had achieved their target of rescuing the girl.

The fighting was over, but Lilith was going through every room on the lower floor of the mansion.

'What are you looking for?' asked Arjuna, curiously.

'Remember when we were here yesterday, and Scarface walked out of that room?' asked Lilith.

'Yes?'

'Well, he wasn't in the room when we first came in, right? Otherwise, he would have come out immediately. He only turned up after a few minutes.'

'Are you implying what I think you are implying?'

Lilith nodded her head and moved towards the room. As they entered, they saw an open trap door. They could see steps leading down. Arjuna and Lilith glanced at each other and then, asking Mylitta to stay there, went down the steps, their swords drawn. The place was dark, too dark for them to know where to put their feet.

'Wait here. I shall be back with a torch,' said Arjuna as he climbed back up the stairs and scrounged around for a torch. He soon found one and, having lit it, descended the steps into the cellar. They could see the tunnel leading off towards the north. They moved forward with Arjuna in the lead. They must have covered a hundred yards or so when they came to an abrupt halt. The tunnel had caved in during the earthquake.

Lilith swore, in a very un-lady-like fashion, in Akkadian.

'Yeah, I feel like swearing too, assuming, that is, that you were swearing. I am not very well up on Babylonian swear words,' said Arjuna.

Lilith smiled mirthlessly and kicked a petulant foot at the mud in front of her.

'You think, it leads to where I think it does?'

Lilith nodded. 'Inside Isin's walls,' she said. 'This proves it. This shows that the attack had support from the highest quarters in Isin.'

Chapter Seventeen

Isin's Folly

The sun was just breaking above the horizon and cast its effulgent rays on the city and its walls, the countryside beyond, and the army assembled there. The rays bounced off the bronze paraphernalia that an army carries, the myriads of bows, arrows, shields, spears, swords and flagstaffs. The sun, not discriminating at all, also shone down on two mounted men who were approaching the army camp at a canter.

They each led another horse behind them. They had continuously switched horses and ridden through the night. A closer look at the men would have shown dark circles around their eyes from lack of sleep and the general tiredness that comes from long hours of riding, even for hardened soldiers.

One of the men was a soldier but the other was not and he seemed worse off than his companion. He sat with his head bowed and occasionally lolling from side to side. It was evident that he was dozing even as his horse was following the lead of the other man's mount.

'Wake up, Sabium,' said Shrutasena in his raspy voice.

'Eh? What?' said Sabium, coming awake with a start.

'We are almost there. That's your army.'

'Oh, all right,' said Sabium, yawning loudly. 'Gosh, my eyes feel all gritty from lack of sleep.'

'Lack of sleep?' queried an amused Shrutasena. 'You have been dozing on that horse for the last hour or so.'

'What's one hour for someone who needs eight to nine hours to feel fresh in the morning?' he asked, with another yawn.

'I am hoping that you are not going to yawn in front of your prince and the king,' said Shrutasena as he slowed his horse down to a gentle trot. It didn't do to surprise an army by riding up to it fast. Soldiers were apt to shoot someone full of arrows and ask questions later.

Upon reaching the camp, they were inevitably stopped by the guards. After much explaining and fast talking on Sabium's part, they were finally escorted to the king's tent. Sabium also requested that a soldier be sent to summon Prince Murabi, as what they had to discuss would interest him as well.

The king wasn't yet awake and Sabium and Shrutasena spent the time freshening up. There was a large wooden casket with water, and they both washed their faces and hair and dried them off with the ends of their tunics.

Prince Murabi arrived as they were at it and called out, 'Sabium! Shrutasena! Have you found the princess?'

'We have news, my prince,' said Sabium.

'Let's wait till we are in front of the king, so you don't have to repeat yourself,' said the prince.

❖

'So, the Larsa dogs are responsible for this outrage,' thundered King Sin-Muballit, the veins in his face bulging, his features contorted with rage. Sabium had just finished telling them about their own fortuitous meeting with the trader at the tavern and the message that he had passed on.

'We will march on Larsa then,' said the king, looking at General Gamil, who had also been called into the tent by prince Murabi, to listen to Sabium's tale. 'Make preparations to move out!'

Even as he gave his order, a soldier entered the tent and whispered something into Murabi's ears.

'Show them in,' said Murabi, his eyes gleaming with excitement.

The soldier went out, and Lilith, Arjuna and Mylitta walked in. Sabium saw Mylitta and, forgetting that he was in front of the king, ran to her and hugged her fiercely, kissing her upturned face repeatedly, saying, 'Oh, thank Marduk you are safe. Thank Marduk you are safe.'

It was Mylitta, who disengaged herself from Sabium, understanding the impropriety of what he was doing. Women seem to have that innate understanding of what is proper and what is not, and so she halted Sabium's kisses and, turning towards the king, bowed to him and said, 'My apologies, Your Majesty. Sabium here seems to have lost his senses.'

Sin-Muballit let a rare smile play on his lips. 'We were also young once, young lady. I can understand why Sabium did what he did.'

This made Mylitta blush prettily as Sabium simply tightened his arm around her and bowed to the king in gratitude.

'How did you find her?' asked Murabi, intruding into the moment.

Lilith gave them a terse explanation of the events that led to locating Mylitta and her rescue.

'We couldn't capture the man who was the leader of the gang alive, Your Majesty,' said Lilith regretfully. The fight was also complicated by the earthquake.

'Oh Marduk. I have never experienced a shaking like that,' exclaimed General Gamil.

'Was there a lot of damage here?' asked Arjuna.

'We were fortunate to be on the ground and only under tents. There were a whole lot of tents that were flattened, but all that did was cause some bruised egos. Soldiers resent being made fun of by their fellow soldiers as they are trying to untangle themselves from under the tent,' said General Gamil with a smile.

'We did find something interesting however,' said Lilith.

'Oh?'

'We found a secret passage into the city.'

'Did you, now?' said Gamil, his smile growing wider by the minute as he rubbed his hands together. Then, turning to the king, he said, 'This new information puts a whole different perspective on things, Sire.'

'What do you mean?' growled, Sin-Muballit. 'We still need to get to Larsa to free Sybella.'

'Yes, of course Sire, but we do not know if she is really there. We only have the word of the trader who says he had the word of a stranger, and, from the looks of it, not a particularly trustworthy stranger at that. We will need to independently verify that what he says is true.'

'Moreover, Sire, the secret entrance into the city is from an abandoned mansion outside the city walls, and which was used by the kidnappers. So, it might well be that Isin is very much involved in the kidnapping and is trying to divert us towards Larsa by throwing suspicion on them?' said Lilith.

'Or it could be that they are *both* involved in it, Isin and Larsa,' added Arjuna. There was silence in the tent for some time.

'Arjuna, Shrutasena and I can go to Larsa and see if we can get into the city, Sire' said Lilith, breaking the silence.

'And what of the Isin cretins?' asked Sin-Muballit.

'We cannot ignore them now and go to Larsa, Your Majesty,' said Gamil, adding, 'If they *are* in cahoots, then we would be caught between the two armies. We will need to subdue Isin before we go around them to Larsa. I do not want a hostile force to my rear.'

'How do we do that?' asked the king.

'It all depends on how Enlil-Bani reacts. If he disavows all knowledge of the kidnapping and lets us into the city, we will merely post a contingent here, large enough to ensure that he doesn't take any unwise decisions when we march on Larsa.'

'And if he does not?'

'Then we will know that he is complicit and will need to subdue him. We now have a way to get into the city on the sly, thanks to Lilith.'

'I don't want to merely take the city,' said Sin-Muballit. 'I want them to fear us so much that they will never even contemplate any such audacity in future. We need to show them that we can smash them at will.'

'And how do we do that, father?' asked Murabi.

'We give them a demonstration of what all these lovely, nice, black weapons that we have from our friends from Hind can do.'

❖

Enlil-Bani climbed onto the top of the ramparts of the northern gates again. He puffed out his cheeks, drawing deep gulps of air into his lungs. *A few more days of doing this and I shall become as fit as I was in my younger days*, he thought.

He gazed down at the army arrayed in front of him. It was a large army; much larger than his and he knew that he couldn't hold out against them for long. He had discussed it with his general, Tayma, who had agreed with this view.

Enlil-Bani was also much put out with a conversation that he had had the previous night. A man had come to his chambers late at night. He had almost fallen asleep when a palace guard had fearfully knocked on the door and opened it, saying that there was someone at the door. Enlil-Bani was about to snap at the guard but, assuming that at this late hour it could only be Erra, he instructed the guard to let him in. There was really no point in venting at the guard for doing his job when he had himself specifically ordered them to show Erra in, regardless of the time.

Enlil-Bani had taken one look at the man and said, 'You are not Erra. Where's Erra? Guards!' he called out. Several guards rushed into the room; their swords pointing menacingly towards the man.

The man had gone down on his knees in fear, shouting, 'I am sorry, Your Majesty. Please forgive me. Erra is dead!'

'What?' asked the king.

'Yes, Sire. Erra is dead. Only a few of us could escape.'

Enlil-Bani's eyes narrowed dangerously as he asked, 'Why don't you tell me what happened?'

The ruffian's tale about the rescue of the princess' companion and his own flight, although sketchy in detail, had made Enlil-Bani think through the night. He had dismissed the man from his room, irritably, and had sent for Tayma. The general and he had sat through the night discussing the ramifications of the news that Erra had brought them.

That the Babylonians would now blame them was evident. Plausible deniability had flown out of the window, once the princess' companion had been found so close to the city. They now had a choice to make. Would they be able to withstand a long siege against this large army or not. Tayma, who had been out inspecting the damage to the city walls when he had been called for, had shaken his head emphatically.

'The earthquake last night has left large cracks in the city walls, making it child's play for any army—let alone one as large as the Babylonians—to tear them down and surge in. There is no way that we can repair the walls in time, Sire,' was Tayma's considered opinion.

'Well, that means we might have only one choice.'

'The Numidians?'

'The Numidians.'

Enlil-Bani's mind came back to the present as he went over his course of action again. The only chance he had was to get an overwhelming victory against the Babylonians in the first skirmish. A victory that would demoralize the opponents. He knew that the Numidians could do that. They had that effect on people. Yes, he would let loose the Numidians on them.

Enlil-Bani, the king of Isin, observed a man approaching the gates. He was a young man and sat tall in the saddle. He had a flag in one hand and the other hand was also held up in a greeting. He stopped when he was about fifty yards from the gates.

Enlil Bani looked around him and saw that his archers had their arrows nocked on their bows. One word from him and the young man would be riddled with arrows. He contemplated it briefly but then decided not to. He had other ways of ensuring that the young man died.

'King Bani,' shouted the young man.

'Who are you?'

'I am Prince Murabi, the man you sent those murderous soldiers of yours, to kill.'

'I don't know what you are talking about,' said Enlil-Bani.

'I am sure you know very well what I mean. Anyway, my task is not to get your confession. It is merely to inform you that this is your last chance to surrender the city to our king, Sin-Muballit. If not, the king will construe that as a sign of your guilt, and we will use force to take the city.'

'Is that so?' asked Enlil-Bani with a mocking laugh. 'And how do you propose to do that?'

The young man let out a mocking laugh of his own. 'Look at your city walls, king. Bal Marduk was kind enough to shake the earth for us last night. Look at the big cracks that Marduk has made in the walls. Do you really think you can defend these?' he pointed towards the cracks.

'You talk big for someone so young,' Enlil-Bani said conversationally. 'By the way, have you ever heard of the Numidians?'

Murabi was unsure of where the conversation was heading but said 'yes' in response. 'We have a large contingent of them now. Have you ever seen a Numidian? Have you ever seen one fight? Here, let me show you.'

He called out to one of the Numidians amassed below, near the gates and asked him to come up beside him. The Numidian ran up effortlessly and stood next to the king, hardly out of breath. He was an impressive specimen. He had a shaved head and was huge, easily over six and a half feet tall, with corded muscles. He was bare bodied and only wore a kind of leather wrap around his hips. The man grabbed a bronze spear leaning against the wall and then proceeded to bend it in two; his biceps bulging and standing out as he did that.

Murabi took in this display of manhood meant to instil fear in him and smiled grimly.

'So, my boy,' said Enlil-Bani. 'I have a contingent full of these magnificent men. And I am going to let them loose on your army. How many of your soldiers, do you think, will ever see Babylon again?' He laughed uproariously as he said that.

Murabi waited for his laughter to die and then said, coldly, 'I see that you are bent on war, but I shall be remiss if I do not do what I was sent to do, that is, give you fair warning. You see those men in the front ranks of my army?'

'Yeah? What of them?'

'Do you notice something different about them?'

'Yes, I do. Their weapons are all black. Have your soldiers forgotten to clean their weapons before they come to war? Look at mine. Do you notice the sun shining brilliantly on their shields and armours?'

'Those are weapons that we have got from Hind. They will cut through your weapons like a sickle through paddy. Do you really think your Numidians would still stand a chance against us?'

Enlil-Bani laughed again. 'Nice trick, kid. There are no weapons that can cut through bronze. Do you really think I am some pimply-faced teenager that I would be taken in by that?'

'It's your funeral,' said the young man, infuriatingly calm. 'I have done my duty and warned you. So, do you want to reconsider your original decision of fighting us?' he asked, politely.

Enlil-Bani didn't reply but whispered something to the archer standing next to him. The man immediately let loose an arrow that whizzed past Murabi's head.

Murabi did not flinch or react in any way.

'Consider that my response,' said Enlil-Bani. 'The next arrow will not miss your head.'

Murabi turned his horse and galloped away towards his army. Immediately, the gates of the city started to swing open and the Numidians poured out in front of the Babylonians.

Murabi watched the Numidians array themselves in a series of straight lines. The sun beat down upon the land and the ebony-coloured, sweat-drenched bodies of the Numidians glistened in its light. They were holding large rectangular shields in front of them and tapping them rhythmically on the ground. Dust flying off the ground, enveloped them in a hazy cloud. They seemed to be doing some sort of a war dance, and their voices could be heard above the din of the shield-beats.

Murabi turned to General Gamil and said, 'Impressive, aren't they?'

'Yes, they are. But let's see how impressive they still look after this.' He asked the orderly beside him to blow a long note on a long, thin trumpet. The response from their side was immediate. The front ranks of the Babylonian army went down on their knees while the archers, who had been placed behind them, lifted their bows in the air, pulled back on their bowstrings and launched their arrows into the skies. The arrows sped up, fighting against that mysterious force that seemed to pull everything back down to the earth. They sped on but eventually gave up the unequal fight, pausing for an instant at their zenith before plunging back, nose first. The same mysterious force that had arrested their upward path now seemed to accelerate them on their way down as they rained upon the Numidians.

The Numidians had not been unaware of what was happening. As soon as the archers came into view and launched their arrows, their leader gave a series of crisp commands. His troops responded by kneeling at once, phalanx style, with their shields held above their heads, except for those in the front rank, who placed their shields in front resulting in the formation of an impenetrable wall. Or at least, that's what they thought.

As the arrows came down, their arrowheads penetrated the bronze shields, causing large cracks to appear on them. Some even penetrated the shields far enough to injure a few of the men who flinched and momentarily brought down their shields, causing fissures to appear in a once solid shield-roof.

The Babylonian archers had followed the first salvo with another and yet another. The incessant rain of arrows, especially those of the second and the following waves, burst through the damaged shields and impaled themselves in the heads and bodies of the Numidians. Enlil-Bani, standing atop the city walls, watched in horror as his prized Numidians were decimated in a matter of minutes. The Numidians died where they knelt, their bodies peppered with arrows that had broken through their seemingly impenetrable shields. Those few who had suffered wounds that were not fatal tried to crawl back towards the gates. It was then that the Babylonian cavalry and infantry charged.

It took Enlil-Bani a minute to gather his wits about him before shouting orders to his archers to target the Babylonians as they neared the city walls. His archers, to their credit, did react, but then, they also had to deal with incoming arrows from the Babylonian archers. Enlil-Bani watched an archer next to him go down with a black arrow lodged in his chest. He pulled out the arrow and looked at the arrowhead curiously, testing its sharpness with his thumb. The arrow was indeed heavier than the ones they used. As he peered over the wall, trying to not make himself a target for the incoming arrows, he saw a scene of utter devastation.

His entire Numidian contingent had been wiped out. Even now, the Babylonians were butchering any soldiers who had managed to survive their deadly arrow barrage. Enlil-Bani knew when he was beaten. He stood up slowly, noticing that the incoming arrows had stopped. He raised both his hands in a gesture of surrender and bowed down to Sin-Muballit in his chariot.

Chapter Eighteen

Larsa's Dilemma

Princess Sybella of Babylon, daughter to King Sin-Muballit, sister to Prince Murabi, sat in a filthy, rat-infested hole underneath a dilapidated mansion inside Larsa. The cell that she had been thrown into had smelled foul when she had first entered it. Now, after a few days of living in it, her own urine and faeces had contributed to adding to the overwhelming stench. She had barely been able to keep down the meagre food that someone or the other delivered to her every few hours. The stench had made her throw up often, but she had still forced herself to eat.

I am Princess Sybella of Babylon, daughter to King Sin-Muballit, sister to Prince Murabi and I shall not let these swine get the better of me, she kept repeating to herself. Whenever she found herself sinking into dejection, she would repeat that line over and over again. It provided her with the strength to face up to her situation.

She thought back to her hurried and whispered conversation with the man who had brought her food for the first time. The Babylonian who had recognized her, and to whom she had entreated to send out a message about her whereabouts. She hadn't seen him since and wondered if he had simply dismissed that from his mind. After all, why would he risk everything to help her, when he was part of the group that had kidnapped her in the first place?

She had grown weak over the past few days. The food that she was given and that she could manage to keep within her was barely enough for sustenance. She spent much of her time sleeping. Sleep brought about by weakness, and which left her in a semi-comatose state. *Thankfully*, she thought.

She found it hard to tell the time. There were no windows, and the only time she could see some light was when someone came along with a torch to push a plate of food through the door. Even then, she couldn't make out if it was day or night.

She heard footsteps outside and an elongated sliver of light from the torch appeared under the door, making the rodents in its path scurry back into the darkness provided by the unlit parts of the room.

The door opened and the light provided by the torch brightened the interior. Sybella's eyes were fixed on the plate of food that the man placed on the floor in front of her. She grabbed it in her hands before the rats could get at it.

'Princess,' said a voice softly.

Sybella looked up into the eyes of the man she had spoken to on the first day.

'You,' she said, drawing in her breath sharply.

The man put a cautionary finger to his lips as he peered nervously back the way he had come and then said,

'Princess, it is done. I have passed the word to a trader from our city. Now we can only wait.'

Hope dawned in Sybella's heart and found its way to her face as it brightened under the flickering light cast by the torch. Hope burned bright within her even as the man closed the door and retreated the way he had come, plunging the room once more into darkness.

'You cannot back out at this late hour, Your Majesty. Not after all the trouble I have been to. We have been to,' the man corrected himself.

Nur-Adad, King of Larsa, looked at him, his eyes wary. He slouched on his throne; his paunch pushing against the fabric of his tunic; his chin resting on one hand. Zabaya had come to see him late in the evening, as was his practice.

Nur-Adad had initially gone along with the scheme outlined by Zabaya as having been proposed by Enlil-Bani. *What was there to lose, after all?* he had asked himself. The scheme, as he saw it, had all the upside for him, without any downside to it. If it succeeded, it would get rid of those pesky Babylonians. If it failed, he could always deny his own involvement.

He still smarted from the defeat by them seven years ago. He had been much younger then, and infinitely more vigorous. But that defeat and the march of time had aged him more quickly than he had thought.

He felt his age now, old and weary. He knew that it was not in him to mount a direct challenge to the Babylonian kingdom again. He would have to leave that to his offspring. His thoughts turned towards them with disgust. How he wished his offspring were those that he could pin his faith on. Unfortunately, they were wastrels, spending more time in whoring and carousing than in learning to run a kingdom. Already, he knew that there were other families in Larsa who were looking to supplant his own.

There were intrigues all around him, and this scheme was a last-ditch effort by him to bring the warring factions to his side. If it worked and the Babylonian royal family could be uprooted, then his own position would be strengthened, and he could even get those two wastrel sons of his to appear palatable to the men of his court.

He had been hoping to hear news of the demise of Sin-Muballit and his family, but Zabaya had eventually appeared with a tale of the utter failure of the venture. To make matters worse, there was the news that the damned princess was now held captive in his city. He had a good mind to kill the lot of them and be done with it. Then, he could deny any involvement in the misadventure. Zabaya had convinced him that there was much to be gained by holding onto the girl and that he could use her as a bargaining chip.

Now, however, he was starting to wonder if he had not been a fool to get convinced by Zabaya's argument. While it had sounded good on the face of it, there were some obvious drawbacks. Chief among them being the prospect of facing a siege of the city by the Babylonian forces. Zabaya had argued that it was a prospect worth pursuing, as the Isiners would come to their aid, allowing them to trap the Babylonians between their armies. That had given him some succour, until now.

Earlier in the evening, a man had arrived from Isin with news of Enlil-Bani's surrender of the city and Erra's death. He had come to share this with Zabaya, who in turn, brought the information to his king. It was when Nur-Adad had expressed his desire to sue for peace with the Babylonians that Zabaya had made that statement.

'I am not convinced. I think that we are way past the time where we could have taken advantage of this. I only see danger now.'

'My king,' said Zabaya, a zealous gleam in his eyes, causing him to look almost unhinged. 'We must *not* let this spoil our plans. We mustn't. I will not allow you to do that,' he said as he stalked out in anger.

Nur-Adad looked at his back as he walked away, in surprise, astonishment and a sense of unease.

Lilith, Arjuna, Shrutasena, and Sabium ducked into a wood near Larsa to shed their telltale soldier's uniforms and don more inconspicuous attire. It was Sabium's idea, of course. They had seen the increasing presence of soldiers as they neared the city. Four travellers on horses that did not look like any that traders would ride was a dead giveaway. They had stopped by a village a mile or so back and bought themselves some garments which they now proceeded to wear.

'I don't think we should enter the city on our horses,' said Sabium.

'I agree,' said Lilith. 'What do you suggest we do with them?'

'There is a tavern near the city with a stable. The owner is known to me. We can leave our horses there and then walk to Larsa. It is only a mile or so away. It would be less conspicuous.'

Dusk saw the four of them approaching the city gates. The group was unusually quiet. Their silence was understandable, given the circumstances. While they had won a victory in Isin, there was the ever-sobering thought at the back of their minds that their princess was being held captive. They did not know if she was alive or dead.

Sabium had another reason to be glum. He and Mylitta had had their first ever fight. Mylitta had insisted on coming with them. The thought of her having been rescued, while her friend and companion was still captive, continued to haunt her. Sabium had been equally firm in dissuading her from joining them. Mylitta's eyes had flashed at him in anger, and it was only Lilith's firm tone in support of Sabium that had decided the issue in his favour. Mylitta had, however, stormed out of the tent that they were in, leaving Sabium looking glum, downcast, and morose. She had not even come to say goodbye to him when they had left Isin.

They walked in pairs with a good twenty yards between them, mingling with the rest of the crowd, to not stand out as a group. Lilith and Arjuna, walked together, following Sabium and Shrutasena.

As they entered the city, Sabium led them off purposefully towards the left. A series of winding, narrow lanes brought them to a sort of guest house. Sabium spoke to the innkeeper and got them rooms towards the back.

'Is there a way to get out of here in a hurry?' murmured Lilith to Sabium.

'There is an exit at the back,' he whispered.

The men offered Lilith one room as they took the other. Lilith protested saying that she didn't mind sharing her room with one of them. Sabium looked slyly at Arjuna and said, 'Why don't you share the room with Lilith, Arjuna?'

Arjuna looked furiously at him, his face reddening, whether with embarrassment or in anger, they couldn't quite say.

'No, I think it would be better if we men stayed together in one room.'

Lilith looked at Arjuna and said, 'I don't really mind, you know.'

'That might be so, but I think we will all be more comfortable this way,' said Arjuna stiffly, even as Sabium sniggered behind his back. Lilith noticed the sniggering and a wicked gleam came into her eyes as she asked Arjuna, 'Are you scared of what people might say?'

Arjuna's face reddened again. He muttered something about it not being proper.

Lilith gave a frustrated sigh as she blew air out of her mouth. 'Oh, come on. We are all adults here,' as she grabbed hold of Arjuna's arm and dragged him towards her room.

Arjuna gave a quick glance back to see Sabium bent over with laughter and even the normally sober Shrutasena showing twinges of a smile on his face. He shook his head exasperatedly and followed Lilith into the room that they were going to share.

❖

They had dinner at the inn and then gathered in Sabium and Shrutasena's room.

'So, what's the plan,' asked Shrutasena.

'What exactly did the trader say again?' asked Arjuna.

'He said that she was being held in an abandoned mansion at the back end of the city,' said Sabium.

'What does "back end of the city" even mean?'

Lilith looked questioningly at Sabium who said, 'I think I know what it means. There is only one place where a person like the man who met the trader could have come from.'

'And that is?'

'The north-western edge of this town. The poorest place. It is a ghetto.'

'Is that why you led us here, to the west?'

'Yeah. I figured that it might be easier to scout that area from here.'

'So, do we go now and scout?' asked Shrutasena.

'No,' Lilith said, her hair loose and flapping around her face. *Very cute*, thought Arjuna, momentarily distracted.

'We don't know this town well enough to go sneaking through it at night. A better idea might be to do a walk through in the morning and mingle amongst the crowd.'

'We need to be dressed for it, then,' said Sabium. 'I will make arrangements for some clothes more suitable for that part of town,' he said, getting up and leaving the room.

Lilith found it difficult to fall asleep that night. Arjuna had pulled his mat to the far end of the room, a respectful distance away from her, and fallen asleep. She could see his chest heaving up and down, evenly. Lilith's eyes softened as she looked at his sleeping form.

She knew how he felt about her, of course. Every woman knows when a man has feelings for her. Men had always been drawn to Lilith, but her formidable reputation as a queen's bodyguard, coupled with her own demeanor, kept them at a distance—yearning wistfully for a glance, a smile, or a word from her.

This was somehow different. Thinking back, she realized that Arjuna had been in love with her since they had first met on the steps leading to the river. Even when she had slapped him, she had noticed the look in his eyes. One of infatuation. She had dismissed him then as just another typical, besotted man. But now, she knew that he wasn't. She wouldn't have opened up to him if she had thought otherwise. She had poured her heart out to him when she had been at her most vulnerable and he hadn't taken advantage of that to press his case.

She remembered pulling her hand away from his, secretly hoping he would take it again. But he hadn't. He had maintained the same respectful distance from her as he was doing now. She knew that Sabium and Shrutasena had both figured out how he felt about her and that they ribbed him in their own ways.

Lilith smiled as she thought of the conversation earlier that evening as they debated how to accommodate the four of them in two rooms. She looked fondly back at Arjuna as she recalled his confusion and hesitance in sharing a room with her. She wondered if he knew how she felt about him.

She paused. Did she know how she felt about him? She sifted through her own feelings about him. Did she love him? She had never known the love of a man before. Always, embittered by her past, she had thought of all men as being the same—callous, selfish and greedy—and had maintained her distance from them. But she had not done so with him. Why had she insisted on his sharing the room with her? Was it purely through altruistic motives? She knew in her heart of hearts that it wasn't so.

She realized with a start that she loved this stranger from her homeland. She loved his strength and his confusion when it came to her. She recalled the look in his eyes when she had regained consciousness in the abandoned mansion after the ceiling had caved in upon her. There was, of course, panic and worry. But there was something else too. He cared for her. He truly did. She couldn't remember the last time that anyone had cared for her. It felt nice. She wondered if she should go over and sleep next to him. And then she decided against it. That wouldn't do. His propriety wouldn't allow it. So, she lay down on her mat, facing him, looking at his silhouette and drifted off to sleep, a smile on her lips and a song in her heart.

Zabaya had been in a foul mood ever since he had returned from the palace. The men stepped around him carefully as he vented at them for the smallest of mistakes. Nur-Adad's pusillanimity disgusted him. *He calls himself a king*, he thought, scornfully. *A toad would make a better king than that old has-been. Hasn't the nerve to see something through to the end and calls himself a king.*

The news of Erra's death had shocked him and filled him with a sense of foreboding. It is not that he had been particularly close to Erra. There was no love lost between them. He had thought of him as a partner in this enterprise and the relationship was strictly professional. However, his death had brought home to him the precariousness of his own position. Nur-Adad's reaction to the latest news had made it amply clear to him that he was on his own. The king would look on him as expendable and wash his hands off him.

Zabaya took a long chug from his cup. *Bloody bad quality liquor at that. I wish I had picked up a flagon from the palace. I am a captain in the army, and I need to put up with these dolts in this shit hole.* He quaffed from the cup again, draining it, and tried to fill it up but the flagon was empty. That sent him into a paroxysm of rage as he yelled and swore—at the king, his men and himself, in that order. He screamed at his men to get him more wine.

He wondered what to do next. Nur-Adad's reaction had left him with very few choices. Should he just kill the girl and be done with it? Bury her body somewhere impossible for anyone to find? And then finish off his men so that none lived to tell the tale?

That would be easy, but that would also let Nur-Adad off easy. His scorn for his king, which had previously manifested itself as mere resentment, was now building up into a full-blown hatred. *After all that I have done for him, he is hanging me out to dry! I wouldn't be surprised if that old fool were to invite Sin-Muballit into the city, arrest me and throw me at his feet. Even if I were to protest to Sin-Muballit that I was merely the instrument and that Nur-Adad was the mastermind, who would take my word against that of the king?*

He sat drinking far into the night, his mind a welter of conflicting emotions. Plans rose and fell on the waves of his thoughts. It was as he was almost falling into a drunken stupor, that he finally figured out what he would do. *Yes, it would be glorious*, he thought. *What a way to go, if go I must!*

Chapter Nineteen

The Stakeout

Lilith and the others waited till the sun was midway up to its zenith before venturing out of the inn. Lilith and Arjuna were impatient to get going, but Sabium had restrained them, explaining that the longer they waited, the busier the streets would be, making it easier to blend in.

Lilith noticed that the city was buzzing with the hum of everyday activity. Traders called out their wares aggressively. Bullock carts, chariots and horses jostled with people for space. The *hyah hyah hyah* of the cart drivers and the *clippety-clop* of the horses added an interesting counterpoint to the shouts from the vendors. Street urchins ran in and around the carts and horses, coming perilously close to getting crushed as they played their little games. There was always the imminent danger of them coming under hooves or wheels, but they seemed to have an uncanny knack for moving away at just the right moment.

As she meandered through the crowd, along with her companions, with Sabium leading the way, the smells of the city hit her, and she crinkled her nose at this olfactory assault.

Each city has a distinctive smell, thought Lilith. The scent of flowers and incense, garbage and urine, smoke from chimneys, vegetables, meat, and stale food all blended into a unique aroma that was unique to Larsa.

Dogs scurried about trying to get at the food rotting away by the sides of the street. They tried to dodge the stones chucked at them by the kids, yelping and howling as an occasional stone or clump of mud found its mark on them. Lilith had always been fond of animals, and she had to reprimand a couple of the kids as they bunged small stones at the dogs.

Lilith and her friends had chosen clothes with a worn-out look, making it easier for them to blend in with the crowd flooding the streets. They followed Sabium as he led them slowly to the north-western end of the city. Lilith noticed that the density of the crowd seemed to increase in direct proportion to the poverty that they saw around them. The streets were that much dirtier now, with heaps of garbage over which flies danced gleefully, dotting the sides.

An occasional drunk or two had passed out among the piles of garbage. Crows gathered in large numbers, pecking away at the refuse, cawing incessantly. Fights, both verbal and physical, broke out frequently among the members of the populace. Short temper was in abundance here and the yelling and screaming seemed to accentuate the overall feeling of despair that seemed to pervade this part of town. Or so it seemed to Lilith.

As they neared the north-western end of the city, she noticed that the houses were typically built close to one another. The houses all resembled each other—flat, squat, blocky and unlovely to look at. However, at the end of one of these lanes, set slightly away from the rest of the houses, was an old mansion. They had almost crossed the street leading up to it when Lilith heard Shrutasena calling out softly.

'Could that be it?' he asked, as she walked back towards him. The others, careful not to appear too interested in it, looked in that direction, one at a time. There were people on the street, and they looked a singularly unfriendly bunch. Dark eyes and darker stares were directed at them. As Lilith chanced a look, she noticed a man come out of the mansion and squint his eyes towards their end of the street. She heard a gasp behind her and swung her head around unhurriedly to see Sabium hurrying away from there, motioning them to follow him.

They paused a hundred yards or so past the street for a whispered conversation.

'It's him!' Sabium whispered, with barely suppressed excitement.

'Who?' asked Arjuna.

'Him. Him! The man who picked up Mylitta.'

'Are you sure?'

'Positively. He had wrapped his turban around his face but in the tussle, it came loose. I got a good look at him. It *is* him.'

They all looked expectantly at Lilith. She was the leader of their group.

'We can't all stay here,' she said, after a pause. 'They will catch on to us in a jiffy. We will need to spell one another. But how do we even stay here to keep a watch on that house?'

They all looked around. It was Arjuna who saw it first.

'There. That building. It looks to be some sort of an inn. Not the sort of inn that I would be seen dead in, though,' he added. 'Perhaps we could get onto the terrace? And keep a look out from there? Or what about one of those windows?' he asked, pointing to the windows overlooking the street and then back at Lilith.

The others nodded in agreement. Lilith decided that Sabium would take the first shift because he knew the man and could get a good look at him.

'Four hours Sabium,' said Arjuna. 'I shall take the next shift and Shrutasena, after that.'

'What about me?' asked Lilith.

'Uh huh. Not you.'

'What?' she flared.

'Hold on. You aren't the most inconspicuous person, you know.'

'What do you mean?' she asked, looking at Arjuna, her eyes narrowing dangerously, her brows furrowed.

'Have you taken a look at yourself in the mirror recently?' he asked with a smile.

Her eyes softened as she understood the import of his words. She still frowned, but her lips curled up in a smile. She punched his arm and turned away, leaving a pleased looking Arjuna.

'All right, Sabium. Get a room up there. I will be back in four hours,' said Arjuna as he and Shrutasena followed her back to their rooms.

❖

'You think Nur-Adad will have his own bunch of Numidians to pit against us?'

The mid-morning sun rose directly in front of them. They had come down south from Isin after leaving a contingent there to ensure that Enlil-Bani didn't suddenly get ideas about a surprise attack on the Babylonian army from the rear. The road down from Isin curved south-east following the flow of the river and so they had veered to the north-west of the city.

They had made good time, covering the intervening distance of about fifty miles in a day and a half. They had bedded down for the night a scant five miles north of Larsa and had started early in the morning today.

Sin-Muballit squinted against the sun, which was shining directly in their faces. The Babylonian king sat in his chariot, trying to get a better view of the city walls.

'How do his city walls look?' he asked his son. 'Did the earthquake cause any damage to their walls like they did in Isin?'

Murabi, who had younger and keener eyes, peered at the walls and then said, 'I think I can see cracks, father. The earthquake was strong enough that it would affect all fort walls, even our own.'

Sin-Muballit grunted.

'I wonder if he has got word about what happened at Isin,' said the young prince.

'He is bound to have, Your Highness,' said General Gamil. 'I am sure their men at Isin would have hared back here to give them news about the destruction of the Isin army.'

'That ought to make them a little more malleable,' murmured Sin-Muballit.

'Yes, Sire, I certainly hope so.'

Sin-Muballit looked around at his army and then back at his son.

'Well, you had better get going then and talk to the king.'

Murabi nodded and kneed his horse forward into a gentle trot, riding towards the city gates with a flag in his hand.

Nur-Adad waddled over to the gates and stopped near the stairs leading up to the ramparts. His scouts had told him early in the morning that the Babylonian army was on the march, and he had been prepared for them to show up by midmorning.

He had spent a considerable portion of the previous night thinking through his options. The account of the man who had brought news from Isin was very disquieting. He kept talking about new kinds of weapons that could penetrate through their own armour. He didn't think there was anything tougher than bronze but apparently, this new metal, whatever it was, could simply scythe through their armour and weapons. He had heard a lot about Isin's Numidian contingent, and to hear about their complete demolition was a wake-up call for him.

That was what had ultimately decided it for him. He could not afford to throw his own troops against the formidable Babylonian army. He would have to wash his hands off the whole affair. But then, he would need a fall guy, and, in his mind, Zabaya fit the bill perfectly. He had dispatched a few soldiers to fetch him.

He climbed the stairs slowly, pausing every two or three steps. At the top, he peered down to see a young man sitting astride a horse. He waved out to him civilly. There was nothing else that he could do.

They had taken to watching the house in pairs. After that first day, they had realized that in case the kidnappers decided to move their prisoner from the house, they would need a way to quickly alert the other members of their group. So Sabium and Shrutasena had paired up, as before, with Arjuna and Lilith mounting guard together. Arjuna had asked Lilith to veil herself while going in and out of the building. It wouldn't make her invisible to the ruffians outside, but it would at least make her slightly more inconspicuous.

There wasn't much that they could do during the long hours of keeping watch over the house. There was little activity. The man that Sabium had seen had not left the house for long. He had taken a couple of trips into the city but had quickly returned each time. They could see other men in the mansion. These came out periodically and loitered around the front of the house but then went back inside quickly.

Arjuna and Lilith enjoyed these quiet moments together. While they had an eye on the house, they started to get to know each other. Arjuna was surprised by Lilith's change in attitude from a sort of strict propriety to an easy openness. Lilith, for her part, revelled in being able to get to know Arjuna. She quizzed him about his home, his family and friends. She broached the subject of any women who he might have waited for him and was secretly delighted when he declared that he had no wife or girlfriend back home. Arjuna had never been in love before, apart from the teenaged infatuation that all kids go through, and Lilith had never had any hope of falling in love, ever. They gently explored each other's minds with their words, hesitantly at first, and then with increasing candour.

Arjuna had taken to calling her 'Chitra' when the others weren't around, and she absolutely loved it. She didn't know what the future held in store for them, but she wanted to enjoy this time, however long it lasted.

They had relieved Sabium and Shrutasena early in the morning. Suddenly, Lilith's attention was diverted from their conversation by the sight of several soldiers moving furtively down the street leading to the mansion.

'Arjuna, look.'

They watched as the soldiers moved stealthily, warning people along the way to keep quiet and move away from the mansion. They reached the mansion and then tried to open the gate softly. The metal creaked stubbornly as they pushed, causing the men to freeze in mid-stride, uncertain whether to continue or not.

'Who do you think they are?' asked Arjuna.

'Look like soldiers.'

'Does this mean that the kidnappers are working on their own?'

'I don't know about that. But it surely implies that there will be no war here ...'

She had barely completed the sentence when the mansion and the street erupted into action. Men poured out of the house with swords and war cries. The soldiers who had expected to catch the men off-guard were themselves caught unawares. They quickly pulled back from the gate as the kidnappers swarmed from inside the mansion. There were a good twenty men or so and they were more than a match for the ten odd soldiers who had approached the street.

The battle was short but decisive. That first rush killed nearly half the soldiers, and as the others realized the peril they were in, they tried to flee back up the street. The kidnappers pursued them and hacked at them from the back as they ran. Three soldiers fell as the knives hurled by their attackers embedded themselves in their backs. Two others managed to escape into the main road and melted into the crowd.

Arjuna and Lilith's eyes swung back towards the mansion and that's when they saw Sybella's kidnapper, the man Sabium had recognized, come out of the house, dragging a woman behind him. There was a veil across her face, but it was obvious to the watchers that it was Princess Sybella.

'Come on!' said Lilith as she jumped up and ran down the stairs and into the street.

'I'll follow them. You get Shrutasena and Sabium,' she ordered Arjuna, who ignored it and moved alongside her.

'Didn't you hear what I said?'

'I did, and I am not going anywhere. If you are going after them, I am coming with you,' he said, his face set and his attitude one that brooked no arguments.

Chapter Twenty

Martyr Without a Cause

It was pure chance that had made Zabaya glance out of the window of the mansion and spot the soldiers sneaking up on them. He had quickly gathered his men and spun them a story about betrayal. The men had not liked that one bit. They had taken up their weapons and charged out, decimating the soldiers, and putting the ones still alive to flight.

That is when Zabaya had dashed down into the dungeon and dragged the princess outside. Sybella was weak from lack of proper nourishment, the travails of the kidnapping, the long journey from Babylon and the many days of having been cooped up in the dungeon. She fell repeatedly, as she was dragged up the stairs mercilessly, by Zabaya. At one point, as she fell again, he bent his face low to hers and screamed,

'Princess, if you don't get on your feet and walk, I shall be forced to slit your throat right here. Understand?'

Sybella had nodded her head fearfully and forced herself back onto her feet, following Zabaya to the door.

Near the door, he had stopped and, unwrapping the cloth that he had tied around his head, had put it over Sybella's head, wrapping the ends across her face as a veil.

He had dragged her down the street on which his mansion was located and then turned into the main road that led towards the western gates of the city. He had got information earlier in the morning that the Babylonian soldiers were marching to it, and he knew that where they were, Nur-Adad was sure to be.

Zabaya's men, gesturing menacingly at everyone, cleared a path for him and Sybella as they walked down the road at a fair clip. Men, women and children got out of the way, hastily. Zabaya had Sybella's right hand gripped firmly in his own as he dragged her onward, towards the city gates.

Behind them, Arjuna and Lilith followed, making sure to stay among the crowd. The kidnappers following Zabaya cast frequent glances behind them, and Lilith and Arjuna dodged through the crowd ensuring that they remained hidden.

It did not take them very long to get to the city gates. Zabaya glanced up and saw Nur-Adad on the ramparts. He seemed to be talking to someone on the other side of the gates. Zabaya gestured to his men to protect the stairs as he dragged Sybella up to the ramparts.

Nur-Adad had been engaged in a conversation with young Murabi, who had asked him to surrender the city, or else.

'Why do you want me to surrender the city, young man? We are already paying tribute to your father and to Babylon. The city gates are being opened for you. You can come in.'

'Bring out my sister then,' insisted the young man.

'Your sister?'

'Yes, we have reliable information that she is being held captive inside the city. Which also means that you and that Isin dog were planning this together.'

Nur-Adad feigned an expression of innocence as he spread his arms wide and shrugged his shoulders.

'I don't know why you would accuse me of that. Even if what you say is true, what does that have to do with me?'

At that very moment, Zabaya reached the top, dragging a moaning Sybella up the stairs.

'You lie, Nur-Adad,' he screamed as he held Sybella in front of him, his left arm around her upper body, his right hand holding a knife against her neck.

Nur-Adad was taken aback. Zabaya had a wild gleam in his eyes. Nur-Adad backed away from him as his bodyguards inserted themselves between him and the crazed man.

'Prince Murabi,' yelled Zabaya, one eye on Nur-Adad's bodyguards, 'the king of Larsa is lying. He was in on it from the start. He knew all about the plan to kill you all in Babylon. Him and that Enlil-Bani of Isin. I was just a mere instrument that they were using.'

Nur-Adad laughed mirthlessly as he looked down at Murabi.

'Prince Murabi, this man is a renegade soldier that I had dismissed from my army a month ago. He left, threatening vengeance against me. It is obvious that this whole episode was his way of getting back at me.'

'Liar!,' yelled Zabaya again. Then, turning to look down at Murabi, he said, 'Prince, I do not lie. I meant every word that I said.'

'If you did, then you would have no hesitation in letting my sister go. Let her go and we shall talk.'

As Zabaya spoke to Murabi, he had moved away from the stairs. Nur-Adad's bodyguards took this opportunity to hustle their king down the stairs and away from the mad man. Zabaya noticed this and realized that he was now stuck on top of the ramparts.

Lilith had reached in front of the city gates, about twenty yards from the stairs leading to the ramparts. She noticed the kidnappers guarding the stairs.

'Arjuna, take some of those soldiers and start attacking those kidnappers.'

'Where are you going?'

'Why, up there, of course,' saying which, she sprinted around the group of soldiers to the other side of the stairs, kicked off her footwear and started to climb up the wall using her fingers and toes. The wall was roughly fifteen feet high and smooth. There were slight gaps between the layers of bricks and smaller cracks that had developed during the earthquake. Lilith used these to pull herself up. Suddenly, her feet slipped, and she dangled desperately, her knuckles wedged into the tiny cracks. Her skin abraded and the back of her knuckles were blood covered.

The muscles in her upper arms screamed with pain, but she held on as she found purchase for her feet again.

She hung there, her body quivering with the effort, but knowing that she had to keep going. She only had another five feet to go, and Lilith scanned the wall to see where she could get some purchase for her fingers. The wall was very smooth at this height except for a small crack slightly above and to the right. It was about three feet above her. Lilith hesitated for a couple of seconds, resting her weary muscles before pushing off with her legs and jumping up and to the right. She searched for that crack with both her hands, but only her right hand found it. She wedged her fingers in and balled them up into a fist as her left hand fell helplessly.

There she hung, her right arm supporting the entire weight of her body. She gritted her teeth and then reached up with her left hand again and this time, wedged the fingers of that hand into the crack as well. Her body weight was distributed across both arms now and that provided some relief to the aching muscles of her right arm. She tried to see if she could wedge her toes into any cracks but there were none to be found, and she gave up that idea. She hung there for a few seconds. For an eternity. She looked up and saw that the top of the wall was a scant two feet above her head. After a brief moment to rest her weary muscles, she released both hands at once and made a final, desperate leap, propelling herself with her powerful, well-trained legs.

This time, both her hands gripped the edge of the wall, and she was able to pull herself up. She lay panting on the ground, her chest heaving, her muscles spent. Her fingernails were torn and bloody, as were the back of her hands and knuckles.

As Lilith scaled the wall, Arjuna fought his way through the kidnappers, steadily whittling down their numbers. His heavy iron sword swung and sang through the air as it found its mark repeatedly. The other Larsa soldiers reacted to the lead provided by him as they attacked in force.

The kidnappers were also at a disadvantage because Nur-Adad's bodyguards, on the stairs, came up behind them and simply knifed the few who stood guard with their backs towards the stairs. The men crumpled up and died almost soundlessly. As the others saw their comrades dropping around them, they threw down their weapons and surrendered.

Arjuna gave them an order to get on their knees and gestured to the other soldiers to stand guard over them. As he looked up again at the ramparts, he saw Lilith get up slowly and take her sword and knife from her waist belt. She had her knife in her left hand and her sword in her right.

Zabaya, who had noticed Nur-Adad escaping down the stairs surrounded by his bodyguards, saw the attack launched by the soldiers against his men. He had not seen Lilith climb the wall behind him but had turned back towards Prince Murabi standing outside the gates. The prince had now been joined by his father, sitting in his chariot.

Zabaya's eyes gleamed, the eyes of a madman. It seemed that whatever fragile string had connected him to reality, however tenuously, had finally snapped. He was now just an animal. A dangerous animal. An animal that had been trapped and that was looking for a way out. He held Sybella against him, hoping to use her body as a shield as the knife against the throat was clutched tighter, drawing blood as it nicked her throat and brought a frightened gasp from her

It was then that Lilith gave voice, 'Release the princess.'

Zabaya turned around quickly to face this new threat. At the same time, Arjuna had run up the stairs from the other side and spoke, 'Give her up. There is no escape. Your men are either dead or have surrendered.'

Zabaya looked back over his shoulders and saw Arjuna standing there, a blood-stained, black sword in his hands. He tightened his grip on his prisoner, his arms crushing her chest and raising an involuntary cry from her, 'Stay away. Or the princess dies.'

'Easy now,' said Lilith. 'If the princess dies, you die too.'

Zabaya laughed. 'You think that scares me, girl? I know that I am dead anyway. You think either Nur-Adad or Sin-Muballit is going to let me live? Not a chance. But, before I die, I shall at least complete my task and kill the princess.'

With that, he moved to draw his knife against her throat. 'No,' screamed Prince Murabi, King Sin-Muballit and Arjuna at the same time. However, for Lilith, it was as if time had slowed down. She saw his hands move, ready to draw the blade across Sybella's throat. Her left hand, which had been drawn behind her back, swept forward in one smooth motion. She didn't have time to change her grip on the knife to throw. Instead, she just let the knife go as she held it. The blade turned over a couple of times, lazily, glinting in the harsh sunlight, before it hit with a muted *thwack* on Zabaya's forehead, penetrating his skull.

Zabaya cried out one last time as his arms around Sybella loosened. She fell to the floor of the rampart even as Zabaya swayed unsteadily on his feet and then took a step before plunging over the side. He was dead before he hit the ground.

Chapter Twenty-One

The Release

A week had passed since the events at Larsa. Arjuna and Lilith entered the palace gates along with Shrutasena. There was a festival-like atmosphere, both in the city as well as inside the palace walls. There were buntings everywhere. The palace was decked with flowers and the fragrance given out by them was heady. It was late in the afternoon and not yet time for the torches to be lit. Several open tents had been constructed next to each other so that the guests could walk through the gardens without the sun beating down on them.

The place was already filled with the invitees. There were a few that Arjuna recognized. Lilith, given the nature of her work, was aware of who they were but had not met them socially. Her escapades during the recent events were now the talk of the town and many of them waved out to her while calling out her name as if they had known her all their lives. Lilith limited herself to gracefully bowing her head at them before walking past.

'You seem to be very popular, suddenly,' noted Arjuna.

Lilith arched her eyebrows at him in response.

'No, really. I saw several young men eyeing you as we walked in.'

'Hmmm. Why do *you* care?' asked Lilith, an impish gleam in her eyes.

Arjuna floundered. 'Well, of course, not that it is any of my business. I just thought I'd inform you of the impact you are having on the young male population in Babylon.'

'I see. And I suppose then that you would be perfectly all right with me latching on to one of those hunky men?'

'Well ... obviously, it is for you to decide,' he concluded, lamely.

Lilith decided to be kind to Arjuna.

'Oh, *pffft*,' she said, with a little snap of her fingers. 'Those men don't stand a chance. I have someone else on my mind.'

'You do?' asked Arjuna, a worried look on his face.

'Mm-hmm,' said Lilith, noticing his discomfiture with the corner of her eyes and suppressing a smile. *Men are so transparent*, she thought. *And so incredibly dense at times*.

Arjuna was wearing his Bharatiya dress while Lilith was wearing a stunning, full length, sleeveless and daringly cut gown in dark green. It complimented the green of her eyes. A person who had no idea about her profession would have placed her as a member of the aristocracy. Only the still-healing wounds on her knuckles, wounds from that mad dash up the Larsa fort walls told a different tale.

Shrutasena, prudently walked a few feet behind them, giving them their space. This was not something that he had wanted to do, but Arjuna had forced him into coming here.

As they neared the heart of the festivities, Arjuna saw Sabium waving out to him. The Babylonian trader had arrived here earlier and was accompanying Mylitta. He was hanging on the outside of a little group that included Mylitta and Princess Sybella. There were several young men gushing around the ladies, and Sabium had been deftly pushed to the periphery of that group. His only consolation was that every so often Mylitta would catch his eyes and flash a dimpled smile at him.

Once, during a quick break from all the gushing young men, she came up to Sabium and whispered in his ears, 'Do stay where I can see you, love. I have *got* to stay beside the princess and only the fact that you are around to catch my eye is preserving my sanity.'

Sabium had preened like a peacock, and any misgivings about young men flocking around the love of his life quickly vanished, replaced by thoughts of what he would do with her once he got her away from the crowd.

He waved to Arjuna and Lilith when he saw them, and as they approached, the crowd of young men around the princess parted as she pushed through to her rescuers.

'Lilith! Arjuna!' she exclaimed, extending her hands towards them and taking one of their hands in each of hers. Mylitta also took this opportunity to make her way to Sabium, ducked under his arm and put her arm around his waist.

'You look stunning Lilith,' said Mylitta. 'All this beauty hidden under those black warrior clothes and that black veil.'

Lilith managed to blush prettily and immediately looked away in confusion. She was not used to the repartee in such social settings.

'We,' Sybella indicated to Mylitta and herself, 'don't know how to thank you enough for what you have done for us.'

'It was my duty, Your Highness,' said Lilith, adding, 'I was honour-bound to help recover you both. I ought not to have allowed the kidnapping to happen in the first place,' her voice laden with genuine emotion.

'Oh, come on now. You can't blame yourself for that? You were tasked with guarding the queen and you did that well enough. None of us could have guessed that Dagan would turn out to be a traitor.'

Lilith refrained from saying anything. She had a lot of stored up guilt over what had happened during the festival, but this wasn't really the time or place to display them. She merely contented herself with bowing to the princess and murmuring, 'You are too kind, Princess.'

'Lilith,' said Sybella, her face serious. 'Can we dispense with the 'Your Highness' and 'Princess' please?'

'I don't think so, Princess. I am still a slave of your mother's, you know,' she said with a smile.

'We will need to do something about that, then,' said Princess Sybella, a look of determination on her face.

Heralds announced the arrival of King Sin-Muballit, emperor of all lands between the two rivers. The king was looking a little peaked, and Sybella quickly left the side of her friends and ran up to her father as she gripped his waist with one hand. The king smiled at her affectionately, draped an arm around her shoulders, and leaned on her for support as he hobbled toward the throne set for him.

'The king seems to have aged over the past few days,' remarked Arjuna quietly to Lilith.

'His health was a concern previously, but the kidnapping of his favourite child seems to have hit him very hard,' she replied.

Sin-Muballit looked around the assembled crowd. The queen sat next to him. Murabi, who had been waiting to the side, stepped forward and whispered something into his father's ears. The attendants asked for quiet as the king was about to speak. An expectant hush settled on the lawns of the palace as Sin-Muballit spoke, his voice low and faint.

'My dear friends, thank you for coming to this event. The last few days have been hard on all of us, especially on these two young ladies here,' indicating Sybella and Mylitta.

'However, thanks to Marduk's grace and the efforts of our valiant soldiers,' he looked at Lilith and General Gamil, 'we have come through this trial by fire, unscathed.'

'We, of course, must also remember to thank our friends from Hind, without whose efforts, the rescue of my dear daughter and her friend, would not have been possible.'

The assembled crowd broke into applause.

Murabi gently interrupted his father just as he was about to resume. 'Father, if I may?'

Sin-Muballit nodded, happy to be able to catch his breath. Even that short speech had left him gasping.

Murabi cut a dashing figure as he surveyed the people gathered in front of him. He had worn his official robes for the occasion, including a turban on his head. The younger ladies in the crowd were eyeing him appreciatively, a fact to which Murabi was completely oblivious.

'Friends,' he began, 'while my father has expressed his thanks to our friends from Hind rather succinctly,' he turned and smiled at his father and said, 'I would like to take this opportunity to expand on that. You see this?' he asked, taking out his black sword.

'This is the sword from Hind, a sword made of metal so powerful that it can cut through every other metal known to us, like a knife through butter . . .'

'Or like a knife across the throat of an Isin dog . . . ' someone shouted crudely, creating a ripple of laughter through the crowd that brought a little smile to Murabi's lips.

'That's right. This, my friends, is something that we have had our eyes on for years. Did I say years? I should say generations, ever since our traders returned from that distant land with stories of the wondrous metal. We have had small samples of it smuggled to us a while ago, of course,' he said, with a twinkle in his eyes, as he glanced at Arjuna, 'but nothing more than that. My dear friend Arjuna's fellow countrymen have steadfastly refused to give us these weapons over the centuries, unwilling perhaps to share this invention with the outside world.'

Murabi paused for effect as he surveyed the crowd. They were listening to him with rapt attention. Even the younger women were concentrating on the story, and not on him.

'Until now. I don't know what magic Sabium and the other traders did, but Prince Arjuna's father agreed to provide us with sufficient quantities of these weapons,' said Murabi as he looked warmly at Arjuna. Arjuna was touched that Murabi did not mention that it was the drying up of trade and the slow death of the river that fed Rohitaka that had led to his father's decision. His perspicacity and propriety, even at such a young age, astounded Arjuna.

'So, yes,' continued Murabi, 'Our victory over Isin, the utter annihilation of their Numidian contingent,' he paused as loud cheers and applause broke out in the crowd. He waited for the applause to die down before continuing, 'The utter and complete annihilation of their Numidian contingent, which eventually led to the king of Larsa opening his gates to us, would not have been possible without these weapons. But did our friends just give us the weapons and leave?' he asked, looking around. 'No, they didn't. They stayed to train us. Every day, Arjuna and Shrutasena trained hundreds of our soldiers in wielding these heavier weapons. *That* is what helped us beat those Isin dogs. And so, for this, once again, I say to you, my friends'—he looked at Arjuna and Shrutasena—'thank you, thank you and thank you.' Arjuna and Shrutasena bowed to him and the king and queen, and then turned towards the rest of the crowd to acknowledge their cheers.

'But wait,' said Murabi, 'there is more,' as the assemblage quietened down. 'They gave us their weapons and they taught us how to fight with them. Is that all they did? When tragedy struck us, when the Isin murderers tried to attack our city during our beloved festival, when the lives of the royal family were in danger, did these men from Hind stay away from the action?'

'No!' arose a united shout from the crowd.

'No, indeed. They fought. Shoulder to shoulder with us. They picked up their swords to protect your king and his family. And for that, I am thankful.'

Cheers broke out again and Arjuna and Shrutasena, bowed again, somewhat embarrassed.

'But wait,' said Murabi, again. 'Was that all they did?' he asked the crowd, now almost playing with them.

'He is good, isn't he?' whispered Lilith to Arjuna, clutching his upper arm. He was aware that she hadn't let go of his arm in a while now. He nodded silently, his attention fixed on Murabi.

'It wasn't,' Murabi said softly. Arjuna marvelled at his capacity to use his voice as an instrument to sway the audience. *What a king he is going to make someday*, he thought.

'These friends of ours,' he flung his hands out expansively towards Arjuna and Shrutasena, 'went in search of my beloved sister, your princess, Sybella, and her companion Mylitta. Did they have to do that?' he asked, his voice rising.

'No!' yelled the crowd.

'But they did it. They went out in search of these two young women. They kept going even when many of us would have given up in despair. They never wavered and they helped to bring back Mylitta first and then Princess Sybella.'

There was a sustained applause after this last remark. Murabi wore a broad smile, waiting for it to subside before continuing, 'You know, dear friends, I have waxed eloquent about our friends from Hind. You must all have thought that I was only talking about these two gentlemen here, Arjuna and Shrutasena, but that is not quite true. When I said "our friends from Hind", I included our own dear Lilith in it, of course.'

The crowd gasped as they heard these words.

'You didn't know that, did you? Lilith is originally from Hind. And so, was it any wonder that it was she who helped save Princess Sybella at Larsa? Who climbed that wall using her bare hands and feet? Who confronted that maddened kidnapper when he was ready to cut Princess Sybella's throat?'

The audience gasped again and Murabi, quite enjoying the reactions that he was eliciting from the crowd, said, 'Yes, you heard me right. The kidnapper had his knife up against Sybella's throat,' and he made a dramatic gesture as if he were holding a knife against his own throat. 'He was going to cut it when our Lilith, not content with scaling a vertical wall, threw her knife with pinpoint accuracy at the kidnapper's forehead and killed him. So, thank you Lilith. Without you, my dear sister wouldn't be here with us and neither would Mylitta.'

The crowd started hooting and cheering as Lilith bowed her head in embarrassment.

'Now,' continued Murabi, apparently still not done, 'You all know Lilith is the head of the queen's bodyguard. But you also know that all the queen's bodyguards are slaves.'

Lilith's eyes grew hard as she dug her nails into the object she was holding, which, at the current moment, was Arjuna's arm. He winced.

Murabi looked at Lilith, his eyes as soft as his voice and said, 'I think that it is time to change that. Mother?'

The queen, who had been listening with pride to her son's oratory, stepped off the throne and approached Lilith, who had left her hold on Arjuna's arm and knelt before the queen. The queen raised her by her shoulders and said,

'Lilith, you have served me well. No queen can ask for a better protector. But I think. It is now time for me to release you from bondage.'

Lilith gasped involuntarily when she heard this and looked at the queen. Her beautiful green eyes filled with tears as she saw the queen take a tablet that Murabi handed to her.

'Lilith, or to use her original name, Chitrangadha—Did I get that right?' she asked, looking at Arjuna, who nodded.

'Chitrangadha, I hereby release you from the bonds of slavery. Here is a tablet that is proof that you are now a free person and no longer a slave.' She handed the tablet to Lilith, who took it with trembling hands, overcome with emotion.

She read the inscription on the tablet and then tucked it into her waistband. She reached out suddenly and hugged Prince Murabi, whispering, 'Thank you' in his ear. The audience roared their approval and Sybella and Mylitta came over and gave long hugs to her.

It was then that the heralds blew their trumpets again and the crowd turned towards the king.

Sin-Muballit had been watching his son's performance with great pride. He struggled to his feet and, waving away the hands of his servant who had reached out to support him, said, 'My dear Babylonians. I have an announcement to make.' The king looked around to make sure that everyone there was listening to him. He needn't have bothered. All their attention was on him.

'I have not been keeping great health for the last couple of years. I don't think that is a surprise to anyone here.' He gave a thin smile and then said, 'The events of the past few days have brought home to me how unfit I am to be your king. No, no, no, I know what I am saying,' he said, as a chorus of disagreements rose from all the people there, led by his son.

'Listen, I think our great city, our great civilization needs a new king. Someone younger, someone more vigorous. Someone like my son.'

'No, father,' protested Murabi.

'Hush, my son,' said Sin-Muballit, with a smile. 'I am still the king.' Then, turning his attention back to the crowd, he said, 'I have decided to abdicate my throne in favour of my son, Murabi. Come here, lad,' he said.

Murabi, his face still reflecting the shock he felt inside, walked up to his father. Sin-Muballit drew his new iron sword, holding it up with both hands before formally handing it over to his son. He then embraced him and, turning to the crowd, shouted, his voice surprisingly strong, 'All hail your new king, Ham-Murabi!'

Chapter Twenty-Two

Homeward Bound

It had been a long night of celebration. They had stuffed themselves with food and drink, though Arjuna, noticing that Lilith had barely touched her wine, had moderated his own drinking. Sabium, Mylitta, Shrutasena, and even the princess were tipsy, having consumed copious quantities of drink. Surprisingly, the young king, Ham-Murabi, had refrained from getting drunk and had limited himself to nursing a single cup of wine.

Arjuna had been quiet through the course of the evening. Given the loquaciousness of the others, he had contented himself with laughing at their jokes, but mainly in casting surreptitious looks at Lilith. He was in love. He knew that now. The thought of leaving Lilith here in Babylon and spending the rest of his life without her filled him with dread.

He spent the night listening to her. Looking at her. Taking in her presence next to him. He had never seen her this uninhibited before. Being set free seemed to have transformed her. Earlier, she had always been reserved, but now, it was as if the floodgates had opened up, and her full personality was out on display. She smiled and laughed a lot more and the many fences that she had erected around her seemed to have been torn down.

Lilith, for her part, was not unaware of Arjuna watching her. She sat next to him, close enough to feel his presence but far enough to maintain a modicum of decorum. However, as the night passed, her self-restraint started to slip. She clutched his arm often and sent what she thought were ample signals to Arjuna for him to make the first move. But the man absolutely refused to do anything.

It was not like he didn't like her. She knew that he liked her, of course. He had made it amply clear over time. The way he looked at her was proof, if proof was required. Not to mention his jealousy at the attention that Lilith had received over the course of the evening from the assorted young men. She had been amused to often catch him glowering at them. *So why doesn't the silly man take a hint and put his arms around me?*

Finally, the group decided to call it a night. As Arjuna got up from the table where they were seated, Lilith placed her hand on his and asked quietly, 'Do you want to take a walk along the river with me?'

Arjuna looked down at her, surprised, and nodded his head.

The two of them said their goodbyes and walked out of the palace gates and towards the river. Lilith continued to attract appreciative stares and wolf whistles from the young men celebrating in the streets. Only her reputation and Arjuna's scowling mien kept them from intruding on their privacy.

They reached the river and started walking along its bank. A cool evening breeze had sprung up. They could see boats bobbing up and down on the river, tied to the many jetties along the riverbank. There were a lot of people sitting on the steps leading down to the water's edge. A few couples could be seen walking alongside the river, the same as them.

Lilith clutched Arjuna's arm as they walked. She decided to broach the subject that was uppermost on her mind.

'So, you and the sergeant will be returning home soon, I suppose?' Arjuna nodded his response.

'I bet you must be missing your home, having been away for so long.'

'Yes, don't you?'

'I don't know. This has been home for a long time now. I have almost forgotten what my original home was like.'

Lilith could feel Arjuna tense, from the way he clenched his arm, before he asked his next question,

'What will you do now? Now that you are no longer the queen's slave?'

'I don't know,' said Lilith, her head bowed.

Arjuna hesitated for a moment before blurting out what he had wanted to ask for a long time: 'Why don't you come with us to Bharat?'

Lilith stopped walking. Arjuna turned towards her and looked her full in the face. Lilith's eyes drilled into his.

'Why?' she asked.

'Why? Why what?' asked Arjuna, confused.

'Why should I come to Bharat? I don't know anyone there. Not anymore.'

'You know us.'

'You are asking me to come to Bharat for you and Shrutasena?' asked Lilith, amused.

'No. I am asking you to come to Bharat for me,' said Arjuna.

Lilith's smiled. A gentle smile. A triumphant smile. She reached out and touched Arjuna's cheek with her right hand.

'Was that so hard to say?'

'What do you mean?'

'Oh,' said Lilith in exasperation, rolling her eyes 'Don't you know, you silly man, that I have been waiting to hear you say that for several weeks now?'

'Wait. What? Really?' said Arjuna, a look of confusion on his face.

Lilith sighed. The longsuffering sigh of every woman who realizes that her man is and will be dumb about some things. She raised her head and kissed a very surprised Arjuna, flush on his mouth. Arjuna was stunned momentarily, before he responded. His arms went around her, and he drew her to him tight. His lips sought hers, hungrily. Their tongues touched, hesitantly, and then explored each other's mouths, drinking deep and trying to quench an insatiable thirst arising out of an unquenchable desire. They stayed that way for a long time.

❖

In the days after the celebration, the Bharatiyas started planning their way back home. The original plan had been for them to take the overland route, through the land of the Ahuras, past the *Upariśyena* mountains, which acted as a gateway to Bharatavarsha, and then down into the plains of Aryavarta. But the new king, Hammurabi, had convinced them that going by ship was a much faster way to travel. Moreover, they wouldn't have to deal with the brigands and smugglers on the land route. Pirates roamed the high seas, no doubt, but none would dare attack a ship as large as theirs The Bharatiyas had agreed to his suggestion. They had spent a month in Babylon, mainly to attend the wedding of Sabium and Mylitta. Sabium's shoulder was still bandaged from the knife wound, but he didn't mind that.

'Makes me look like a war hero,' he told Arjuna.

Lilith had thrown herself enthusiastically into the whole affair, on the bride's side. It had been years since she had taken part in a wedding, and Arjuna suspected that it was perhaps some deep-seated womanly desire that was expressing itself in this fashion. Not that Arjuna knew all that much about how women thought in any case.

The wedding itself had been a gala affair with the participation of Princess Sybella and the royal family. The new king had himself attended all the ceremonies for the man who had helped save his sister and had spared no expense on his behalf.

One evening, as Arjuna and Shrutasena were walking with Sabium along the banks of the Euphrates, two days before the wedding, Sabium had asked Arjuna,

'Why don't you ask Lilith to marry you? You know you want to. And you know that she does too.'

Arjuna had thought about it and then broached the subject with Lilith that very evening as she came to meet him on the steps leading to the river, behind the Esagila. It was an idyllic evening with the hullabaloo of the day giving way to the quiet of the night. A few boats plied on the river, but most had either dropped anchor mid-river or had moored themselves to the various piers along the riverbank. Tiny pinpricks of light could be seen coming from the boats. The crowd that usually thronged the Esagila had also thinned out and it was only lovers, in pairs, who infested the riverbank now. People like them.

'So, Chitra?'

'Mmm?' she asked, nestled comfortably against him, her head on his shoulders.

'I have been thinking.'

'Yes, good to do that from time to time. Keeps the brain from atrophying,' she said, a smile implicit in her voice.

He playfully slapped her on the arm.

'I am serious.'

'All right, I am listening.'

'Do you . . . I mean, would you . . . I mean to say . . . have you thought . . . ' he floundered.

Lilith moved her head off his shoulders, looked at him and asked, 'Are you by any chance asking me to marry you?'

'Why . . . yes,' said Arjuna, relief writ large on his face. 'That's exactly it.'

Lilith laughed delightedly. 'Oh, you silly man.'

'Well?'

'Well, what?'

'Will you?'

Lilith rolled her eyes. 'Why are men so dumb?' she asked looking up at the sky.

'My dear silly, stupid, love. Of course, I will . . .'

Arjuna's face brightened as he grabbed her and kissed her fiercely. When they separated, both slightly out of breath, Lilith said, ' . . . but not here.'

'What do you mean?'

'I want to get married back home.'

'Surashtra?'

'Surashtra. Rohitaka. I don't care. But in Bharat.'

Arjuna nodded and hugged her again.

The wedding had lasted through the day and well into the night with much singing, drinking and carousing.

'Quite different from our weddings, isn't it?' asked Shrutasena.

He had not joined in the singing but had gone about putting away impressive quantities of liquor. There had been an impromptu competition of arm wrestling among the more boisterous of the men. Shrutasena had dominated the competition. His arms were the size of many a young man's thighs and they came a cropper as they went up against him.

Lilith had forced Arjuna to join in the dancing and they, along with the bride and groom, Sybella and Murabi, had danced far into the night.

As Sabium and Mylitta had bid them goodnight, with a giggling Mylitta dragging Sabium off to their wedding chambers, the others had sat talking. An element of sombreness had crept into the conversation as it veered around to the Bharatiyas sailing home. Everyone there understood that they would likely never see each other again, and there were many moist eyes among them.

They started off in the royal boat exactly a week later. King Hammurabi and Princess Sybella gathered at the riverbank next to the Esagila to bid farewell to their friends. Earlier, they had all been to Esagila to pray to Lord Bal Marduk and get his blessings for the long journey back.

'I didn't think you were a devotee of Bal Marduk,' whispered Lilith as they bowed in front of the deity.

Arjuna shrugged.

'*Ekam satya, viprah bahuda vadanti,*' he said.

Before they boarded the vessel, Sybella, Mylitta and Lilith clung to each other in a long embrace with much crying and sniffling. Sabium, his eyes moist, hugged Arjuna and Shrutasena fiercely and then stepped back, drawing Mylitta away from the huddle and consoling her as she sobbed into his chest. King Hammurabi, forgetting his royal decorum, hugged first Arjuna and then Shrutasena. When he came to Lilith, he took her hands and kissed her gently on her cheeks. Then, turning to Arjuna, he said, 'Take care of her, my friend. She took care of my mother

---

* *Truth is one. The wise call it by many names.*

and our family for a long time. She deserves someone to care for her now.'

Arjuna nodded as he took Lilith's hand and they boarded the vessel. The plan was for them to sail down the river to the 'Bitter Sea' as the Assyrians called it. They would then board a larger vessel to make their way home to Bharat.

As the boat pulled away, they waved goodbye to their friends one last time. They kept waving until the distance shrank those on shore to such an extent that they could barely discern one person from the other. Eventually, as they took a bend in the river, their friends were lost from view.

The boat remained quiet for a long time as they sorted through memories of the past few months—or, in Lilith's case, years. She kept turning back, to catch a last glimpse of a city that had both enslaved and freed her. Which had also given her a life of dignity. Arjuna sat beside her, holding her hands, giving her whatever strength that he could.

Chitrangadha and Arjuna sat at the bow of the ship, watching the sun dip below the sea to their right. The sea was placid today and there was just a gentle swell as the ship cut through the water. The sails were up, billowing as they caught the wind effortlessly. The ship dipped and rose along with the swell causing a gentle, rocking motion that enveloped the couple in its embrace. The rays of the sun glittered and almost seemed to bounce off the waters into the eyes of the watchers, casting a silvery patina on the surface of the water.

Arjuna was sitting with his legs spread out in front of him and his back resting against a flag mast. Chitra had nestled herself between his legs, her body leaning back against his, her head resting on his chest. His arms were wrapped tightly around her while hers lay on top of his. Occasionally, she would reach out with one hand to run her fingers through his hair, or to reach up and give him a kiss as he bent down, unasked.

She was struck by her own lack of inhibition in demonstrating her affection and love for him. She had never done that with anyone. Not since she had been kidnapped, at least. It felt good, she admitted to herself. It felt good to finally connect with another person without putting up barriers. She had had a few friends among her own kind of course. The other bodyguards were her friends, although, given that she was the leader, there was always a bit of reserve in the way they behaved with her. She, on her part, was friendly, without opening herself up to them in an uninhibited manner.

With Arjuna, she felt no need to put up a facade. What Arjuna saw was the original Chitrangadha, not Lilith. He called her Chitra now. Lilith was gone and she loved it. Loved hearing the name that her father had used. A name that she had almost buried under layer upon layer of scabs formed from the wounds inflicted on her by the world and her own circumstances.

With his usual tact and delicacy, Shrutasena had settled near the stern, joining some of the crew in games of *chaturanga** on a board scratched into the boat's floor, subtly granting the couple some much-needed privacy.

The ship sliced through the water, drawing closer to its port of call. The trip had been uneventful. As Murabi had surmised, pirates had stayed away from them, given the size of the ship and the fact that there were a considerable number of burly soldiers as part of the crew. Murabi had ensured that his friends would not be hassled during their trip, and so it had proved.

The ship had hugged the coastline, keeping it to their port side as it had travelled, so as to not get blown off course. They had gone due east for a long time before turning south, following the contours of the land. Chitra and Arjuna had spent the days getting to know each other better. They had discussed their childhood, the relative beauty of their places of birth, their hopes and dreams. They spoke of their future together—their love for children, how many they would have, and where they would raise them. In short, they had the same conversation countless lovers on the brink of marriage had shared through the ages.

Arjuna had tried to broach the topic of Chitrangada's uncle. Did she want to take revenge on him? He was ready to take their army from Rohitaka and mount an attack against her uncle's clan, but she had demurred.

'It is strange, you know. While I was a slave in Babylon, the only thing that kept me going through those initial

---

* Chess

years was revenge. Revenge against my dastardly uncle
for doing what he had done to me. I dreamt about it. I
planned it meticulously. I used to think about it constantly.
Of how I would make him pay. Of how I would humiliate
him, perhaps tonsure his head, put him on a donkey and
parade him around the place. Of how I would impoverish
his family and run them out of the palace. My heart filled
with pleasure as I constructed my mental images of him
and his family roaming around the land in torn clothes,
envious of the riches that I would have. I wouldn't let them
die, of course. Death would be an easy release for them. I
wanted them to suffer and to feel the pain of being torn
away from all that they held dear to them.'

'But?'

'Why do you think there is a "but"?' she asked, squinting
up at him, to avoid the midday sun that shone directly
over them.

'There always is. It was building up to the "but",'
Arjuna said, and she laughed delightedly, taking pleasure
from the fact that he could read her mind so well.

'But,' she continued, 'ever since I have found you, those
thoughts have vanished from my mind.'

'Ever since you found me? Or ever since you got your
freedom from slavery?'

'Ever since I found you,' she said, firmly. 'Or maybe the
answer to both those questions is one and the same.'

'What will you do in Surashtra when we reach there?'

'I don't know. Perhaps, pay them a visit. Let them
know that I am alive and well.'

'Wouldn't it be dangerous?'

She chuckled and pulled his arms around her. 'I think we can handle any danger that they can throw our way, love.'

They had spent the days in happy togetherness, in the sort of bliss that comes to people in love, just once in their life, if they are lucky.

The ship had continued its way south along the Bharatiya coastline. Gradually, however, the sunny days had given way to stormy weather. The sea had become increasingly rough. The sun was hardly to be seen as thick, roiling, dark masses of black clouds rolled in from the south-west. It had been raining non-stop for almost a week now. They spent most of their time in the covered area in the middle of the deck or below, sheltering from the rain.

The ship was no longer cutting through calm seas. The swells were no longer gentle. There were huge peaks and troughs that the ship alternately topped and then plunged into at impossibly crazy angles. Water swept over the decks every time the ship went down into one of the troughs and then struggled to come up again, shuddering under the weight of the water. Eventually, the ship would shake the water off itself, almost like a dog after a bath, and then ride the wave to the top, only to repeat the whole process again.

The seamen seemed to shrug this off as normal and went about their duties. But the landlubbers, the soldiers, spent a considerable portion of their time emptying their stomachs into the sea. Shrutasena, as unmistakably a land creature as they come, was unusually vocal about his discomfort.

'Blast this. I would have taken three extra months of travel through land infested by brigands, to this,' he said, holding on for dear life as the ship prepared to plunge again to the bottom of the next trough.

They were now approaching the point where they had to round the jutting headland leading into the port of Surashtra, but the weather took an even worse turn—if that was even possible. The rain pounded down harder, and the ocean turned into a churning, boiling cauldron of furious currents and eddies, tossing the ship like a toy in the grip of a wrathful, petulant child bent on destruction.

The wind had come up very strongly and even while quartering the sails, the ship was having a tough time maintaining its course. The travellers huddled together below deck, fear writ large on their faces. Chitra and Arjuna held on to each other for comfort. A sort of tearing and rending sound started to be heard above the sound of the waves lashing the ship, the high-pitched whine of the hurricane raging outside and the sound of thunder. It seemed as if the ship was groaning in the throes of agony as it was tossed this way and that by an unforgiving ocean.

Time stood still for the travellers as they were thrown around the interiors of the ship. They heard cracking sounds as some of the boards gave away. Water began seeping into the ship, as not all of it drained off the deck when the vessel rose from the depths of a trough. The interior of the ship started filling with water. The seamen distributed a few vessels and pails to the travellers to start bailing out the water in an altogether futile attempt at avoiding the inevitable. The quantity of water pouring in defeated the feeble attempts of those trying to bail it out. As the ship grew heavier, it also grew more sluggish, and its ability to come out of every succeeding trough became less and less.

The captain came below decks, his face grim.

'You all need to come up now,' he shouted, his voice barely reaching them above the surrounding din. 'The ship is doomed. We are not going to make it.'

As they trooped up clutching the handrail along the stairs, he handed each of them a stout piece of wood. When he came to Chitra and Arjuna, he shook his head ruefully and said, 'I am sorry. I had promised my king that I will see you safely through to your country but who can account for what the Gods will?' He pointed to the raging waves with his left hand, while his right clutched the handrail tightly to keep from being swept into the sea.

The ship started listing to its side more and more with each passing moment. A despairing cry was heard as one of the soldiers, who had momentarily lost his grip on a rope that he was clutching, was swept off the deck into the waters by the force of the waves lashing over them.

Chitra, Arjuna and Shrutasena clung to each other. Chitra, who was the strongest swimmer of the lot, gave them some last-minute instructions, 'Remember to hold on to the pieces of wood. Do not fight the current but go with it. Ride the wave, as it were.'

They had tethered themselves to a short length of rope so that they would at least be together. Chitra ran her fingers over the tablet Murabi had handed her. It was hung around her neck like a pendant with a string along with some beads. She had had a couple of holes drilled into it so she could wear it as an ornament. Arjuna noticed the gesture and shouted into her ear, 'Don't worry. The Gods wouldn't have allowed you to get away from there only to take your life here.'

Chitra clutched the tablet tighter, her lips moving in prayer.

Eventually, what they had feared came to pass. The ship, lurching like a drunken sailor at port and finding it increasingly difficult to right herself after every dunking in a trough, gave up the fight. One moment, the passengers clung to beams and ropes for support; the next, the ship shattered beneath them, hurling them into the churning, frothing cauldron of the sea.

Chapter Twenty-Three

The Sea

Morning offered a strange scene. The sea was calm, with a faint ripple of waves across the surface. A large, flat piece of wood floated on top with three exhausted people asleep on it and, for all practical purposes, dead to the world.

Chitra, Arjuna and Shutrasena had fallen into the kind of slumber that only comes to those whose bodies have been utterly spent, battered and exhausted. The night, for them, had been one long struggle for survival. When the ship had come apart and they had been dumped into the waters, the three of them had thanked their foresight in tying themselves together with the piece of rope. It allowed them to support each other. Arjuna was the weakest swimmer of the lot, and Chitra and Shrutasena took turns helping him keep his head above the water.

It was Shrutasena who took the lead. He manoeuvred them into the troughs. He taught them how to duck under and through the waves breaking over them. It was tough work. The stinging rain lashed them through the night, save for a fleeting respite when they passed through the

storm's eye. Arjuna and Chitra had assumed that the worst
was over, but it was Shrutasena, with his experience, who
had told them that it was but a passing phase and that they
needed to remain vigilant.

They had initially seen other heads bobbing about in
the water, but gradually they had gotten separated from
them. They had no way of knowing whether the others
had survived or simply been pulled under or had just lost
the will to fight. They had come upon a larger wooden
board, broad enough for one person to get onto, and they
had taken turns. At the very least, it eased their aching
muscles and granted them some much-needed rest.

They kept paddling through the night, a stubborn
refusal to give up. It helped that all three were soldiers and
giving up didn't come easily to them. Had they been alone,
perhaps they might have been tempted to give up, but their
togetherness kept that thought at bay. They continued
paddling and ducking underneath waves, weaving their
way from trough to trough. In the brief lull offered as
they passed through the eye of the storm, Shrutasena even
found the energy to joke, 'At least we don't have to worry
about getting eaten by sharks.'

'Why not?' asked Arjuna.

'They would already have dived deep along with all
the other aquatic creatures to take shelter from the storm.
They are sure to find all the food they need down there.'

Eventually, this storm too had passed, like every
storm that individuals go through in life. The easing of
the pelting rain had been their first indication that they
had survived the worst of the storm. The swells had also

gradually diminished in size. It was then that they had
spied the much larger piece of their ship floating a scant
hundred yards or so away from them. They had all paddled
furiously toward it, then climbed aboard and collapsed,
utterly spent.

Shrutasena was the first one to wake up sometime around
noon. He sat up and looked around him. The sea stretched
as far as his eyes could see in all directions. He shook
Chitra and Arjuna awake, and they sat up slowly.

'Do you see any other survivors around?' asked Chitra.

'No,' said Shrutasena.

'Perhaps they drifted further away or . . .'

'Or maybe they just gave up the fight and are dead,'
said Shrutasena. 'We are lucky that we are together. We
had one another to depend on. The others on the ship
were alone. The mind can play tricks on a person when he
feels that he is facing insurmountable odds. The wish to
give up can be overpowering at times.'

Arjuna gave a small grin as he looked from Chitra to
Shrutasena and said, 'Well, at least *we* survived the storm.'

Shrutasena nodded but then added grimly, 'We might
have survived the storm, but we are by no means out of
trouble. For one, we do not have any water to drink.'

He saw them look longingly at the water around them
and said, 'No.'

'No what?' asked Arjuna.

'No to drinking that water,' he said indicating the sea.
'Drinking that is a sure way to die.'

Chitra and Arjuna's faces fell as they heard this.

'Secondly,' continued the veteran, 'we don't have any food. I am not sure how long we can survive without either of those.'

'You are all cheer, today,' said Arjuna with a grin. 'We survived the storm, didn't we? I am sure we can survive this as well.'

He stood up slowly, holding on to Chitra's hand for support and surveyed the horizon all around.

'I can't see any land though.'

'Yes, I noticed that too,' said Shrutasena, dryly

'We could be anywhere now,' said Arjuna.

'Not really,' responded Shrutasena. 'The winds were from the south-west yesterday and the storm itself seemed to be a result of the monsoons. As you know, the monsoons come up from the south-west and so I am hoping that it wouldn't have taken us too far out from the coast.'

'How do you know so much about the sea?' asked Arjuna.

'I had a friend who was fascinated by stories of the sea that we heard from merchants and traders. He left home around the time that I joined the army. He would come back periodically with tales of the lands that he had seen.'

'How come I haven't ever met him then?'

'He left when you were very young.'

'And now?'

'He hasn't come back for over twenty years.'

'Oh. Do you know what might have become of him?'

'Look around you, Arjuna. Who knows how many sailors lie in its depths? My friend might have gone down with his ship, or he might have settled down in a faraway land. Perhaps, he found himself a girl somewhere and is living out his life there.'

Shrutasena sighed as his mind went racing back to retrieve memories of his friend. Chitra, noticing his mood, tried to turn it back to more practical matters.

'The coast has to be to our east, yes?' asked Chitra.

'Yes,' said Shrutasena, waking up from his reverie.

'Then all we need to do is move towards the east.'

'How do you propose we do that?'

'These boards,' she gestured to the ones they had with them when thrown into the sea and had clung to, even after finding the much larger raft.

'We can row using these, or at least paddle with them,' she said, squinting her eyes, as she looked critically at the suitability of the boards as oars.

They took turns at paddling, two at a time, keeping the sun at their backs. They began by taking breaks every quarter of an hour, but the lack of food and water eventually shortened the spells of paddling to five minutes each. Their hands blistered from the rough boards. Their throats were parched, and it made it difficult for them to swallow their own spit. Their lips chapped and cracked under the searing heat. Night brought with it some relief, at least from the heat, but the lack of food and water was beginning to take its toll on them, fit as they were. They lay sprawled on the raft, splitting headaches pounding, huddled together and still tethered by the rope—just in case one of them rolled off.

❖

They lay there immobile now. Too spent to even pretend to try and steer their raft towards the east. The sea took them whichever way it wanted as the ripples on its surface drove the raft forward. This was the third day after the storm. Humans can survive without food for a long time, but water is vital to our survival. And that, they did not have. Slowly, the terrible heat dried out their bodies. They sank into a kind of stupor that was worse than any induced by liquor.

Their limbs refused to move. Their throats had nearly closed. They lay in a dead faint, waiting for the end. They slipped in and out of consciousness. Arjuna's eyes opened of their own accord, suddenly. He was too weak to even sit up. He moved his head from one side to the other with great difficulty to first look at Chitra and Shrutasena, and then towards the horizon, to the east. The sun had moved slightly off the vertical towards the west and Arjuna had to squint his eyes as he tried to see if he could spot land.

There was just that flat expanse of water, yet again. As he moved his head back into a neutral position, he noticed a dark form flying high above and passing in front of the sun, then wheeling away. *That is beautiful*, he thought. *I wonder what it would be like to fly away into the sky. Like the devas* do, on their mounts. Like Karthikeya† and his peacock or Narayana‡ and Garuda§.* He squinted his eyes again as he tried to follow the path of the bird. *That does look like*

---

* Celestial beings
† God Karthikeya
‡ Another name for Vishnu
§ An eagle and God Vishnu's mount

Garuda. Am I dead already? Has the Lord come on his divine
mount to take me away?

There was some strand of thought that was tugging
away at the edges of his brain. Some thought that was
stubborn and insistent and didn't allow him to concentrate
on the eagle that was flying above him. He tried to ignore
it, but it was incessant, persistent and unrelenting. He
was starting to get quite annoyed by it. He could not
concentrate on the flight path of the bird because of this
annoying thought in his brain. He decided to give it his
attention so that it would leave him in peace.

And then it hit him. A bird. A bird! A bird here could
mean only one thing. That they were close to land. He had
heard that from someone—he couldn't recall who, where,
or even how long ago. He wanted to leap and scream for
joy but his body refused to cooperate. He tried to call out
to Chitra and Shrutasena and share the good news, but he
could barely get a croak past his vocal cords. He looked up
again at the bird and noticed that it had been joined by a
few more. A smile creased his face as he sank back into
unconsciousness.

Arjuna's eyes opened again. He looked up, hoping to see
the bird but his view was blocked. It was dark and he
couldn't even see the stars. He was feeling much better—
now able to swallow his spit for the first time in what felt
like ages. He raised himself up on his left arm and realized
that he was sleeping on something soft. He peered through
mucus-glazed eyes and noticed Chitra and Shrutasena on

either side of him. He sank back into his bed and then broke into a wide smile. He was sleeping on a bed.

He ran his fingers along the edges of the bed until it encountered something hard and unyielding. Earth! They were on land!

Chapter Twenty-Four

Surashtra

The next morning saw them all sitting up as men and women entered the little hut. Arjuna noticed that they were lying on very rudimentary beds filled with hay. The folks who entered were hardy and wiry, with cheerful faces. The women came in bearing bowls of porridge and large mud cups filled with coconut water and buttermilk.

An old man—clearly the leader, judging by the way the others deferred to him—sat down beside them and gestured for the women to set the bowls and cups before the survivors.

'Eat and drink, please.'

Chitra looked at him and voiced the question on everyone's mind, 'How did you find us?'

The old man laughed uproariously—something they would soon learn he did often.

'Our men were out fishing, and they saw the raft. We had seen several pieces of wood that had floated into our village and knew that ships must have gone down in the storm. It is a miracle that you three survived. But we can talk about that later. I would like you all to eat and drink first. We must replenish the water that your body has lost over the last few days.'

'Did you feed us something last night?' asked Arjuna.

'Why do you ask?' asked the old man, a twinkle in his eyes.

'My throat doesn't feel like it has been stuck together.'

The man laughed that infectious laugh of his again.

'We force-fed you some coconut water. Like we do for kids, with the little feeding cup. Our men thought you were dead when they pulled you off the raft into the boats.'

'We would have been if you hadn't found us. The last thing I remember is the birds circling high above us, wheeling away against the backdrop of the sun,' said Arjuna.

They spent a few days in the village, regaining their strength. The girls in that community took to Chitra and she was often missing for the entirety of the day. She taught them the rudiments of fighting and they shared all their stories with her. One evening, Chitra returned with them, dressed in their local skirts and wearing a necklace made of seashells.

'Well, well,' murmured Arjuna appreciatively. 'You do look nice.'

Chitra smiled and tossed her hair at him provocatively, the way she had seen the local girls do at their beaus. Arjuna grabbed her arm and pulled her to him, his lips seeking hers as his arms tightened around her waist.

Their dalliance was interrupted by the shuffling of feet. Chitra broke away from Arjuna and looked to see a little girl standing there, holding a bracelet made from seashells. She walked up to Chitra and shyly handed it to her.

'Did you make this for me?' she asked.

The child nodded her head.

Chitra took the bracelet and then drawing the child to her, kissed her cheeks. She put the bracelet on her right wrist and then reached up to her neck and lifted the tablet given to her by Murabi from it. She showed it to the girl who reached and touched it solemnly, running her fingers across the cuneiform script.

'You like it?'

The child nodded her head again, giving a shy smile.

'It's yours. Here. Let me put it on you.' Chitra took it and put it around the young girl's neck. The girl took the tablet in her hands and then gave Chitra a tight hug before running off. She stopped a few feet from them and looked back at Chitra. Then, giving her a wide smile, she ran away.

Arjuna, who had been watching this silently, looked questioningly at Chitra.

'You gave away the tablet? I thought it meant a lot to you.'

'It did.'

'But?'

'Being that close to death changes one's perspective. Chitra has finally left Lilith behind.'

They left the village the next day. The young women of the village were all teary-eyed, hugging Chitra repeatedly. The usually smiling men, including the gregarious old headman, were solemn as they bid farewell to the three of them. They plied them with food for their way. Arjuna and Shrutasena had quizzed them about the road to Surashtra. It looked like the storm and the resultant drift had taken them a hundred and fifty miles south, to this marshy land. There were several little islands here and the fishermen had taken them to the mainland from one of the islands.

'Just walk straight up north till you get to Bharukachcha*. You can then take a boat from there to cross the small gulf and once across, Surashtra is a day's walk from there.' The old man then asked them hesitantly, 'Do you have someone there you need to meet?'

'Not really. She,' Arjuna said indicating Chitra, 'is from that town and hasn't been back in a number of years.'

'Do you have someone you love there, miss?' asked the old man, quite serious.

Chitra gave him a puzzled look. 'Not really, why?'

'We have heard some worrying news from there, miss. I don't know if you are aware, but over the past year or so, there have been several massive earthquakes in Bharatavarsha. We have felt it even when out in the sea. The sea has lashed out at us, whenever that happens.'

'What have you heard, grandpa?' she asked.

'We heard that one of the earthquakes destroyed Surashtra. We have met a lot of people who have fled that land and are coming down south now.'

Arjuna reached out and took Chitra's hand as she remained quiet.

---

* Modern Bharuch

'We shall go anyway,' he told the old man. 'The rumours might well have been exaggerated.'

The old man nodded silently and clasped their hands. Chitra bent down to touch his feet in respect. The old man raised her up and then kissed her forehead and hugged her. They took their leave and moved north towards Surashtra.

The route to Bharukachcha was straightforward, at least at first. The path was supposed to head north along the coastline. The ravages caused by the recent storm were in evidence. Freshly uprooted trees lay on the ground, their mud-encased roots in the air, resembling giants who had been slaughtered. The path was waterlogged, and the trio waded through knee-high water at several places. The flooding had been intense, and water had breached inhabited areas. Snakes swam through the water, and while Shrutasena assured them that these were water snakes and hence, not poisonous, Chitra and Arjuna still stepped warily as soon as they saw them.

They saw several families standing on the roofs of their dwellings. The lower portions of their houses were completely submerged. The hurricane had caused many trees to shed their fruits. Coconut trees were devoid of coconuts as the fruits lay on the ground or floated on water.

'I think we ought to move inland a bit and then try and find an alternative route,' said Shrutasena and the others agreed.

They walked eastwards for a mile or so until they reached relatively dry land. The earth was still wet and damp, but the sea hadn't invaded this far inland. There was no defined path or road here and they had to move through the woods, creating their own path.

'We won't have to watch out for wild beasts at least,' said Shrutasena.

'How so?' asked Chitra.

'The rains. Water holes deep in the jungle will be full. The animals do not have to come this far to the edge of the woods for water.'

Progress was slow given the lack of familiarity with the land and the route. They had to take frequent detours as they found themselves reaching dead ends where dense undergrowth blocked their path. Arjuna and Chitra did not seem to mind it though. This was a time for discovery of each other's minds and bodies. Shrutasena, showing his usual tact, had told them the first night that he would sleep a hundred yards or so away so that they were not all caught unawares at the same time, in case of emergency. He had then walked away out of sight of where Arjuna and Chitra had bedded down for the night. This had now become his practice.

The nights were surprisingly cool in the forest. Arjuna and Chitra usually made passionate love and then lay entwined, talking dreamily of this and that. They always got an early start in the morning and walked towards the place where Shrutasena was resting only to find him ready and waiting for them. The first couple of times, Arjuna had a sheepish look on his face. But with time, all three of them had gotten used to their arrangement.

They spoke a lot during the day. They spoke of many things, social, religious and political. Arjuna was in awe of

Chitra's quick mind. It was during one of these discussions that she said, 'I have been meaning to ask you for the longest time about iron. How come you folks have it and nobody else does? Where do you get it from?'

'There is a ridge near ancient Hastinapura where we find the ore. We are able to melt that to remove the impurities,' said Arjuna.

'If that is so, why don't others do the same? Use that ore?' Chitra asked. 'How do we typically get metal from ore?'

'Using heat? We heat it until the metal melts, and impurities stand out and can be removed.'

'Correct. But how do we give the heat?'

'Through our kilns.'

'Does the heat melt the kilns?'

'Of course not. Just the metal. Copper or whatever.'

'We have found that the heat required to melt iron ore is much greater than that required to melt copper.'

'Mmhmm.'

'The heat that is required is so high that it would even melt the soil in the regular kiln.'

'So then how do you do it?' asked Chitra.

'We have a special kind of limestone available in our area. Right now, that seems to be the only thing that can withstand the heat required to melt iron.'

'Aha. So, you have a source for both the ore and the material to make the special kilns required.'

Arjuna gave a beatific smile in response.

'How long have you all had this?' Chitra asked.

'For well over a thousand years. Why do you think Raja Yudhishthira was able to conquer the rest of Bharatavarsha so easily? Why do you think Arjuna was undefeated in battle? Agreed that he was supremely talented, but it helped that his arrows could go through the armour of his enemies while his own armour, made of iron, could stop theirs.'

'And do you remember how Jarasandha was killed?'

'Yes, I have heard the story in my childhood. Didn't Bhima fight and kill him? And also, how Krishna split a twig to show him how to finally defeat Jarasandha.'

'Yes, but the folklore in our area is that Bhima defeated Jarasandha because Bhima's mace was made of iron while Jarasandha's was not.*'

Chitra mused on this for a while before saying animatedly, 'Oh, and that idol of Bhima's which Lord Krishna is supposed to have made and kept in front of King Dhritrashtra? Wasn't that supposed to have been made of iron and didn't King Dhritrashtra embrace it and turn it to dust? How could Dhritrashtra turn an iron idol to dust?'

'Well, that idol was actually made from the same soil that the iron comes from. I suspect that that might have something to do with the legend of Dhritrashtra crushing an iron idol of Bhima's.

'That finally makes sense to me,' said Chitra. 'I have been thinking of that story ever since you folks landed up in Babylon with your iron weaponry. Have been meaning to ask you that for ages but somehow, it always skipped my mind.'

---

*In the great Indian epic, the Mahabharata, a powerful king of Magadha, Jarasandha, was killed by the Pandava Bhima in a one-on-one battle.

'I am sure that what we both have been up to the past few weeks would also have caused it to skip your mind,' said Arujna.

Chitra blushed prettily and then swatted at his arm, playfully.

'Anyway, that's why we keep it a secret. The location of that ridge where the ore comes from is known only to a select few of our *rishis*.'

'Makes sense.'

'We had even refrained from giving or trading our iron weapons with anyone for over a thousand years.'

'Why now?'

'We don't have a choice. Ma Sarasvati is drying up. Some say that she has gone underground, unhappy with the *adharma* that abounds in the world now. Anyway, the city has been in decline for over 200 years now. There isn't much trade, and this was a way to raise some much-needed money. I have a feeling that we will have to leave the city at some point in time. Very soon.'

Chitra drew her breath in sharply.

'Abandon it?'

'Yes,' said Arjuna, with a rueful nod of his head.

They reached the Narmada River a month later. The monsoons had well and truly arrived, and the river was in spate. It had rained for almost the entire duration of their journey. They had made makeshift dresses that would give

---

* Sages/Philosophers/Scientists

them some respite from the rain as they walked. They had made these from banana leaves interwoven with leaves from coconut trees. They had seen the local farmers use them and had copied their design. It served them pretty well, keeping most of the rain off them during the day.

Bedding down for the night was a problem since the ground was wet and damp. They found large banyan trees for shelter and slept beneath their coconut and banana-leaf rain protectors. It was not particularly comfortable, but they were soldiers and could take the rough with the smooth.

As they neared Bharukachcha, they veered left to walk back towards the coast. They saw a lot of new settlements along the way, with people building huts in profusion. They stopped near one of these settlements to ask if someone could take them through the gulf up to Surashtra.

'Surashtra? Haven't you heard?', asked a beefy looking man, busy erecting a hut.

'Heard what?'

'About Surashtra.'

'What of it?'

'There isn't one anymore.'

'What?' asked Chitra, disbelievingly.

'What do you mean?' asked Arjuna

'What I said. There was a terrible storm a few days ago.'

'Yes, we know about the storm. We were caught in it,' said Arjuna.

The man looked up from what he was doing and said, 'Well friends, you are incredibly lucky then.'

'What happened to Surashtra?'

'The sea reached in and gobbled it up,' he said, with the air of one stating the most obvious thing in the world.

It was Arjuna's turn this time to say, 'What?'

'That's right, my friend. One day, there was Surashtra. The next day, the sea.'

'What happened to all the people there?' asked Chitra.

'What do you think happened, lady?'

'They are all dead?'

'Nearly all of them. There might have been a few out in their boats and ships who found refuge along the coast, but if you are really looking to visit the town of Surashtra, you need not. Like I said, it doesn't exist anymore.'

'But surely, the sea would have receded after the storm?'

The man put down his tools and looked at Chitra. A look tinged with understanding at her loss.

'That is where this storm was different, sister. The storm alone might not have caused this much havoc but there was also an earthquake. Didn't you feel it?'

'We were in the middle of the sea. Didn't feel anything,' said Chitra.

'You were in the middle of the sea during the storm and still survived? The Gods must look on you with special favour.'

'About Surashtra though …'

'Yes. Like I said, the earthquake along with the storm has done something to the land. The sea has not … not receded. Surashtra has gone under water. Perhaps, sometime in future, the sea will go back. Hopefully.'

Chitra was quiet. Arjuna moved to her and put his arm around her. She buried her head against his chest and sobbed, her body shaking. The man building the hut muttered a few words of commiseration and walked a few paces away from them. Shrutasena looked distraught as he watched Chitra sob. Arjuna held her tight and ran his hand gently through her hair. He let her sob it out. Eventually, Chitra looked up at Arjuna, with tear-laden eyes.

'I am sorry,' she said.

'Don't be. It was your home.'

She sniffed and wiped her nose and eyes on her cummerbund.

'Yes. That's where my father and mother were cremated. I was looking forward to revisiting the places associated with my childhood. It's all gone now,' she said, a tear escaping her eyes and trickling down her cheek.

'Do you still want to hire a boat and go there? Perhaps the man is wrong? The sea might have receded,' Said Arjuna.

She shook her head vehemently.

'No. I don't want to go there and see the place submerged. If the city still exists, we will come to know about it, and I can always come back later.'

'All right,' said Arjuna. 'We'll do it your way, if that's what you want.'

'That's what I want.'

'We had better be on our way to Rohitaka then,' said Shrutasena, adding, 'We have a long way to go.'

Chapter Twenty-Five

Rohitaka

They moved north-east from Bharukachcha. They had asked around for the fastest route to Rohitaka. The longer but better-known route was through Ujjaini and across the land until the road intersected the *Uttarapatha*[*] and then turn up the road as it ran north-west.

The other route was to go straight up north, skirting the great desert to the west until one came to the ancient bed of the Sarasvati River and then follow the riverbed upstream. They decided on the latter route. The monsoons had not yet come this far north, and travel was much easier for them here than it had been through the forests in the *Dakshinapatha*[†].

Chitra's eyes had lost their earlier sparkle. It was plain to the others that she was still mourning the loss of her childhood home. As usual, Shrutasena gave the couple

---

[*] Ancient northern road. Now known as the Grand Trunk Road.
[†] The old southern route.

space, but Arjuna stayed close, walking beside her with her hand in his, careful not to intrude on her sorrow.

As they moved further up north, they felt the earth shake quite often, with tremors that lasted for minutes at a time. They had taken to sleeping on open ground, under the skies, even if it rained. It was a safer option than sleeping under trees, given the number of trees they had noticed crashing down due to the earthquakes. They had fashioned wooden spears and bows and used those to hunt for their food. Game was aplenty and deer and goat meat, cooked over a fire, made for an adequate meal.

'Have you ever experienced these many earthquakes in such a short period of time, before?' Arjuna asked Shrutasena.

'Never. This is really strange.'

About a month out from Bharukachcha, they came across the dry, ancient bed of the Sarasvati River and turned east, following its path.

'Well, at least we will be able to eat properly at one of the many cities dotting the riverbed,' said Arjuna, longingly, adding, 'It has been a while since we ate a properly cooked and seasoned meal. What do you say, Chitra?'

Chitra looked at him with a faraway expression. It was obvious that she had not heard the question. Arjuna repeated it for her.

'Yes, it would be nice to eat a meal cooked by someone else, for a change,' she said quietly.

They had walked on the riverbed and even bedded down for the night on the sand there. They found that convenient since a little digging got them drinking water. They came upon several small, abandoned villages.

'Looks like people have given up any hope of the river flowing again and moved,' said Shrutasena, pointing to yet another small collection of brick houses that showed every sign of having been abandoned. Arjuna nodded grimly. He was remembering how his own city's sheen had gone down over the past several decades. Or so he had been told by the old men of his city.

The abandoned villages had a forlorn, haunted look about them. Like the ghosts of generations past looked down sorrowfully at what was left now of their homes. The wind whipped through their little streets. It blew over broken vessels, furniture and toys snapped in half or fragmented lying on the ground, abandoned where they had fallen. Cracked and splintered wheels lay by the side of the streets. These told a tale of the departure of not just the people but the souls of these villages.

It was another ten days later that they came upon the big city of Kalibangan. They looked in dismay at what had been a once thriving city, now reduced to an empty shell. The city had been entirely abandoned, at least for a few months. As they got off the riverbed and walked its lonely streets, they noticed the widespread damage caused to the buildings.

Several of them had collapsed in a heap. The once neat streets were piled with rubble and dust.

Arjuna had been here a few years earlier, accompanying a trade delegation. He remembered to have eaten at a shop that had served the yummiest deer meat that he had ever had. He walked the streets looking for it and finally came upon the restaurant. It had collapsed of course.

Chitra bent down and picked something up from the street.

'Look.' She held a small, square seal in her hand, that had some writing on it and a figure of an *ekashrnga*, a unicorn. 'What are these?'

'Seals that identify the tradesmen,' said Shrutasena. 'This one's name was Shantideva. The unicorn marked him as coming from the northern regions of Bharatavarsha.'

Chitra let the seal drop to the ground.

'Not keeping it?' asked Arjuna.

Chitra shook her head. 'Doesn't feel right to take it from this place. It belongs here.'

Shrutasena, who had walked a few feet ahead, called out to them and pointed to the citadel that lay to one end of the city. It had completely collapsed. As they walked from the upper to the lower town, they noticed the same mix of dilapidation and rubble that had confronted them in the little villages that they had come across along the way. The only difference lay in scale.

'To think that people lived here for thousands of years. Grew up, ate, played, worked, prayed, loved, raised kids, shared their hopes and dreams. Think of the millennia of memories that lived on because of the people who lived here. Look at that soot-covered hearth, still showing signs of the last meal that had been cooked on it. Look at these streets and marketplaces that would have been a beehive of activity. Traders calling out their wares. Women haggling with them. Children playing hopscotch in the streets.

Chariots rumbling through them. Horse and bullock drawn carts trundling through the lanes. Potters making those lovely pots with the beautiful designs. Beadmakers lovingly making the necklaces that are so prized in distant places like Babylon.

All of it, gone, just like that. Who knows? In a mere hundred years, this place might be nothing more than a memory. A millennium, hence, not even that. I wonder what our descendants who stumble upon this place a few thousand years later will think of it. Will they look at these places with dry-eyed practicality? What will they infer as they look at the remains of the houses and pottery and seals. Will they wonder what the lives of the people who lived here for ages would have been like? Or will the millennia wipe out all traces of the lives and memories of these people?

If that is so, why do we humans even worry about anything? After all, all life ends in death. Do we know what comes next? There are any number of philosophies, but can we say for sure whether they are true or not? If the ultimate reality is death and dissolution, of the gradual fading away from memory till even the wisps of smoke rising from our burning bodies mingle with the clouds, and all remnants of our having lived on this earth are lost forever, when even the memories of our existence, cease to be, why do we strive to achieve whatever little we can, in our humdrum everyday lives?'

Chitra stopped. Her face had been animated as she had soliloquized. Arjuna and Shrutasena had not heard her say more than a sentence or two over the last month and stood stunned at her eloquence.

She continued softly.

'I remember the priests chanting *"shvetavaraha kalpe, vaivasvata manavantare"* which, as you know, means that we are in the fifty-first year of Brahma's life. We are told that after a hundred years of his life, the universe dissolves and is reconstituted. If everything we know is ephemeral, even the universe, what exactly are we here for? What is the point of all our struggles? We are fairly sure that individual lives don't matter. Do civilizations matter? Do all our lives collectively matter? All the things that we humans individually or collectively do, ultimately mean nothing to the Gods. Or do they? Is all this just *maya** as the *puranas†* tell us? Is nothing real? I can now understand why our great sages went away to the mountains to meditate.'

Arjuna and Shrutasena gave each other a look of worry and concern. Arjuna took Chitra's hand and said, 'My love. I am not a philosopher to be able to answer your questions. I understand where it comes from. Having your childhood home obliterated and then seeing a series of abandoned villages and cities could not have been easy. I am sure every single person, at some or the other point in their lives, has felt as you are feeling. The futility of it all. But as Lord Krishna said in the Gita, all we humans can do is our duty, our dharma, without worrying about the fruits of our action or what that action begets. We can't give up on life just because it has suddenly become hard, or because we have faced incredible losses. We *have* to figure out a

---

* Illusion
† Ancient Indian texts on history

way to cope and move on and keep living, till the breath leaves our body. Isn't that what we have all been taught as soldiers? Not to ever give up, but to keep fighting until our very last breath?'

Chitra did not reply, but removed her hand from his, and snaked it around his waist, as she leaned against him. The trio walked silently through the city and then resumed their journey further east. Towards Rohitaka.

It was five days later that they reached Rohitaka, around mid-afternoon. Arjuna's mind had, for some reason, been uneasy. He couldn't really put his finger on it, but that uneasiness had grown throughout their journey and as they neared Rohitaka, he felt it more and more. They had got out of the riverbed and were now walking along the banks. There was still some residual water in the riverbed, but Arjuna noticed that the water seemed to be standing still. He looked further upstream and could not see any water flowing down.

'That's strange,' he murmured.

'You said something?' asked Chitra.

'That,' he said, pointing to the river. 'That is strange.' Chitra appeared confused. 'I don't get it. What is strange?'

'The river isn't flowing,' Shrutasena chimed in.

'Didn't you both tell me that the Sarasvati's flow had gone down?'

'Gone down, yes. But not stopped completely.' They walked faster now with Arjuna leading the way.

'This is even stranger,' he said.

'What now?' asked Chitra

'Where are the people?'

Shrutasena stopped as if he had been made physically immobile.

'You are right. Where are the people? At this time of the day, there should have been washermen and women washing clothes, little children running around and trying to keep the heat at bay by jumping into the pools of water. I don't see any of that.'

They hurried into the city from the western end, where an air of desolation hung heavy, as if it had been long forsaken. Similar to Kalibangan, there was no one there. No children playing in the streets. No women talking to each other across their balconies. No traders hawking their wares through the streets in their carts or selling them in the marketplaces. There were no sounds of the copper or iron smiths working on their metals of choice. There was no smoke emanating from any of the houses or from the chimneys of the brick kilns. Temple bells did not ring out and neither did the bells around the necks of the cows.

There was no smell of incense or flowers in the air. None at all of food being sold on the streets. All they could smell was dust.

'They have abandoned the place,' said Arjuna with a quiver in his voice. 'But why?' he said, looking around. They passed a large area with a square stone gate.

'What's that?' asked Chitra.

'The cemetery,' replied Arjuna, opening the gate and walking in. The first thing he noticed was the number of freshly dug graves.

'Looks like many people have died recently. He went near a mound that was much larger than the other and read the sign on top of it. It consisted of five names, obviously the names of the people who had died. Shrutasena sank to his haunches in front of it and bowed his head in prayer.

Arjuna came up to him and went down on his knees. He recognized the names as well.

'Shantideva's family,' he whispered.

Shrutasena nodded.

'Wonder how all of them died.'

'Earthquake,' replied Shrutasena.

Chitra slipped her arm around his and held on to it tight. Shrutasena, pointed to the citadel and said, 'Look!'

The tower of the citadel was missing. Arjuna freed his arm from Chitra's and started running. He had to dodge the rubble and debris on the streets, a result of the breaking of the houses along the road. It was evident that a huge earthquake had struck the land and demolished the city. Arjuna slowed down to climb over a large stone before he entered the gates leading to the citadel. He then raced on up with Chitra and Shrutasena following him in his mad dash. They ran hard, their lungs almost bursting with the effort, their hopes getting eroded along the journey to the top.

Chitra and Shrutasena had momentarily lost sight of Arjuna as they ran a few paces behind him. They reached the top and saw Arjuna standing there, his hands on his hips, looking at the destroyed remnants of his home.

As they stood beside him, sharing his sorrow, they heard a sound from inside.

'Pa?' Arjuna called out.

Chapter Twenty-Six

Finale

An old man walked out of the ruins of the citadel. Arjuna and Shrutasena drew in a sharp breath.

'Bhagadutta!' Arjuna called out, rushing to the old man and steadying him as he descended the steps before the citadel.

'What are you doing here all alone?'

The old man squinted, peering at him. 'Who? Arjuna? Is that you, my boy?'

'Yes, grandpa.'

'What are you doing here?' asked the old man.

'I should be asking you the same question. What are you doing here all alone? And where is everybody?'

The old man slowly lowered himself onto a large stone pillar that was lying on its side. The exertion of climbing down those three steps seemed to have taken it out of him. Arjuna remembered a time when everyone, other than his father and mother, had been in mortal terror of Bhagadutta. He ran the citadel like a sergeant runs his unit. The kids, Arjuna included, had all felt the sting of his lashings, both from his sharp tongue and the bamboo cane he always carried.

The old man caught his breath and then looked back up at the trio.

'That is Shrutasena, is it?' he asked.

'Yes, uncle,' said the veteran soldier.

The old man nodded. 'And who is this young lady?'

'She and I are going to get married, grandpa,' replied Arjuna.

'Married, you say? Good, good. It is good to get married. Have lots of kids.'

'Don't let the family die out. I never got married, you know. Couldn't afford to. And didn't have the time, what with running this place and everything.' Bhagadutta said before falling silent again.

'You didn't answer my question, grandpa,' said Arjuna.

'Which question? You will need to remind me. My memory is not what it used to be.'

'Where is everybody?'

'Oh, they are gone.'

'Yes, I see that they are gone,' said Arjuna with exaggerated patience, 'but where? And why?'

'Why? The earthquakes, of course. Where? I don't know. I am here. They went somewhere off towards the east,' Bhagadutta waved his arms vaguely in that general direction.

'What happened, uncle? We have had earthquakes before but have never abandoned our place. Why did they decide to go now?' asked Shrutasena.

'We haven't had earthquakes like this before,' the old man bristled. 'These were enormous earthquakes.

The very mountains shook and fell. The earth tore itself. There are giant cracks now and going deep where there was only flat land before. And then the river stopped flowing. It was the young kids who noticed it first. They told some of the elders, who then came up here to tell your father,' he said, looking at Arjuna.

'And?'

'And your father went down to see if what the kids were saying was true. It was. The river had stopped. Maybe the Gods were angry with us or Ma Sarasvati decided to go under, as she did during the times of the Mahabharata. Lord Krishna's brother, Balarama mentions that the river had dived underground at places.'

'Yes, I know about that, but the river resurfaced later. Are you telling me that now it doesn't?'

'That's exactly what I am telling you,' wheezed the old man. 'We sent a few men upriver to see where it was going under. They came back a month later to tell us that the river had changed its course. It was diverting its waters into the Yamuna now and from there to Ma Ganga. It looks like the mothers Sarasvati, Yamuna and Ganga are coming together, further up north and to the east.'

'So, the earthquake was actually large enough to change the very course of the river,' said Shrutasena to Arjuna. Then, looking at Bhagadutta, he asked, 'How long ago was this big earthquake, uncle?'

'It was a few months ago,' he replied, vaguely.

The three of them looked at each other.

'At about the time we had that earthquake in Babylon, I suppose,' said Chitra, softly.

'Yes. And that, we felt was a big earthquake. If the earthquake originated in Bharatavarsha, and what we felt there was just the effect of that earthquake, it is no wonder that the course of the river got rearranged.'

Arjuna turned to Bhagadutta, who had closed his eyes and was humming a tune to himself.

'Grandpa,' he said gently. 'Did they leave soon afterwards?'

'Eh?' asked the old man, opening his eyes. 'What did you say?'

Arjuna repeated the question.

'No. No. They didn't leave immediately. There was a lot of discussion. A lot. And then they fought and argued some more. Some wanted to go immediately. Others wanted to stay. But eventually, the side that wanted to leave won. It consisted of all the traders, and once the traders decided to leave, everyone else knew that the city was doomed.'

'When was that?'

'About a month ago.'

'Why are you here then?' asked Chitra.

'My dear, at my age, I didn't want to go elsewhere and start a life there. Everything I know is here. My ancestors lived and died here. I can still walk to their graves or their cremation sites and pay my respects. They left me enough food to last for a year. I am an old man. I don't eat much. And I don't plan on living out the year. I know that I won't last that long.'

'Don't you get lonely?' she persisted.

'When you get to my age, child, you will feel lonely even in a crowd. All my friends are gone. Dead. All I am left with are memories. Whether I am alone or in a crowd, those memories keep me company. So here I am, living out my last days in the one place that I know I can call home. I walk the empty hallways, remembering the good times, when these halls reverberated with the smells and sounds of a more vibrant past. I relive those days when the place hummed with activity, when you kids,' he looked at Arjuna and continued, 'ran around the place, creating havoc and giving some work to my stick.'

He doubled up as silent laughter wracked his body. Then, wiping the tears from his eyes, he continued, 'Yes, I have my memories. Don't need anything else now. You kids should go, though. Nothing for you here. Your father told me that you would come and that I was to tell you to follow them east. He said that they would leave word along the way so that you would be able to find them. His plan was to settle somewhere on the banks of the Ganga River. "I want to settle on the banks of the river that now carries the water of Ma Sarasvati" is how he put it.'

Arjuna sported a glum look as he listened to the old man. Chitra slipped her hand in his and clasped it tight. He turned towards her and asked, 'Do you want me to show you around the house? It might be the last look I have of this place,' he said, wistfully.

She squeezed his hand in reply.

'I shall also go and take a look at what remains of my place, I suppose,' said Shrutasena.

'To see if your wife has missed something?' asked Chitra with a smile.

Shrutasena gave a weak smile in return. 'My wife died a long time back.'

'Oh, I am sorry.'

'You couldn't have known. I just want to get one last look at the place, that's all.'

He turned and made his way down, as Arjuna and Chitra went into the main palace. Bhagadutta followed them inside, slowly.

❖

Arjuna led Chitra through the house, pointing out various things to her. The house was stripped of almost everything. There was no furniture to be seen anywhere. There were, however, little trinkets that are always missed when someone moves from a place—a small toy here, a bead there. A cup or two and a flagon left behind. There was only one room on the ground floor that had its full complement of furniture, and it was clear that these had been left behind for Bhagadutta.

'This is a huge house,' remarked Chitra.

'Don't tell me that yours wasn't in Surashtra?'

'Not as big as this!'

'Well, this *is* a bigger city than that small town of yours,' said Arjuna with a smile, pulling her leg.

'My small *town* was prettier than this monstrosity of yours,' remonstrated Chitra, bristling.

Arjuna laughed and pulled her to him, slipping his arm around her waist and kissing her soundly.

'How many other girls have you kissed in these rooms?' Arjuna made pretence of trying to remember.

'Let me see. Hmmm. Wait. Hold on. I will need to count.' Chitra punched him in his chest.

'Ouch,' he exclaimed, rubbing the area with his free hand. 'None actually.'

'Huh. Like I believe that. A prince and not having half the women in the town after him?'

'Why only half?'

'I suspect that the other half were either married or too young.'

Arjuna chuckled. 'You make me sound like my namesake from a thousand years ago.'

'Well, yes. He did go about the place getting married a lot, didn't he?'

'The similarities stop at the name, in this case. I have led a blameless existence,' he said, pulling her to him and kissing her again.

Shrutasena had walked down from the citadel to the eastern end of town where his modest home was. He lived—had lived—in a lane filled with the quarters of his comrades. The street had always presented a chaotic appearance, with children using the streets for their games and the women of the houses sitting at the doorsteps, exchanging gossip with one another.

The lane, however, wore a lonesome look—bereft of noise, of the clamour that underpinned a thriving city. As Shrutasena walked past the houses of his comrades, he peered into a couple of them. A lot of them had crumbled. Some of the walls had collapsed fully. There were a few houses that still remained standing, precariously. He wistfully remembered the good times he had spent there—the drinking, the eating and the laughter. Mostly, he remembered the laughter. And the food.

It was strange. He couldn't remember the many conversations they had had over the years. But he remembered the food that he had eaten in every house. Ever since his wife had passed away, the wives of his comrades had fed him. Every day. Every single meal. He had protested with them. Told them that he was capable of cooking his meals, but they would hear none of it.

He remembered the corn breads, the spicy chickpeas, the oven-baked naans that he dipped into the thick gravy and ate, licking his fingers—not just to show his appreciation for the food but also because it was so delicious.

The buttered dal, spiced with chillies and herbs, the waft of ghee emanating from the scented rice. These were what he now remembered. They triggered memories for him. Memories not of conversations, but of long evenings spent in these various houses. Evenings spent trying to forget the memories of his wife. Of their time together.

It was strange. It had been so long now since she was gone that he had almost forgotten her face. He could remember the smells. The smell of her skin after she had had a bath, or of the time they spent making love. But his memories of the exact contours of her face were starting to fade.

He finally reached his place. His house was one of those that was still standing, miraculously. There were cracks in the walls but none large enough to bring the structure down. He walked in slowly and stood in the middle of the front room. There was nothing there. They had taken all his things, obviously, expecting him to return and follow them to wherever they had relocated. He walked to the small room that he used as his sleeping quarters. There wasn't anything there either. He had only had a mattress made of cotton and a wooden pallet on which he had placed the mattress. Both were gone.

Shrutasena stood still, surveying the remains of the years of his life. Nothing. Just bare floors and walls. *Nothing lasts*, he thought. *If even my memories are starting to get fuzzy, what do I say of inanimate things, which only meant more to me because of my association with them?*

It was as he was musing thus that he felt the earth shake so violently that he was thrown to the ground. Mud and plaster from the ceiling started raining down upon him. Shrutasena rose from the floor, unsteady on his feet, struggling for balance as he swayed with the movement. He moved quickly towards the front of the house, keen to get out before the roof came down on him. The house was shaking violently, and he could see new cracks appearing in the walls while the older ones started to widen. He realized that he didn't have much time and rushed out. Just as he cleared the doorway, he heard a *crrrraaaack* followed by a resounding thud as the roof came down. Immediately the walls gave way, and the house collapsed in on itself.

Shrutasena turned around and saw that his house was now just so much rubble. All around him, houses were starting to fall. It was then that he looked up towards the citadel and gasped in horror. He started running towards it, as fast as his legs could carry him.

❖

The earthquake struck when Arjuna and Chitra were on the first floor, towards the back of the palace. The front of the citadel, which had already been weakened by the force of earlier earthquakes simply collapsed in a heap upon the hapless Bhagadutta. Mercifully for him, death was near instantaneous as huge blocks of stone and masonry fell on him. Not even a cry could emanate before the stones crushed the life out of him. Bhagadutta died exactly where he had wanted to die, in the house that he had dedicated himself to looking after for over half a century.

Chitra and Arjuna had grabbed onto each other when the earthquake had struck as masonry started falling on and around them.

'The stairs,' Arjuna yelled, pulling her towards it. Suddenly, they felt the whole floor move as it gave away. As they fell on the floor, the roof above them began to cave in. Arjuna instinctively pushed Chitra down under him, shielding her body with his.

They landed with a thud as the floor now rested on the ground. Even before they could get up and try to scramble away, the roof crashed around them. A huge beam fell on Arjuna's legs, near his ankles, shearing them away cleanly, as if cut with a sharp sword. Arjuna felt no pain, nor did he realize what had happened. He only knew that his legs were trapped. The beam had formed a sort of hollow in which they lay. Without the beam, he knew that they would have been crushed to death.

He had rolled off Chitra's body after the roof had come down and saw that she was lying there immobile. A thin trickle of blood was visible on her forehead where she had probably cracked her head.

'Chitra! Chitra!' he cried out. He put his finger under her nostrils and could sense her breath. He nudged and prodded her into wakefulness.

Chitra opened her eyes slowly and looked at him. She started coughing almost immediately. The air was filled with dust and mud particles that they were now inhaling. She looked around, moving her head with great difficulty and noticed that they were completely hemmed in. She raised her hands, placed them on the block across the beam bearing down on them and pushed. Arjuna followed her example and did the same, but the block wouldn't budge.

'We are stuck,' she said again, falling into paroxysms of coughing.

Arjuna understood that they would soon run out of air. He tried desperately to find some way to dig through, to give themselves a way to get some fresh air, but to no avail. They were well and truly trapped.

Shrutasena ran like he hadn't in a long time. The earth was still shaking and that made it all the more difficult as he dodged around stones and rubble, wending his way up to the citadel. The gates to the citadel, along with the walls, had collapsed and he had a tough time scrambling over them. His breath was coming out in gasps. His fingers and knuckles became bloody and raw, as the skin scraped off them in his attempt to crawl over the collapsed fort walls.

He eventually got over and started on the path to the citadel. He stopped short as he noticed that the entire citadel had collapsed. Where a two-storey mansion had stood before, there was now only a giant mound of rubble.

'Arjuna! Chitra!' he cried as he started climbing atop the mound. He crossed the place where the doorway to the citadel had stood, and cried out 'Bhagadutta' once but soon understood that chances of the old man surviving were very slim. He had no idea where Chitra and Arjuna might be underneath all the mud and stones and masonry.

He kept calling out to them, hoping to hear their voices again and again as he scrambled over the top.

The air was getting fouler and fouler. Arjuna knew that the dust they were breathing in would settle in their lungs. It was not good. Their breathing was becoming more and more laboured. He held Chitra's left hand with his.

'Looks like this is it, eh?' asked Chitra.

'Don't speak like that. We have to see Ma Ganga, remember?'

Chitra smiled wanly even as she gasped for breath.

'I somehow doubt that, love.'

'Shrutasena will find us,' said Arjuna confidently.

'Even he can't dig through all of this to get to us,' she indicated the masonry tumbled over and around them. The ground had stopped moving now, but that hadn't improved their position one bit.

'If this is it, I have no regrets,' said Chitra with a satisfied look in her eyes as she gazed at Arjuna.

'None?'

'None. I never thought that I would find a man to care for me or that I would come back to my homeland.'

'It isn't over yet,' said Arjuna, less confident now. It was then that Chitra suddenly stiffened and put her fingers on Arjuna's lips.

'Shhhh. Did you hear that?'

'What?'

'Listen!'

They listened. First, the silence all around them, broken occasionally by the creaking and cracking sounds as the rubble settled around and on them. Eventually they heard a voice crying out, 'Arjuna! Chitra!'

'Here! Shrutasena! Here!' Arjuna yelled back and Chitra followed.

They heard the voice move away from there, and in despair, started yelling and screaming. Chitra looked around their little space to see if she could find anything to bang against the beam. She spied a broken pot to her right and pulled at it until it came free from the clasp of the masonry. She lifted it up and started hitting rhythmically against the beam. It rained down more mud and plaster on them, but she kept going.

'Arjuna? Chitra?' They heard the voice now, much closer to them and filled with more certainty than desperation.

'Shrutasena! Can you hear us?'

'Oh, thank Indra, Varuna and Rudra that you are alive!'

His voice seemed to come from somewhere to Chitra's right.

'I can't see you.'

'We are trapped,' yelled Arjuna. 'Can you dig us out?'

'Let me see if I can get something to try and dig you out,' he said, scrambling away in search of anything—iron or even a wooden plank—that could help extricate them. He searched feverishly, getting increasingly frustrated as he could find nothing there.

He went back to where he had last heard their voices.

'Arjuna. I shall go down to the main town and get some implements from there. I remember seeing some iron rods near the smithy.'

Shrutasena took the same route again as he had used to come into the citadel. He scrambled over the broken fort walls and ran as fast as he could, to the smithy. He noticed an iron rod lying there, and hefting it in his hands, started back towards where his friends were trapped.

Scrambling over the fort walls again was easier with the iron rod acting as a staff. He reached the pile of mound that had been the citadel and walked around the area where Chitra and Arjuna were buried.

'Arjuna, I have an iron bar with me. Hold on. I shall dig you both out soon.'

He thought he heard a muffled response from Arjuna, but he couldn't be sure. Shrutasena started to dig in a frenzy. His palms started to blister as he used the iron to get to his friends. He had no idea how deep they were under all the rubble. He lost track of time. The sun beat down upon him, but he didn't care, nor did his pace slacken as he dug, halting periodically to remove the debris. Every so often, he would call out to his friends. Their voices, in reply, would reassure him and he would get started again.

However, he noticed that their voices were getting feebler and feebler, and he dug with renewed frenzy, yelling at them constantly. Reassuring them that he was almost there. That he would have them free. His arms tired. Sweat poured off his body. His breath was ragged, but fear for his friends' fate fueled him with superhuman stamina as he kept digging.

The sun was just beginning to dip below the horizon when Shrutasena broke through the last layer. He had come out right on top of them. He could see their faces. Arjuna's face was turned to his right, as if he wanted his last sight in the world to be that of Chitra. She was looking straight up. Arjuna's right hand was holding Chitra's left.

Shrutasena knelt near the opening and called out softly, 'Arjuna? Chitra?'

There was no response. There couldn't be. They had run out of air and their time on earth. Shrutasena, normally a stoic man, broke down and sobbed, hunched over, beating his fists on the ground, again and again.

Shrutasena looked down into the grave that he had spent the better part of two hours digging. He had spent the whole of the previous night lying near the place where Arjuna and Chitra lay. It was too dark for him to do anything. He had briefly considered covering up the spot where they lay and make that their final resting place. But for some reason, he couldn't bring himself to do that.

Night had fallen suddenly, and he lay down on the rubble, unwilling to leave them there, lest some animal or rodent disturb his friends' rest.

He got up early the next morning, just as the sun cleared the horizon and went to work. He took the iron rod and made his way to the cemetery. There, not far from the family of five, he started digging a grave. Just a single grave, large enough for both his friends. They had died together, and he didn't want to separate them. It had taken him a good couple of hours to dig the grave deep enough. He had a feeling that there might be other graves beneath the one that he had just dug. But it was too late to care about that now.

He went back to the citadel, having found a route that didn't involve him scrambling over large mounds of the fort wall's rubble. He started to widen the hole that he had initially dug to get to his friends. That took him more time since he had to dig around the beam that had fallen across them. He eventually managed to create an opening large enough to hop in and stand within that enclosed space. He tried to lift Arjuna out but found that his feet were pinned by that giant block of stone. It took him a while, but he used the iron rod as a lever to nudge the block off Arjuna's feet. It was then that he noticed his feet were missing below the ankles. He had obviously bled out from his wound. The blood had congealed and coagulated into a dark brown mass around his legs.

Shrutasena hefted him up and carried him across his back and shoulders, down to the cemetery and laid him down inside the grave. He then went back and picked Chitra up in his arms and carried her down to the cemetery, his face grim and set, his eyes filled with tears and with sorrow. He had no children of his own, but what he felt for these two was probably the closest he had ever come to paternalistic feelings. Tears that had initially remained contained within his eyes threatened to spill over, and eventually did. They ran down from his eyes and into his grizzled beard.

He laid her to rest beside Arjuna, just as he had found them—Chitra on her back to Arjuna's right, his head tilted towards her. He placed Chitra's left hand in Arjuna's and then looked around for some gift to put into the grave along with them. He walked back towards some of the houses and went in, trying to find something, anything, to place in their grave. In one of the houses, he found a small pot with some marbles and a few pieces of beads. That would have to do.

He carried them back to the grave and deposited the pot to Chitra's right. The sun was now higher up in the sky and starting to really beat down on the land. Small insects and mosquitoes had started to land on the mortal remains of his friends and Shrutasena knew that he could not afford to dally. He went down on his knees and then gently kissed Arjuna's and Chitra's foreheads. He passed his hand over their heads in benediction and then got up and bowed to them. He looked at their faces once again. Chitra's face seemed to reflect a serenity that was in contrast to her gloom the past few weeks. As if she had finally found her peace. Arjuna's face seemed to have a little smile of contentedness. Like his life had achieved its purpose.

Shrutasena climbed out of the grave and, taking the makeshift wooden shovel he had used along with the iron rod to dig, started shovelling the mud back into the grave, filling it. It took him a while but he persisted. Sweat and tears streamed down his face, and he paused frequently to wipe them away. Eventually, he was done. He picked up the iron rod, and turning his back on the grave, walked slowly but surely towards the eastern edge of the city.

At its outskirts, Shrutasena took one last lingering look at the desolate city. Then, with his face still reflecting the sorrow in his heart, he walked eastwards. He would find his king and let him know where his son lay.

The sun beat down on the deserted city. It would continue to do so for millennia.

Epilogue

The team of researchers from the Deccan College had been working for over two years at the site and had discovered a large cemetery, now named as RGR07, in typical dry, academic style. There had been numerous graves that they had discovered, almost every one of them containing a single skeleton. Their biggest discovery to date had been a large set of graves containing five different skeletons, obviously a large family.

This morning had begun the same as many such mornings with junior researchers gently cleaning around the many skeletons, trying to see if the earth around them hid other remains or objects that might have been buried with them. They had found the usual collection of pots, beads and shells that were interred along with the bodies.

Two young researchers were supervising a dig inside the trench, creatively named B4, in the hopes of finding some more graves. The dig had been started a week earlier and much earth had been removed in the process. As the dig went deeper, it also got slower, with the researchers urging the men digging to be careful as their shovels bit into the earth.

The researchers were talking to each other, wondering whether to continue the dig in this spot or to move on when one of the diggers called out to them in Hindi.

'*Saheb, kuch mila.*' (Sir, found something.)

The young men jumped down into the area, excitedly, and bent to take a look. They spied what looked like the tibia or shin bone. However, it seemed to be missing the entire ankle and foot. They asked the diggers to step aside, and then, taking their brushes, knelt down to gently begin cleaning away the mud.

They lost track of time as the skeleton started to emerge from the mud accumulated over millennia. As one of the men crawled backwards to get at the mud around the skeleton's right hand, he felt a sharp, throbbing pain as his knee stubbed against a protruding object. He looked angrily at it, his first instinct being to grab it and hurl it away from him. That's when the years of training under his diligent professors kicked in. He peered keenly at the object and then shouted excitedly to his colleague.

'Looks like we have another one here!'

The young men scampered around like excited puppies as they now started to clear away the mud around the second skeleton.

'Look to see if there are any more and if we have to extend the dig,' said one to the other, but they couldn't find anymore.

They stared excitedly at each other. A double burial was rare. Really rare. This could be something extraordinary.

It took them nearly a week to clear away the mud around both the skeletons. Their professor had come down from the college after they excitedly called him that first night about their discovery. The skeletons were lying face up, with the head of the larger skeleton turned towards the one lying to the right.

The professor looked carefully at the skeletons. There seemed to be no sign of any injuries, broken bones, apart from the missing feet on the taller skeleton. He would send samples over to his Korean colleagues, he decided, to date the specimens and get some expert opinion on how the couple might have died.

The grave was marked as BR11, completing the address of the couple's final resting place: RGR07/B4/BR11. The taller, footless skeleton was designated 11A, and the smaller one, 11B.

The paper on the finding was published in September of 2018. The conclusion by the researchers was that the burial was that of a couple, with 11A being the remains of a male and 11B, those of a female. The couple seemed to have died around the same time and been buried together. The researchers could not find *any evidence of trauma or specific or non-specific pathological lesions in the skeletons*.

Arjuna and Chitra still lay together, even after the passage of nearly four millennia.

---

* DOI: 10.5115/acb.2018.51.3.200

Acknowledgements

A book exists not just because of the author but also thanks to a host of others who have supported them throughout the journey of completing it.

First and foremost, I want to acknowledge my wife and children, who have patiently endured my stealing time away from them to write this book. It's the immediate family that bears the brunt of an author's tantrums as they navigate the stress of writing—grappling with writer's block, endless revisions and everything in between. I couldn't have done it without them. They are the wind beneath my sails.

It is very difficult to thank one's parents—for what does one not thank them? Apart from everything else that I owe to them, including my existence, I want to thank Appa and Amma for inculcating in me a solid work ethic and a love for education and books. My special thanks to Appa for being the very first reader of my work as a writer. He has always been the first reader of every one of my books, and his words of encouragement mean a lot to me.

My elder daughter was the second person to read this book, and her heartfelt reaction convinced me that it was worth publishing. My special thanks to her for that. I would also like to thank my younger daughter for being a sport and creating the Babylon map at the last moment.

My sincere thanks to Lipika Bhushan for agreeing to be my agent and for guiding me on the path to publishing this book. My thanks to Penguin Random House India for selecting this book for publication. Thanks to Gurveen Chadha for recognizing something in my writing and recommending the book to her internal team. My sincere gratitude to Nikita Dahiya for shepherding it from draft to print and to Aninda Das for guiding it through multiple rounds of editing.

I am deeply indebted to the many established authors—Amish Tripathi, Ashwin Sanghi, Abhas Maldahiyar, Anand Ranganathan, Abhinav Agarwal, Sunanda Vashisht, Ratul Chakraborty, Deepak M.R., Shivakumar, Anand Narasimhan, S. Venkatesh, Sanjeev Sanyal, Smita Barooah and Dimple Kaul—who generously offered words of encouragement for the book.

Special thanks to Pranshu Saxena for his ideas regarding iron and mining that played a crucial role in this book. Thanks also to Dr Amruta Natu of Bhandarkar Oriental Research Institute (BORI) for digging up the old papers about the discovery of the tablet near Bombay and sending it to me.

Chance plays a significant role in the birth of any work of art. My visit to BORI was one such moment, and I am deeply grateful to providence for guiding me.

Lastly, and perhaps most importantly, I bow to Ma Sarasvati—without whose benevolence none of this would have been possible.

Scan QR code to access the
Penguin Random House India website